# THE LOVELY WICKED RAIN

# THE LOVELY WICKED RAIN

SCOTT WILLIAM CARTER

FLYING RAVEN
PRESS

FOR L.B.

PROVING THAT THOSE WHO
TEACH, CAN ALSO DO


THE LOVELY WICKED RAIN

For more about Flying Raven Press, please visit our web site at
*http://www.flyingravenpress.com*

ISBN-10  0692230165
ISBN-13  978-0692230169

Printed in the United States of America
Flying Raven Press paperback edition, June 2014

*Chapter 1*

It was raining. It was a hard rain. It was not a drizzle or a mist, so often the case on the Oregon coast, but a loud, powerful, torrential downpour—rattling the windows that circled the little room, crackling on the aluminum roof a few feet above their heads, rising and falling with the moaning of the wind but never subsiding for long. This was a rain full of rage and single-minded purpose, so awful and awe-inspiring that the only sensible thing to do was to pretend it didn't exist.

They were in the turret, just the two of them, arguing about politics or sports or something else equally inane, having to raise their voices obscenely to be heard over the racket. The actual conversation didn't matter. It was a distraction. There were a couple of times when Gage, glass of bourbon in one hand, his finger raised to make a point with the other, realized the absurdity of sitting in this bubble of glass and sticks, four stories up on the edge of a bluff overlooking the Pacific Ocean while a ferocious storm raged outside, but he didn't let himself linger on the thought for long.

If he let himself think about the storm, he invariably thought about Zoe out in it. If he let himself think about Zoe, his thoughts turned to the ear-ringing argument they'd had that morning. If he relived the argument, he was forced to reckon once again with the simple fact that she was leaving in a little over a week—and not at all where he had hoped she would go.

"I'm sure she's fine," Alex said.

Gage turned to him, his rumpled old companion with the big bags under his eyes and the pocket full of ballpoint pens. The single beaded lamp on the end table between their two leather chairs created an intimate sphere of light, as if they were huddling over a campfire. All of Alex's many books, filling the shelves between each of the dark windows in the hexagonal room, were invisible to them except for the smell: leather and old paper. A former FBI agent, proprietor of Books and Oddities, and co-owner of the Turret House Bed and Breakfast, Alex Cortez had been Gage's friend since Gage dropped out of the FBI academy more than twenty years earlier—an outcome in which Alex, one of his instructors at the time, had played a significant role.

Gage was sometimes still surprised how their friendship had endured, especially with the twenty-year age difference. He didn't make friends easily. In fact, he didn't make friends.

"Who's fine?" he asked.

Alex considered Gage the way he might have considered a lewd joke book that had been misfiled in his bookstore in the children's section—with skeptical bewilderment. The lamplight gleamed on his mostly bald head. What Alex lacked in scalp hair he made up for with his thick gray mustache.

"I wasn't thinking about her," Gage said.

"Right."

"I wasn't."

"Then what were we talking about?"

"What's that? I can't hear you. It's raining outside, if you haven't noticed."

"I noticed! I asked you what we were talking about."

"Hmm. It was something about the last election."

"Actually," Alex said, "*you* were talking about the last election. Ten minutes ago I changed the subject to whether we'll ever get a pro football team in Portland. Your response was to talk about campaign-finance reform."

"It could be relevant," Gage said.

"Maybe we should talk about the elephant in the room."

"Do we have to? I mean, I already know you live a double life as a cross-dressing cocktail waitress at the casino, Alex. Your secret is safe with me."

"The *other* elephant in the room. The recently turned eighteen-year-old girl who's just about to leave for college."

"Woman," Gage said.

"What's that?"

"Woman! She'd kill you if she knew you called her a girl."

"Woman, fine. The woman who decided to attend our local community college this fall against your wishes."

"It wasn't against my wishes," Gage said.

"Right."

"It wasn't!"

"Didn't you tell her you'd pay her way, but only if she went to OSU or Willamette University or some other reputable four-year school?"

"I don't recall."

"Didn't you also tell her that if she enrolled at Barnacle Bluffs Community College, she was going to have to find another place to stay?"

"What's that?"

"You heard me!"

"Geez, you don't have to shout. It may be raining, but I'm not deaf."

"You're impossible."

"Janet used to say the same thing," Gage said.

This got Alex to shut his trap in a hurry. Gage knew it was a bum move, bringing up Gage's own murdered wife as a conversation stopper, but he wasn't in the mood to play the part of the patient to Alex's psychiatrist. His friend's wry grin waned, eyes softening, and for a moment Gage thought he might have made things worse by inviting a stroll down those dark alleys of his past, but Alex merely nodded. He took a sip from his wine then, staring at what was left of the merlot, quickly drained the glass.

He stood, slightly wobbly, the lamplight catching every crease and ridge in Alex's face, his skin like a newspaper someone had crinkled into a ball then tried to straighten the best they could.

"I think I'll get another glass," he said. "Want a refresher on that bourbon?"

"Tempting," Gage said, "but I better get going. Zoe might be back by now."

"You know, if you had a phone like the rest of the civilized world, you could call her and find out."

"I heard cell phones cause cancer."

"You don't even have a landline."

"I heard landlines cause cancer."

"All right, all right. There's no winning with you. Come on, I'll see you out. If Eve knew I was up here in hurricane-force winds, I'd be sleeping on the couch for a week."

Gage started to rise, but then he heard an odd pop from out in the storm—a distinctive bang, a sound nearly engulfed by the roar of the wind. Both he and Alex stopped, turning to the dark windows.

"Did you—?" Alex began.

"Yeah," Gage said.

"It sounded like—"

"I know."

What followed was a mad rush down the turret's winding metal staircase, the two of them stumbling through the parlor to the sliding glass door that led to the patch of yard behind the building. Gage lurched through the rain on the pea-gravel path, his right knee throbbing, before he realized he'd left his cane by the chair upstairs.

Too late. He did his best sprint-lurch toward the edge of the bluff, where the ivy clung to the stone wall like writhing vipers. The glow lanterns that lined the path blinked in and out of the black swirl of night. Rain whipped about him from all directions, running into his eyes, soaking his hair, ice cold dribbling down his back. No jacket, no hat, just polo shirt, jeans, and leather boots—he was already drenched.

The wind roared in his ears. Even on a bum leg, he was ahead of Alex, whose gasping breaths fell farther behind. On his way, Gage groped for the Beretta and found he'd left it at home.

Careless. Lately, he'd allowed himself to fall into the comforting stupor of books and bourbon. What if somebody had come for Zoe? It wouldn't have been the first time.

Down the first staircase to the beach he went, pain knife-flaring in his knee, hard turn on the landing, then bobbling the rest of the way down to the driftwood that collected at the bottom— and there Gage was, staggering across the sand, heartbeat in his ears almost as loud as the wind. He couldn't even hear the ocean, though the salty smell of it was stronger. He blinked to clear the water from his eyes, but it was no use. All he saw was one big black smear.

Was there somebody out there? He wiped at his eyes with his fingers, squinting into the wind. The ocean was a black ribbon, the beach below it a slightly less black ribbon, the sand littered with the uneven shapes of logs, kelp, and other flotsam.

He was standing there trying to get his bearings when another loud *crack* penetrated the wall of sound. Then another. And another.

There was no mistaking them for what they were now. Alex, breathing hard, was just catching up, and he had a cell phone to his ear.

"Gunshots!" Alex shouted into the receiver. The iPhone screen rippled blue on his cheek. "That's what I said. My address is—"

And the rest was lost to the storm, because Gage, thinking he spotted a person sitting on a log not far way, bolted in that direction. Alex called after him, but Gage didn't stop.

Fifty yards away. Then forty. Definitely a person. A young man, maybe. Definitely a young man, though with the slender physique of a woman. Twenty yards away and the young man, a spindly figure in a black hoodie, turned his pale face Gage's way— like a blurry white thumbprint on the night.

When the young man turned his face, he also turned his

body far enough that Gage saw the gun.

It was a snub-nosed revolver, a .38 Smith & Wesson by the looks of it, and the kid held it in his lap as if only half-aware of it—as if it were merely a pair of sunglasses or binoculars, some harmless object rather than a weapon. There was no sign the kid had even fired it, nor was there anyone else he might have fired *at*. Now that he'd been seen, Gage slowed and raised his hands. His own heart thudded in his ears.

"You all right, son?" Gage asked.

The kid stared back with his ghostly face, showing no sign of acknowledgment. There was something familiar about him. Gage had seen him somewhere before, he was sure of it. Inching his way forward, arms still raised, Gage kept his gaze fixed on the kid's gun hand, alert to any sign of movement. He was within ten yards, and though there was a chance he could get there before the kid got off a shot, it was more than likely he'd have to do something along the way to distract him. Kick up sand, maybe? Or throw something. But what did he have on him but his wallet? Here, for once, a cell phone might come in handy purely as an object for throwing.

The kid watched impassively, neither reaching for the revolver nor showing any other sign of hostility. His eyes were sunken and shadowed like the sockets of a skull. He was gaunt and pencil-thin, his water-soaked hoodie and jeans probably weighing more than he did. The dark bangs visible beneath the hood stuck to his forehead like strands of yard.

When Gage was within ten feet, the kid turned to stare at the ocean. Gage crept closer. Water dribbled into his eyes, off his ears, down his neck. His face was already numb. Five feet now. Then three. He circled to the boy's left side, toward the gun, reaching for it. Almost had it. A few more inches.

"Fucking loser," the kid said suddenly.

Gage froze, right hand outstretched, fingers nearly to the boy's gun hand. The kid had said the words just barely loud enough to be heard above the wind, but with so much hatred that it stopped Gage dead in his tracks.

"Gonna do it," the kid said. "Gonna do it one of these days."

Slowly but firmly, Gage placed his hand on top of the kid's gun hand. He expected an attempt to pull away, but the kid didn't even flinch. Gage knew he had fairly large hands—gorilla hands, Janet had once called them—but even so, the kid's still seemed small and dainty, soft and pliant like a toddler's hand.

"Why don't you give me the revolver, son?"

The kid didn't respond. The hoodie clung to the hard ridges of his ribs. Sirens, still distant, penetrated the wall of wind. Keeping his right hand firmly pressed on the kid's hand, Gage used his left to pry the gun free. It was surprisingly easy. As if he were holding an explosive device, Gage moved the gun, at arm's length, slowly away from the boy.

The kid gazed up him, eggshell skin catching what little light there was, and Gage was sure of it now. He knew this kid. One of Zoe's classmates. She'd studied with him a few times, calculus or economics, part of a study group. In the darkness, he could not make out the kid's features clearly, but he remembered effeminate lips, soft eyes, and the kind of stooped gait of somebody shouldering the burden of a lifetime of abuse from his classmates.

The kid might have been crying, but there was so much water on his face, it was impossible to tell.

"You're Zoe's dad," the kid said.

"Something like that," Gage said.

"Am I going to jail for this?"

"Not if this is the worst you've done."

"Some people deserve to die."

"Very true. I've known some of them. Did you kill somebody, son?"

The kid mumbled something. Gage, leaning closer, asked him to repeat it. The kid shook his head and turned back to the ocean. Gage tried to remember a name, but it didn't come. The sirens were so close, the police car must have been up near the Turret House. Alex, cell phone still in hand, appeared to their right, and Gage held the revolver out to him. Alex took it and backed away.

"Let's go inside," Gage said to boy.

There was no response. Gage placed his hand on the boy's shoulder, and it was both sharp and weak like wet cardboard. His hand was only there a second when the boy responded with a convulsive shudder, as if he'd been holding it back and all it took was Gage's touch to release it.

"I'm a coward," the kid said.

## Chapter 2

The kid's name was Jeremiah. He mumbled it to them as they trudged up the steps, his voice mostly swallowed by the storm, but enough fragments of sound made it to Gage's ears that it jogged his memory. Of course. Jeremiah Cooper. His father was Arne Cooper, who coached football at the high school—a huge, broad-shouldered man, pretty much the opposite of his son. Zoe had pointed out Arne when Gage accompanied her to parents' night at one of the home games, and the only reason he remembered it at all was because she'd said, "That guy on the sidelines there, the Bobcats coach—that's Jeremiah's dad. A real asshole."

Gage hadn't wanted to waste the evening finding out *why* she thought Arne Cooper was an asshole—especially since she was the one who'd asked Gage to go to the game, a Halley's Comet–type rarity in itself—so he'd let the comment pass. But he still remembered how intensely she'd voiced this opinion. Even for Zoe, who was often intense, her tone had surprised him.

Exposed on the steps, they were battered by the rain and wind from all sides. Gage's polo shirt and jeans were so soaked, they felt like a second skin, reptilian maybe, something to be sloughed off when the sun finally showed its face. He blinked away the droplets crowding his eyes. Each time he took a step, a searing jolt shot up his right knee. Most of the time, he managed to get by with what remained of his knee without this kind of agony, but then most of the time he didn't try to do the forty-yard dash in a November storm.

He saw the sweep of red lights on the rail at the top of the stairs and then, when they reached the landing, the blurry shape of the police cruiser parked on the street next to the Turret House. No sirens. Red beams rotated across the grass and gravel like helicopter blades. Rain streaked the headlight beams. A tall man in a trench coat jogged toward them, hand poised at his side as if ready to pull a gun from a holster.

The kid, behind Alex but in front of Gage, hesitated, and Gage gave him a gentle push from behind.

The man in the trench coat slowed, wary, and when the weak light hit the man's gaunt face just right, Gage saw that it was indeed Percy Quinn—police chief, Mr. Rogers look-a-like, and general thorn in Gage's side in any matters related to the law. Quinn's hand strayed from his hidden holster, but only barely. His eyes, underneath those bushy black eyebrows of his, searched the kid's face, then looked at Gage. Quinn's thinning gray hair lay flat and wet against his glistening scalp.

"Gage," he said, "what the hell is going on?"

"Good to see you too, Chief."

"Madge said you called in gunshots on the beach. I was on my way home."

"You sound a bit cranky today, Percy. Is it the weather?"

"Gage—"

"My mistake," Alex piped in behind Gage. He held up the iPhone. "I'm the one who called it in. I thought I heard gunshots, but I was wrong."

"It must have been the thunder," Gage said.

"There hasn't been any thunder," Quinn said.

"Well, then it must have been something else. We're going inside to get some hot cocoa. You want to join us?"

"Gage, I'm not in the mood for—"

"We'll even toss in some marshmallows."

"Gage—"

"Not a fan of marshmallows?"

Water dripped from Quinn's enormous black eyebrows, running down the hard lines of his face like water flowing through ravines. The red lights of the police car continued their rhythmic sweep. Gage prodded Jeremiah forward, but the chief put his hand gently on the kid's shoulder.

"Hold on there, son," he said. "I recognize you. Jerry Cooper, isn't it?"

The kid responded with an ever-so-slight tip of his chin.

"Anything you want to tell me, son?"

"No."

"Everything all right at home?"

"Yes, sir."

"Mind telling me what you were doing out there?"

"Just walking," Jeremiah said.

"Just walking?"

The kid nodded. Quinn looked at Gage, who shrugged.

"All done?" Gage said.

"I don't like this," Quinn said. "I don't like this at all."

"Sorry to trouble you."

Quinn stared, unblinking. The rain spotted his trench coat like the splatter on a Jackson Pollock painting. Shaking his head, Quinn turned and slumped away into the rain, toward his police cruiser. "It's what you've been doing ever since you got to this damn town," he said, loud enough for Gage to hear. "Troubling me."


SOGGY SHOES AND SOCKS were discarded at the door. Towels were provided. There was no hot cocoa, but there was hot lemon tea—Eve, Alex's wife, already had it on the stove, as she did most nights for any guests who might want it. She had three steaming mugs laid out on the dining room table before they'd even settled Jeremiah into one of the chairs. He sagged into it like a pile of wet laundry, head bowed so low that the white towel she'd draped over his neck was in danger of sliding off. Water trickled from his hair onto the red silk tablecloth. He stared morosely into his mug, steam billowing across his face.

Beethoven played from the stereo in the other room, just loud enough to be heard over the storm. Gage, taking the seat across the table, watched the boy. Eve also watched him from the kitchen archway, her Mediterranean complexion looking even darker in the dim room, especially with the light from the kitchen behind her. She made no move to turn on the lamp. Gage heard Alex, still in the foyer by the front door, talking to someone on the phone.

"Do you like it when people call you Jerry?" Gage asked.

The kid looked up, confused. "What?"

"Quinn—the chief, he called you Jerry. Do you like that?"

"I don't know."

"You don't know or you don't care?"

"I don't know."

"Or you don't want to say?"

The kid shrugged. He looked back into his mug, as if he could divine the answer there.

"Okay, then," Gage said. "I'll call you Jerry. Is that all right, Jerry?"

"Whatever."

"If you don't like it," Gage said, "you should tell people. Then they'll stop."

Jeremiah looked up, and Gage thought he saw a flash of anger there. It was a relief. Finally, a bit of life.

"Is that what you do?" Jeremiah asked pointedly. "Like, if somebody calls you Gary instead of Garrison?"

"Nope. I just punch them in the nose. Believe me, they never do it a second time."

For just a moment, Gage thought the kid might smile. There was the tiniest flicker of it, a near subliminal blip, but if the lips curled up at all, they made up for it by curling downward even more. Still, Gage took that as proof enough, just as a scientist took a distant star's gravitational wobble as proof that a planet was in orbit around it. If the kid could laugh, or even show the potential for it, there was hope.

"You want to tell me what you were doing with the revolver?" Gage asked.

Jeremiah shrugged.

"I'd like to help you," Gage said.

"I don't know."

"You don't know if you want me to help you?"

Another shrug. He was still transfixed by the steam rising from his tea, but he hadn't taken a sip. Gage took a sip of his and found the lemon flavor wonderful and sweet, which was no surprise, since everything Eve made was wonderful and sweet. Eve returned briefly with some baklava, depositing the glass plate on the table near the boy. He didn't eat this either. Gage, mindful of the few extra pounds he'd put on lately, resisted for five seconds before giving in. He did manage to prevent himself from eating Jeremiah's portion at least. The crispy exterior of the baklava was still warm, and the blueberry filling just tart enough to give it a little extra kick.

"Can I have my gun back?" Jeremiah asked.

"Are you asking me or the tea?"

"Huh?"

"It'd be easier if you look at me when you talk to me."

Jeremiah glanced up, but it appeared to take an enormous effort to keep his head in that position, as if invisible rubber bands connected his chin to the table. His head was cocked to the side, and his chin was tipped slightly down. It was the kind of expression that would have gotten most women to cross to the other side of the street.

"Don't hurt yourself," Gage said.

"Huh?"

"Never mind. Tell you what. You tell me where you got the revolver and what you planned to do with it, and I'll think about giving it back to you."

Jeremiah's eyes, already glassy, appeared to recede away from Gage. The steam from the cup continued its dance across the kid's face. They weren't getting anywhere.

"I can't help you unless you trust me," Gage said.

There might have been a nod there, or it might have been in Gage's imagination. It was impossible to say. The rain picked up, a ferocious roar, and Jeremiah turned and stared at the dark window at the end of the hall. Gage was tempted to ask if the kid was going to eat the baklava, but he restrained himself.

"I like the rain," Jeremiah said. "Do you like the rain, Gary?"

This got a smile out of Gage. The obvious poke with his name was another good sign that there was still life in the kid.

"I wouldn't have moved to Oregon if it bothered me, Jerry. But rain like this—I'll be honest, it scares the crap out of me."

"Not me," Jeremiah said. "I like it especially like this. I think it's lovely."

"You don't say."

"Lovely and wicked."

"There's two words you don't often hear together," Gage said.

They were really going now. It was almost like they were having a conversation. Gage was debating about asking Jeremiah what his favorite color was, but then he heard the front door open in the other room, voices murmuring, then Zoe and Alex appeared in the dining room.

As she made a beeline for Jeremiah, Zoe barely glanced in Gage's direction, but there was enough hostility in that one glance to last a lifetime. Pow. A real punch to it. Just as quickly, as she looked at Jeremiah, her expression changed to one of motherly concern. Her hair, black with a few indigo streaks, was cut short and spiky. She was dressed in her usual goth-hybrid garb—black jeans, black garage-band T-shirt, black eye shadow—but she'd left most of her bling at home, something he noticed lately she'd been doing more. Some silver hoop earrings and a tiny diamond nose stud were her only facial adornments.

Dark spots from the rain speckled her black clothes. Her pale face and arms gleamed with moisture. She swiveled around the seat next to Jeremiah, sitting in it so her knees pressed up against him. She cupped her hand around his neck, pulling him a little closer, leaning into his ear, an intimate gesture. Jeremiah didn't look at her even then, but Gage did see the skin around his eyes quiver.

When Zoe spoke, it was a whisper, too soft for Gage to hear over the rain crackling on the roof. The kid shook his head. She said something else. He shook his head again. Zoe glared at Gage defiantly.

"What did you do to him?" she said.

"Me?"

"He wants to go home."

"I have a few more questions first."

"You can ask him later."

Without waiting for his reply, she stood abruptly and gestured for Jeremiah to do the same. After a brief glance in Gage's direction, he rose and meekly accompanied her, her guiding him by the arm as she might a blind man. He was a full head taller than Zoe, but somehow he seemed shorter. Before Gage could think of something to say, they were out the front door and driving down the road in Zoe's Toyota. He was still feeling the draft from the front door when the sound of the Toyota's engine faded to silence.

Alex held up his hands apologetically. "I called her because I thought she might be able to help."

"It's all right," Gage said.

"Hope I didn't screw things up."

Gage gazed into what remained of his tea. Maybe the kid was right to look for answers there. It was just as good as anywhere else.

"Screw what up?" he said. "I don't even know what happened."

"Well, we've still got the revolver at least," Alex said. "Now he can't hurt someone. Maybe that's the one good thing we've done."

"Maybe you're right," Gage said, though he was left with the nagging feeling that somehow they might have made things worse.

## Chapter 3

The storm broke a little after two in the morning. By then, Gage was back in his house above the highway, having drifted off in his armchair by the wood stove, a crossword book in his lap and his hand still cupping a pencil. The storm did not die off slowly; it was an abrupt change, a 180-degree swing from moaning wind and pounding rain to … silence. The difference was so immediate, in fact, that Gage snapped awake, still in the thrall of a dream where Janet and his old girlfriend Carmen were arm wrestling for the right to bear his child. He didn't know what the dream meant, but he was disappointed he wasn't going to find out who won—not so much the arm wrestling, but how they reacted to the outcome.

Since neither of them had wanted children, he wasn't even sure how they were defining a win.

He poked his head into Zoe's room and saw her asleep on top of the covers and under a copy of *Rolling Stone*, headphones on, music blaring. With no cane, using the walls for support, he crept inside and turned off her iPhone, covered her with the afghan her grandmother Mattie had made her before she died, and turned off the lights on the way out. He liked doing things like that. He'd done it dozens of times in the two years she'd been living with him, and he felt a pang of sadness that he wouldn't get to do it much longer.

He may have wanted Zoe to go to a good university, with all the opportunities it provided, but that didn't mean he wanted her to leave. If there was a contradiction in there somewhere, he refused to acknowledge it.

A few hours of fitful sleep later, he woke to the sound of someone knocking on his front door. It was such a hard, forceful pounding that he was up and out of bed before the first knocks were even finished, heart thudding in his ears, all the sleepiness gone by the time he hobbled into the front hall. He was already opening the door when he realized he'd forgotten not only his cane, but his robe too. He was standing there in nothing but his boxers.

No gun either. Stupid. What if another one of his old pals from the Italian Mafia in New York had shown up to pay him a visit?

Fortunately, the person standing on his porch was neither Italian nor Mafia—not unless you counted high school sports as Mafia, which, in a small town like Barnacle Bluffs, may not have been far from the truth.

Arne Cooper filled most of the stoop outside Gage's door. He was big and broad, thick in the chest and stomach, his green Bearcats windbreaker zipped so high that only a glimpse of his white T-shirt showed beneath. The jacket fit him as tight as paint on a barrel. What was left of his reddish brown hair, just a fringe, was slicked straight back, and his eyebrows were nearly invisible. A fine mist hung over the arborvitae bordering Gage's gravel driveway. Arne's bald head glistened like a polished egg. The only physical trait he shared with his son was his pale skin.

"I hear you have something that belongs to me," he said, smacking his gum. He stood close enough that Gage caught a whiff of spearmint. Behind Arne was a big black Ford Expedition so shiny and bright, it looked like it had just rolled off the lot.

"Excuse me?"

"I'm Arne Cooper."

He said it as if he expected a salute. Gage didn't like the

tough-guy act. And in his experience, anyone who had that attitude wasn't really tough when it came down to it—not when it really mattered, anyway.

"I'm sorry," he said, "I know I called a plumber, but I wasn't expecting you until—"

"Jerry's my son," Arne said with a sigh.

"Ah."

"He says you have my revolver."

"He says correctly."

Arne raised his thin eyebrows and went on chewing his gum. Gage had no gum and didn't feel like raising his eyebrows, so he simply stood there. It was hard to look imposing in boxers, especially when he was facing off against someone as big as a grain silo, but he did his best.

"I'd kinda like my gun back, champ," Arne said.

"That's a reasonable request."

"Okay. So why don't you go get it then?"

"I will. Eventually."

"Eventually?"

"That's right," Gage said.

"Listen, champ—"

"Champ. I like that. Feel like I should be wearing boxing gloves. Or at least chewing some gum. Not really much into the gum-chewing thing, sadly."

Arne blinked a few times and went on smacking his gum. He had the kind of blank stare that could have either meant there was nothing going on behind those eyes, or that there was plenty going on but he'd learned to hide it behind a flat stare for optimal intimidation. Gage wasn't sure which it was, though his experience led him to believe it was most likely the former, people being the eggplants they generally were.

"I don't get you," Arne said.

"Well, that makes two of us. I don't get me either."

"You some kind of comedian?"

"I do like to make jokes. I find it lowers my blood pressure."

Arne shook his head. "You're Zoe's dad," he said, as if that explained everything. "Look, pal—"

"Pal. Even better than champ."

"—I just want my piece, okay? Jerry shouldna taken it, he's been punished like he knows he would be, and now I got to make sure it's locked up better. But I don't got all day to make chitchat, so if you could just hustle your ass and get it for me, I'd 'preciate it."

"No," Gage said.

This finally got Arne to stop chewing his gum. "What?"

"I said no."

"You won't get my gun?"

"No, I won't hustle my ass. Especially for you. And if you talk like that to me again, you can get the hell off my property."

"Hey now. Easy. I just want what's mine."

"I don't even know if the gun is yours. Maybe it's stolen."

Arne's face flushed bright pink. Because of the paleness of his skin, it didn't take much pink to be noticeable, and this was a real doozy.

"What the hell!" he said. "Now you're calling me a thief?"

"No. I'm saying you *may* be a thief. There's a difference."

"Listen, sport, if you don't—"

"Sport! Pal, champ—we have the complete trifecta!"

"Get me my damn gun!"

"Nope. And I think it's time for you to go."

"I don't get you! What the hell do you want anyway?"

"I was going to ask you some questions about Jeremiah. But now I'm not in the mood. You should leave."

Arne leaned in closer, his jaw clenched, eyes dark and intense. "Man, if you don't go get me my gun right now ..."

"Yes?" Gage said.

"It won't be pretty."

"Oh, that's too bad. I'm a fan of pretty."

This apparently was all the kidding around Arne Cooper could take. He lunged for Gage, not really a punch or a grab, more of a clumsy push. This was not a man who was used to fighting people who put up much resistance. Gage, who was always underestimated because of his limp and his general slouched demeanor, dodged to the side and clamped his hand on Arne's wrist, yanking him toward him, farther into the house.

Once he had the bigger man off-balance, executing the next move was relatively easy. With a pivot and a twist, he had Arne's arm up and behind him, the wrist bent to apply just the right amount of pressure to paralyze his opponent. Still, Arne tried to squirm free, so Gage tweaked his wrist just a little. He spun Arne around, facing the door, never relinquishing the pressure.

"Hey! Hey!" Arne cried.

"Just relax," Gage said.

"How can I—how can I relax when you got my damn arm bent?"

Gage was close enough to Arne's back that he could smell him, a mixture of musky animal sweat and a minty deodorant. With each little movement of Arne's body, his windbreaker squeaked and rustled.

"Let me go!" Arne shouted.

"Not yet," Gage said. "I want an apology."

"A what?"

"You heard me. I want you to apologize for being an asshole."

"I don't believe this! You have to be out of your—"

Gage responded with another tweak of the wrist, this one sharp enough that Arne stopped mid-sentence with a yelp.

"Try again," Gage said.

"Fine! I'm sorry!"

"Sorry for what?"

"Let me go!"

"Try again. Sorry for what?"

"I swear, if you don't—*owww!*"

"Try again!"

"Fine! Fine! I'm sorry—sorry for being an asshole!"

"Much better," Gage said.

He shoved Arne out the door. To make sure the man couldn't swivel right around and attack him—his sheer size, in such close quarters, would give him an advantage now that he knew the man he was fighting with was no patsy—Gage stepped on Arne's right foot, just enough to cause him to stumble. A lighter man might have been able to catch himself, but a freight train like Arne Cooper really didn't stand a chance against the law of gravity. He bobbled off the porch until his legs buckled and sent him sprawling on the gravel.

With some effort, Arne pried himself off the ground. His face was bloated and red, and bits of gravel and dirt stuck to his jacket and jeans. He took a single lurching step toward Gage and stopped, grabbing his wrist and glaring with as much hatred as Gage had ever seen anyone look at him—and he'd dealt with quite an assortment of nasty characters over the years.

"Asshole!" Arne cried.

"Now, now," Gage said. "Let's not go down that road again."

"I'm going to get the damn chief of police, that's what I'm going to do!"

"Sounds good. He's a dear friend of mine."

"Yeah! Well—well, we'll see!"

With that witty retort out of the way, he retreated to his black Expedition. The door slammed, the engine roared, and the tires spit up gravel as Arne Cooper made his hasty departure, giving Gage a middle-fingered salute on his way past. In return, Gage offered up his best pearly white smile. He was still watching the trailing gravel smoke, enjoying the way it dissipated into the morning mist, when he heard the creak of floorboards behind him.

Turning, he saw Zoe leaning against the wall, dressed in black sweatpants and a sleeveless gray Radiohead T-shirt. Her smile was even broader than the one Gage had given Arne.

"That was *awesome*," she said.

GAGE HAD JUST ENOUGH TIME to shower, dress, and make a pot of coffee before Percy Quinn showed up on his doorstep—looking even more dour than usual in his gray trench coat, hands stuffed deep into the pockets, shaking his head before Gage had even said a word. Zoe had left for a morning walk on the beach a few minutes earlier.

"Cream?" Gage asked, handing him a mug.

"You know I take it black," Quinn said.

"I always figure it's rude not to ask."

"When have you ever worried about being rude?"

"Oh, I worry about it all the time. But worrying about it and being able to stop myself are two different things. I'm a rude addict."

"You're an asshole addict is what you are."

"I'm not even sure what that means, but it makes me feel all warm and fuzzy inside when you talk to me that way."

The two of them settled at the kitchen table. The bright morning light, shining through the high windows in the A-frame, was not kind to Gage's dusty bookshelves, torn and discolored leather furniture, and threadbare carpet. There were so many magazines, crossword-puzzle books, and newspapers piled on the table that it took Quinn a moment to spot the .38 sitting in the middle of it, nose pointed toward the far wall.

"That it?" Quinn said.

"Yep."

"You put it out here to give it to me?"

"Yep."

"You could have just given it to him and saved me a trip."

"That's true."

"But you didn't."

"Nope."

Quinn sighed. He picked up the revolver, checked the safety, then slipped it into the pocket of his trench coat. He took a sip of his coffee. Gage took a sip of his—with a dash of Irish cream, just the way he liked it. Irish cream may not have been all that manly, but he'd stopped worrying about being manly years ago. Not that he ever worried about it much. In his experience, men who worried about being manly were missing the point of being men.

"Arne says you stole it from him," Quinn said. "He wants to press charges."

"You want to take me down to the station and book me?"

"How about you just start with how you came about having it in your possession."

"Oh, I'm pretty sure you already know the answer to that question, Chief."

"The kid gave it to you?"

"He has a name. It's Jeremiah."

"I thought he went by Jerry?"

"Nope."

"Huh. All these years, I've been calling him Jerry."

"Says more about you than him."

Quinn's big eyebrows dropped, his eyes narrowing. "What's that supposed to mean?"

"It means that you made an assumption instead of making the effort to find out what he preferred. Don't feel too bad though. That's what most people do."

"He could have just corrected me," Quinn said.

"I suppose that's true, Perry."

"You know my first name is Percy."

"Oh, is that what you prefer?"

They stared at each other over the table, steam rising from their coffee mugs. It wasn't a staring contest as much as the inevitable outcome of two men who shared little in common and quickly ran out of things to say. The room was filled not so much with anger and hostility as resignation and world-weariness. Here they were again. The universe always seemed to conspire to bring them together despite their best intentions to stay as far from one another as possible. With a shrug, Quinn took another sip from his coffee, then stood.

"Well," he said.

"Give my best to your wife. Her migraines gotten any better?"

"A little. Gage, listen."

"Uh-oh, that sounded serious."

"Just a warning. People in this town really like Arne Cooper. You've got to know that."

"It must be his winning personality," Gage said.

"It has more to do with him winning the Class 4A state football championships two out of the last five years."

"Or it could be that," Gage said.

"I'm just saying, it might be best not to get on his bad side."

"Might be too late for that."

"Yeah, but I know you. You can't leave things alone. I'm just saying you might want to leave it alone this time."

"Leave what alone? There's nothing there."

"That's what I mean. There's nothing there right now. Then you'll make all that nothing into something, and I'll have all kinds of trouble on my hands."

"I love it when you talk in riddles."

"This town isn't all that sure about you, Gage. You've brought it a bunch of bad publicity the last few years. So far, you're tolerated. But they can turn on you in a hurry."

"Does that mean I'll have to drop out of my Tuesday book club at the public library? I was so looking forward to the discussion on *Anna Karenina*."

Quinn sighed. He studied Gage the way he might study a nasty stain on his carpet, one he couldn't get rid of no matter how hard he tried. That's what Gage was, after all. A stain. A stain on the city. Gage had no illusions about that. And that was just fine by him. He didn't need Barnacle Bluffs any more than it needed him. It was just a place to live. If it wasn't for Zoe, he could leave on a whim. But until the day came when Zoe wasn't part of the equation, Gage wasn't going anywhere.

On his way out the door, Quinn said over his shoulder, "Just don't make things any worse with Arne, okay? If you can do that at least, I'd appreciate it."

"I'll do my best," Gage said.

Though Gage knew, the way he always knew these things, that there was a good chance he and Arne Cooper would be running into each other again.

## Chapter 4

It took a fair amount of convincing and cajoling, but Gage managed to persuade Zoe to let him drop her off at the apartment building next to the community college. Her Toyota was in the shop anyway—the brakes were on their last legs—and she needed a ride. Things weren't exactly back to normal between them, but they were at least on speaking terms, and he couldn't bear the thought of her slipping out of his house without so much as a handshake.

"Not too late to change your mind," Gage said, speaking loud enough to be heard over the wind. "I hear Eugene is beautiful this time of year."

She flashed him the evil eye before returning her attention to the highway, clutching the black duffel bag in her lap a little tighter. She tapped her sandals against the floorboard in a fast beat, a nervous twitch that wasn't at all like her. Seeing her nervous made *him* nervous. The way she sat in the van's passenger seat, hunched and still, made her seem small and girlish, as if she were on her way to her first day of kindergarten instead of college. He also noted with some amusement that though she was dressed in her usual black jeans and black T-shirt, her spiky hair was its normal brown and she wore only a single nose stud, an emerald so small it could have been a mole.

The sun gleamed so brightly on the highway that Gage had to squint, even wearing sunglasses. The ocean, a rich aquamarine, was as still as an oil painting. For a late September day on the Oregon coast, especially at not even ten in the morning, it was unusually warm. They drove with the windows down, the cool air whipping through the van. The Volkswagen's engine was obnoxiously loud, the rumble punctuating the occasional disturbing clang. Zoe had been pestering him to take it into the shop for weeks, but she said nothing today. She wasn't even listening to her iPod.

Just beyond the edge of town, past the Horseshoe Mall where Alex's bookstore was located, they crossed the single-lane bridge over the marshy inlet and reached Old Timer Road. They turned east, away from the ocean, and drove past the city's fenced-in power station, a storage center, and a marine mechanic before crossing into a dense cluster of Douglas firs. After they scaled a short but steep hill, the forest opened into a clearing.

With a half-dozen squat, rectangular buildings connected by patchy lawns and cracked sidewalks, Barnacle Bluffs Community College looked more like an oversize high school than a junior college, though the thick forest surrounding it all gave the place the feel of a fairy tale. Most of the cars, and there were plenty of them, were clustered around the largest of the buildings, a big tan monstrosity at the edge of campus. It was five stories, ivy choking the windows on the bottom floor, the tiny decks on the upper floors boxed in with rusty black iron rails.

"That's it," Zoe said.

"Looks like a prison," Gage said.

"It's just a place to sleep."

"And there's no cafeteria?"

Zoe sighed. "No. I told you. It's more like an apartment. I'll have to cook my own food."

"When have you ever cooked?"

She didn't dignify this with an answer. He parked behind a blue Ford Escort. There were people everywhere—mostly young people carrying boxes, TVs, and stereos, but a fair amount of parents as well. Two girls carrying suitcases walked past on the sidewalk, saw Zoe, and waved. She waved back.

"Know them?" Gage asked.

"Nope," Zoe said.

Outside, it smelled of fir and moss and damp earth; he couldn't even smell the ocean. They could have been in the foothills of the Cascades rather than a short hop to the beach. Between the two of them, they were able to get all Zoe's things in one load. It wasn't much. She lugged two suitcases in addition to the hiking pack on her back and the duffel bag slung over her shoulder. He carried two large cardboard boxes, one stacked on top of the other, each helpfully labeled *ZOE'S STUFF* in black marker. The first step with his right knee, though, was murder.

"You sure?" Zoe said. "What about your cane?"

"I'm fine," Gage said.

"I don't want you to hurt—"

"I said I'm fine."

He clearly wasn't fine—it was as if he had a bag of crushed glass inside his knee—but he wasn't about to admit it to Zoe.

Limping past a blue Suburban, he saw a pretty young woman in tight jeans and a sleeveless yellow blouse that bared her midriff struggling to retrieve a mini fridge from the back. A spindly young man watched. Or at least Gage assumed he was watching. His hair, shoe-polish black, hung so low on his face that Gage couldn't see his eyes. It was long on the sides and in the back as well, wispy, the kind of hair that didn't look good on men. He wore a long gray trench coat over a plain white T-shirt, the lapels covered with various colorful buttons.

At first glance, he thought the young woman was his girlfriend, judging by her teenybopper outfit, slim figure, and the stylish cut of her chestnut hair. Even when he got a better look at her face and saw the telltale giveaways of age that even an expert makeup job couldn't hide completely, he would have pegged her as a slightly older sister until the young man spoke.

"Mom," he pleaded softly, "I can do it."

"I got it, I got it!" she snapped at him.

"Mom—"

"*Shh!*"

She was so small and frail—it was a toss-up which of them was thinner, her or her son—that it was as if she were trying to wrestle a tank out of the back of the Suburban. She put it down hard enough that the metal clanged like a bell, drawing the attention of people around them.

The woman saw Gage and smiled. He smiled back and tried to hide his limp as he trudged along the sidewalk. He debated about offering to help her, but he knew that it was one thing for him to grit his teeth and carry a few boxes; it was another to carry a fridge. Better to smile politely and walk on past. Zoe, however, stopped next to the boy.

"Hi," she said.

If the kid glanced at her, the mop of black hair made it impossible to tell. Without moving his head, he mumbled a hello. He was quite short, shorter than Zoe, and thinner than her as well. His baby face probably would have given him trouble even getting into a PG-13 movie. Even the trench coat did little to give him any bulk. The buttons, Gage saw, pictured characters from various science-fiction television shows: Chewbacca, Mr. Spock, Rod Serling, and many others Gage didn't recognize.

"You Connor?" Zoe said.

Now the kid glanced at her. "Yeah. How'd you know?"

"Jeremiah."

"Oh," Connor said, brightening a little. "He here yet?"

"I don't know. I'm Zoe, by the way. I'm one of his best friends."

"Cool," Connor said.

It was a very fast, whispered exchange. He seemed to be shrinking into his trench coat.

"Who's Jeremiah?" the woman asked.

"My friend," Connor said.

"The one you met at the *Star Wars* convention?"

"*Star Trek*," Connor corrected her, not even attempting to hide his disdain.

"Oh, right." She looked from Zoe to Gage. "I'm Berry, by the way. Bernadette, actually, but everybody calls me ... Are you okay?"

It took Gage a second to realize she was talking to him. Even putting most of his weight on his left leg, the pain in his right knee was almost unbearable, but he thought he'd been doing a pretty job of hiding it. No such luck, apparently. He desperately wanted to set the boxes on the ground, but now that she'd called him out, he couldn't bring himself to do it.

"Just fine," he said.

"You don't look fine. Your face is all ... sweaty."

"It's just a little warm, that's all."

"This is Garrison," Zoe said. "He's my stepdad."

"Oh! Well, nice to meet you, Garrison. You have nice eyes."

"Mom," Connor pleaded.

"Well, he does!"

The way Berry said it, it wasn't like she was just complimenting Gage's eyes. It was as if she was saying she wanted to meet at a hotel later. The assertive sexuality combined with her girlish appearance was an odd combination. Gage guessed she was at least in her early thirties, which wasn't outside the realm of possibility for him, but he still felt a certain amount of skeeviness even considering the possibility, mostly because of how she dressed. It was like fantasizing about a high school cheerleader.

"We're from Waldport," she said. "You two live in Barnacle Bluffs?"

"That's right," Gage said.

"It's nice that there's an adult nearby. I should get your number if there's ever an emergency."

"Mom," Connor admonished her. "I *am* an adult now."

"Oh, of course sweetie. I just meant an *older* adult. Let me get my purse. I'll give you my card. It's got my work number on it—I'm a massage therapist—but that's really the best way to get ahold of me. You have a cell phone?"

Zoe snickered. "He's morally opposed to them."

"What?" Berry said.

Before Gage could explain, someone shouted *"Connor!"* behind them. It was a familiar voice. They turned and spotted Jeremiah across the parking lot, carrying a giant blue plastic tote. Except for his hair, which was reddish brown and even shorter than the last time Gage had seen him, he could have been Connor's twin. He was dressed in a similar trench coat, complete with buttons, and he was smiling like a kid who'd just come down Christmas morning to piles of presents. That was what surprised Gage the most, the smile, since he couldn't remember Jeremiah *ever* smiling. And certainly not like that, with such pure and unadulterated joy.

Connor replied with a high-wattage smile of his own, lifting his slim hand in a wave.

There were hundreds of people in the parking lot, but it was a private moment shared by just the two of them. It lasted only a second. Carrying a blue tote of his own, dressed in his usual ill-fitting green windbreaker, Arne Cooper stepped next to his son. People often used the expression "cast a shadow over the proceedings," but this was one case when it appeared to be literally true.

Arne, hulking and huge, the kind of man who probably ate school buses for breakfast, towered over his son, and it was a sad thing to watch Jeremiah wilt before their eyes—eyes drooping, shoulders slumping, the smile withering and leaving the same blank mask. Arne stared across the parking lot and met their gaze, zeroing in on Gage. No blank mask on that one. All kinds of fear and hatred flickered across the big man's face before he turned away, nudging his son in the back, prodding him to continue walking. Gage sighed.

"I hear Eugene is beautiful this time of year," he said.

*Chapter 5*

For nearly five years, before Zoe came to live with him, Gage had been comfortable with an empty house. In fact, except for the ten years he'd been married to Janet, he'd spent most of his life alone. He expected to be comfortable with loneliness again, as he always was. It wasn't that he didn't miss people—he still missed Janet so much it ached, a hole that could never be filled—but he knew how to deal with it. He didn't fight loneliness, as so many people did. He simply embraced it. Some, including his dear friend Alex, might even say he wallowed in it.

But this was different. For the first few days after Zoe's departure, he tried to find comfort in his routines. He walked to the little corner grocery down the hill in the morning, picking up the *Oregonian* (and the *Bugle*, if it was out that day), any newsmagazines he hadn't read, and a couple of poppy-seed muffins. Maybe the night's dinner, if he needed it. He worked his way through a crossword puzzle. He read his books, usually history with the occasional novel thrown in for variety. He took a nap. He did some afternoon chores, either projects outside, like fixing the rain gutter or trimming the rhoddies, or indoor cleaning, which he detested. He took an evening walk on the beach and had an early bourbon, varying the order depending on his mood. At night, he usually fell asleep reading in his chair. The weather made little difference in these routines. On the Oregon coast, it could change in the span of five minutes anyway.

That was his life. Sometimes he'd visit Alex at the bookstore, maybe even pick up a couple of Subway sandwiches and have lunch with him. There was the occasional case, of course, but those were few and far between, mostly by his choice. He didn't need to work, either for money or personal satisfaction. The insurance money from Janet's death would take care of him indefinitely as long as he lived frugally, and he knew no other way to live. And personal satisfaction? He'd left the man who needed that back in New York.

So it was with some surprise that none of his old routines worked. Or perhaps *worked* wasn't the right word. They didn't *fit*. There were too many other routines that were now missing. There was no teenage girl to rouse out of bed in the morning, to make breakfast for, or to take to school when she invariably missed the bus—which both of them knew she did on purpose. When she returned, there was no afternoon chat about the stupidity of the American educational system, the small-minded teachers, the classmates who had no other aspirations than getting drunk or laid on a Friday night. No peaceful evenings with him reading the *New Yorker* in his recliner and her doing her homework at the kitchen table. No arguments about getting a phone, a TV, or, his personal favorite, some kind of life for himself.

He'd been aware of these other routines, of course, but he'd thought that he'd simply expand or add in others to replace them, that the rest of his life, which had contracted to make space for Zoe, would expand again in her absence. But now he found that those other routines, the ones involving Zoe, hadn't merely been additions. They'd changed his other routines too. Each piece of his life had been woven inextricably around the other parts of his life like a tight-knit sweater. Remove a few stray threads and the whole thing might unravel.

Little by little, Gage was unraveling. He could feel it. Whether squinting at a crossword or hobbling along the beach, she was almost always in his thoughts, and not in a way others had been, even Janet. He worried about Zoe. While he worried about others, too, it was not the same kind of worry. This was the kind of worry that made him walk out of the grocery store and halfway home before he realized he hadn't bought anything. It was the kind of worry that had him writing the wrong words in the crossword puzzle boxes, even if they didn't fit. It was the kind of worry that made him edgy and depressed and aware of his loneliness in a way that didn't feel comfortable anymore.

He took more walks, to the point where his bad knee throbbed painfully all night long. He hung out at Books and Oddities so much that Alex asked him if he wanted a part-time job. He even played poker a few nights at the casino, something he'd had no interest in since his college days. He drank more bourbon. Nothing worked.

The only thing that gave him a momentary reprieve from his anxiousness was when Zoe visited, which she did more frequently than she probably should have. Once or twice a week, at least, she swung by to say hello in her patched-up Toyota Corolla, to check on him, to see how he was getting along. While this made him feel better in the short term, he felt her absence even more keenly after she left. He wished he could talk to her daily, even for a few minutes. He was so desperate, he even contemplated getting a phone.

A month passed this way. Then another. The sporadic sunny day was replaced with the sporadic overcast day. The rest of the time it rained. It rained all the way into November. It was raining on a Thursday morning when he was sitting in his recliner reading the *Atlantic*, a light rain—hardly more than a gray mist outside his windows, but still a rain—coming down when there was a tapping on his front door.

He hobbled to the front door, his right knee seizing up on him, and peered through the peephole. A woman in jeans and a gray sweatshirt stood on his stoop. It was always difficult to see much through the aged, opaque glass, but he caught a glimpse of olive skin and raven hair and eyes the color of emeralds at the bottom of a pond. There was something familiar about her. When he opened the door, he remembered from where.

"Karen Pantelli," he said.

"Hello, Garrison," she said.

A cool breeze ruffled her short hair; the hair was so wispy and fine that it wouldn't have taken much to ruffle it. The rest of her body was just as wispy, slight of build, small-boned. In the baggy gray sweatshirt, plain and without any logos at all, she could have been mistaken for a boy at first glance—but only at first glance, and only from a distance. Her face was definitely feminine, strikingly feminine, with high cheekbones and full, rich lips. She stood with her hands shoved into the pockets of her jeans. Her tennis shoes, which might have once been white, were gray and worn, coated with sand.

A tan Honda Civic was parked on the far side of the gravel parking lot—or at least it seemed beige at first glance. After studying it a moment, he saw that it might have been white, just caked with three or four layers of dirt and dust.

"Are you on a case?" Gage asked.

"Not this time. I'm on vacation."

"The FBI lets you take vacations?"

Most people would have smiled at this, or at least grinned momentarily, but Karen Pantelli wasn't really one for smiling. However, what she lacked in the language of smiling, she made up for in the extensive vocabulary just in her eyes. They glimmered in amusement, so fast he would have missed it if he'd glanced away, like a tiny ripple in a still lake.

"I would have called first," she said, "but you don't have a phone."

"So people tell me."

"I hope it's okay …"

"Oh, sure. I was just working on my cuticles. You want to come in?"

She nodded. He let her into his house. Fortunately, the place wasn't too much of a disaster, some mail on the kitchen counter, some recently folded clothes on the couch, a little dust here and there, but nothing out of the ordinary for a bachelor. He was even decently presentable himself, dressed in a navy blue polo shirt and faded jeans. He was barefoot, but then it was his house and he hadn't been expecting company.

She stood in the foyer, looking small and uncertain, hands clasped in front of her.

"Last time you were here," he said, "I pulled a gun on you."

"It's okay," she said. "I didn't take it personally."

"Well, that's good. I probably would have. Want some coffee?"

She nodded. While he set to work, she leaned against the counter, watching him. She may not have pulled a gun on him, but those eyes of hers were just about as unnerving as twin riflescopes. The first time he'd met her, after Angela was murdered in Barnacle Bluffs by the God's Wrath cult, he remembered thinking how many suspects must have broken down in the interrogation room under the spell of those eyes. Her partner, a big black man with the height and wingspan of a professional basketball player, might have been the more physically intimidating of the two, but he had nothing on her eyes.

Gage poured the coffee grounds into the filter. Even the smell of the beans, the sharp snap of it, was enough to give him a jolt. "You come all the way to Barnacle Bluffs just for a vacation?"

"No, I'm on a road trip."

"Oh yeah? Where'd you start?"

"Florida."

"Wow, coast to coast. How long have you been—"

"A month."

"A month! The FBI's vacation policy is certainly generous these days."

She nodded again, and this time her eyes took on a distant cast. She looked down. He was almost glad for the reprieve, her gaze was so intense. While he finished getting the coffee started and retrieved some mugs from the cabinet, she traced lazy circles with her finger on one of the white counter tiles. Just when the silence was getting uncomfortable, she started to talk, and it was like the floodgates opened.

"At first, I just wanted to spend some time in Miami," she said, her voice soft and flat, like the tape recording of someone reading turned low. "A couple days in the sun. That sort of thing. Then I thought I might drive over to Atlanta and visit my sister. And after visiting with her, I planned on driving home to Philadelphia, but when I got in the car I started driving west instead. Taking my time. You know, seeing some things. Mount Rushmore. The Grand Canyon. Yellowstone. Even a few days in Disneyland. Then I ended up here. It wasn't really planned."

"You do all that in a rental car?"

"No, I bought the Civic in Atlanta. Was in the market for one anyway. Gets me around."

She turned the mug in small circles on the countertop. A shaft of morning light from the kitchen window reflected off the white porcelain mug and painted a slash of light on the counter. He could tell there was a lot more she wanted to say, but whatever it was, she wasn't saying it now.

"You in town just one day?" Gage asked.

"A couple of days," she said.

"Oh."

"Maybe longer."

"I see."

"I was thinking ... maybe we could, you know, see the sights."

"The sights?"

"The things to see on the Oregon coast. Touristy stuff. If you have time. I mean, I don't want to impose."

"I'm not much of a tour guide," Gage said.

"Okay. It was just an idea."

"It's a good idea. I'm just the wrong guy for it."

"Okay."

More turning of the mug. He filled it with coffee. She took a sip, then turned the mug some more. He caught the muted rumble, outside and down the hill, of an eighteen-wheeler chugging its way up Highway 101. What was he doing? This was a beautiful woman, and he was trying to scare her off? The light wasn't just shining on her coffee mug. It was also shining on the cut of her cheekbone, the sharp angle of it. He was struck with the impulse to reach out and trace his finger along that cheekbone. He imagined her skin felt like slightly polished oak, smooth but still a bit rough, waiting for a few more passes with the sander. She glanced up and saw him looking.

"Well, I should probably go," she said.

"Oh."

"Miles to go, places to see."

"Right."

"Figured I'd head up to the Astoria Column. You ever been there?"

"No, I'm afraid not."

"Heard it's quite a sight. They say it's the best view of the Columbia River."

"I've heard that too."

She held his gaze for a few seconds. In his mind, he jumped in and asked if she wanted to go to lunch. Or dinner. Something. Was he really going to just let her leave like this? Her eyes did this little dancing jig, searching left and right, trying to tease out his thoughts, but he didn't even know his own thoughts. He didn't know what he was doing at all.

"Thanks for the coffee," she said, smiling halfheartedly.

"Sure."

He saw her to the door, doing his best not to hobble. Whenever he *tried* not to hobble, it only seemed to make things worse, giving him a herky-jerky Frankenstein lurch. She reached for his door. Trying to be a gentleman, he reached ahead of her. This brought them much closer together, an intimate level of closeness. He saw tiny freckles on her nose. He saw pebbles of gold in her green eyes. He saw tiny creases in her bottom lip, like wrinkles in red silk.

Their faces were only inches apart. He smiled. He expected a smile in return, a way to break the tension, but instead he suddenly found her lips pressed against his lips, her cold nose pressed against his skin, her hands cupping both sides of his face. The kiss lasted only a few seconds, but it was long enough to set his heart racing, to taste the coffee on her lips, to catch a whiff of the jasmine perfume she was wearing. It was long enough to obliterate all his thoughts.

She pulled away even faster than she'd leaned in, eyes wide, the cool demeanor gone.

"I'm sorry," she said.

"No."

"I shouldn't have done that."

"It's okay. Really."

"I don't know what I was thinking. I can't—I can't believe I did that."

"Karen—"

"It's not like me. I'm sorry. I'm not myself."

She started out the door. He caught her arm. She looked at him, and the woman looking back was not some hardened FBI agent, somebody who'd seen more than her share of life's cruelties, but a naive little girl as fragile as a glass doll. Now that she was looking at him, words failed him. He'd acted on impulse, believing he couldn't let her bolt out of there, but now he didn't know what to say.

They were looking at each other like that when he heard the crunch of gravel at the bottom of his drive, tires spinning, a V-8 engine groaning as it dropped into first. He and Karen stepped away from each other. A blue police cruiser rounded the corner, the sun glaring on the front windshield. The car skidded to a stop and Percy Quinn hopped out, dressed in a blue argyle sweater and charcoal gray slacks. He looked as if he was ready to teach a Sunday-school class rather than run a police department.

"One of these days," Gage said, "I'm going to have to put a security gate at the bottom of my—"

"No time for jokes," Quinn said. "You need to come with me now."

"What?"

"The college. There's been a murder."

The revolution of the earth must have stopped, because there was no other way to explain the terrible lurch in Gage's stomach. "Zoe," he said.

"No. But she found him, and she's asking for you."

"Found who?"

"I'll tell you in the car."

"Who's dead, Chief!"

"A boy named Connor Fleicher."

An image of the boy with the *Star Trek* buttons and the long black bangs flashed through Gage's mind. Jeremiah's friend. "Do they know who—?"

"No. But Gage, it was a small revolver to the chest. Could have been a .38. And Jerry—*Jeremiah*—he's missing."

"Oh no."

For the first time, Quinn noted Karen's presence and did a double take. "You," he said. "My God, the FBI moves fast."

"I'm on vacation," Karen said.

"Lucky for you," Quinn said. "Gage, let's go."

"All right. Let me grab my shoes."

He turned into the house, and this time it was Karen who grabbed his arm. He expected a heartfelt good-bye, maybe another apology, and the look of desperation in her eyes seemed to foreshadow just such a remark—which was why he was so surprised by what she actually said.

"Can I come?"

*Chapter 6*

Sunlight glared on the open highway, lancing off the windshields of the cars that pulled to the side to let them pass. A chalky blue sky stretched overhead, the clouds vaporous and thin, and the ocean, glimpsed between the buildings and in the open stretches, was a mirror image of the sky receding to a dark blue band along the horizon. Gage picked up fragments from the steady stream of voices on Quinn's hand radio, but from the backseat and with the radio's volume turned low, he couldn't make out the words, just the breathless excitement of it all.

A dozen police cruisers, two ambulances, and a fire truck already packed the street and the lawn outside the tan monstrosity of an apartment building. None of the lights were flashing. Yellow police tape cordoned off the area, a wide berth fifty feet around, and three uniformed cops kept an already sizable crowd at bay.

Quinn doubled-parked behind another cruiser. Getting out of the car, cane in hand, Gage noted that the digital clock on the dashboard showed that it was just after ten. Even with the sun showing its face this morning, the dome of Douglas firs surrounding the campus gave the air a cool enough bite that he felt it even through his leather jacket.

"When did this happen?" he asked Quinn.

"I don't know yet," Quinn said. "I got the call five minutes before I stopped at your place. Sometime last night."

"Why isn't the whole campus on lockdown?"

"Just the building is. There hasn't been any sign of a shooter."

Gage wasn't impressed. There shouldn't be a crowd at all. A couple of reporters—a young Asian man and a middle-age woman who bore a striking resemblance to Martha Stewart—shouted questions at Quinn, but he headed straight for the building as if pulled by a magnet. A uniformed cop lifted the tape, and the three of them ducked underneath. There were no TV trucks yet, but Gage guessed that by noon at the latest, if not eleven, both the Portland and Eugene stations would be present. A shooting at a school, whatever the kind, was catnip to the press.

The wet grass squished beneath the soles of Gage's black leather shoes. He was careful where he placed his cane. Karen trailed just behind Gage and Quinn. When Quinn had agreed to let her accompany them, he said it was under the condition that as long as she wasn't acting as a representative of the FBI, she needed to keep her mouth shut. She hadn't said a word since they left Gage's place.

A female police officer in a baseball cap opened the door when they approached the building. She whispered something to Quinn and he nodded. Their shoes squeaked on the tiled entryway. A menagerie of posters greeted them, so many posters that only a few spots of the carpeted blue wall could be seen. Gage heard muffled crying from the hall to his right, and when he looked, he saw two cops leaning into one of the rooms in the middle. The rest of the doors were closed. The narrow hall, the whiff of disinfectant, and the flat, fluorescent lighting gave the building the ambience of an old hospital.

"Officers are going door to door," Quinn said, "checking with the kids and making sure they're okay. Come on, it's on the third floor."

Quinn and Karen double-stepped their way up, prompting Gage to forgo the cane to keep pace. Big mistake. The first flight was painful on Gage's knee, the second flight excruciating torture. The third floor was much like the first, but there were a lot more cops, six of them lining the hall. A couple of male paramedics pushed an empty gurney past them. Gage saw Zoe sitting on a folding chair in the hall, face buried in her hands, her legs pulled up under her baggy black T-shirt. Two detectives in gray trench coats crouched on either side of her.

Brisbane and Trenton. Gage knew them well. Brisbane was short and rumpled, his pale scalp clinging to the last few threads of gray hair like the last leaves on an oak heading into winter. Trenton's stylized swirl of hair appeared blood red under the harsh fluorescent light. Even crouching, Trenton towered over his partner, his knobby knees sticking out at odd angles. Zoe was nodding through her hands while the detectives murmured to her. Seeing this, Gage felt the back of his neck burn.

"You're questioning her without me present?" Gage snapped.

"Gage," Quinn warned.

"It ends now."

Zoe, hearing them, sprang out of her chair and threw herself into Gage's arms. Pink cotton pajama bottoms, cut off at the knees, jutted out of the bottom of her black T-shirt. She was barefoot, her toenails painted black. They weren't the hugging type, either of them, but this one felt good. She pressed the side of her face against his leather jacket.

"It's—it's awful—" she stuttered.

"It's okay," he said.

"Walked—walked in—"

"We don't have to talk about it now."

She started crying. That, for Zoe, was even more shocking than the hug. He patted her back and waited for the storm to pass. Quinn joined Brisbane and Trenton outside the open door, conferring momentarily before all three stepped into the room.

Zoe, sniffling, wiped at her eyes. Her black mascara—something he thought she'd given up months ago—smeared at the corners, leaking down the sides of her face. Standing behind him, Karen produced a tissue from her pocket and handed it to Zoe, who accepted it gratefully.

"Thanks," Zoe said.

"No worries," Karen said.

"You look kinda familiar," Zoe said.

"This is Karen Pantelli," Gage said. "You may remember her from when she was here a year ago. She works for the FBI, though she's on vacation. Now, tell me exactly what happened."

"I just walked in and there he was," Zoe said. "All that blood."

"This morning?"

"About—about an hour ago."

"Easy."

She took a deep, shuddering breath. "Once in while the three of us go to breakfast at the cafeteria. I knocked—knocked on his door, and that's when I saw it was just slightly open. I said his name and he didn't answer. I opened—opened it—and—and—"

"All right," Gage said, patting her shoulder, "let's hold off on the rest. Will you be okay for a few minutes?"

There was a bit of reluctance to her nod, but it would have to do. Leaving her leaning against the wall, he and Karen stepped into the open dorm room. He saw the kid, Connor, right away, seated in a beige office chair at the little built-in desk by the window—or a chair that might have once been beige, because there was so much blood trailing down the backside that it was hard to tell.

Naked from the waist up, Connor's bony back was streaked with blood. He still sat upright, though his chin rested on his chest. The bullet hole was a messy smear in the middle of all that black hair. The blood was contained to the one little corner of the room, but there was a lot of it—and other bits, too, orange and white stuff that could have been flesh or bone. Red splatters coated the huge computer monitor, the black drapes decorated with stars, and the yellow-pine desk. Judging by the putrid stink, his bowels had let go of their contents into his *Star Wars* pajama bottoms.

With Quinn, Trenton, and Brisbane, plus two uniformed cops already in the room, the addition of Gage and Karen made for a tight fit. Gathered as they were near the door, elbow to elbow, it was as if they'd paid twenty-five cents for a peep show at a carnival.

"Nobody touch anything," Quinn said. "We're waiting for the forensic team out of Newport."

"Joys of a small town," Gage said.

"Save the jokes, pal."

"He didn't die right away," Gage said, and he felt a twist in his gut at the thought of Connor's final moments of agony. "His heart went on pumping. Otherwise there wouldn't have been so much blood."

Trenton, his red hair nearly scraping the low ceiling, snorted. "What are you, CSI Barnacle Bluffs?"

"He's right," Karen said. "And judging by the way some of the blood has already dried, this happened fairly early last night."

"You his partner now?" Trenton snapped. "The FBI doing cutbacks?"

"Just traveling through," Karen said.

Gage surveyed the room. He figured he had only a few seconds before Quinn realized there was no reason Gage and Karen should be there. Posters from various science-fiction shows—*Battlestar Galactica, Doctor Who,* and the like—decorated the walls. *Red Dwarf?* He'd never heard of that one. Models of *Star Trek* and *Star Wars* ships hung from the ceiling on white thread. Except for a single-person bed, which was a twisted mess of white sheets with a plain brown bedspread bunched at the bottom, the room was neat and tidy. It was *impressively* neat and tidy, considering how packed it was with books—both textbooks and paperbacks, all of them shelved neatly on the homemade bookshelves that had been constructed out of cinder blocks and unfinished pine. A small entertainment center—old boxy TV on top, stacks of DVDs beneath—along with the white mini fridge somehow also fit into the room.

"Kid never saw it coming," Gage said.

"Brilliant observation," Trenton said. "Unless he had eyes in the back of his head, that would have been tough."

"Don't you have some traffic tickets to give out?" Gage said.

Quinn sighed and leveled a finger at Gage and Karen. "All right, you two need to get the hell out of here. You can stay with Zoe until we're finished talking to her."

"Not without a lawyer present, you won't," Gage said.

"What the hell, Gage, she's not even a suspect."

"Yeah, that's what you say now. But if she was the first to find Connor, then I know what that means."

"Fine," Quinn said. "Take her home. If I need her, I'll call her down to the station and you can bring your damn law—"

He was interrupted by a burst of static on his radio, followed by a breathless, high-pitched squawk: *"Chief! We have him—in the cafeteria! Come quick! He's … he's got a gun!"*

Quinn, eyes flaring wide, brought the radio to his mouth, but Gage was already on the move. There was only one *him* it could be. Jeremiah Cooper. It wasn't until he heard the radio that Gage realized that this was the one person they all should have been asking about and yet nobody had. Brisbane shouted after Gage, but Gage knew how all this would play out unless someone intervened.

On his way past, he told Zoe to wait right there. By the time she asked where he was going, Gage was skidding down the stairwell, gritting his teeth at the needlepoint pain shooting through his knee. Karen followed close behind, then Brisbane and Trenton, then Quinn, all of them bursting through the door and onto the grass.

Gage, not knowing the campus at all, was at a loss at which way to go, and before he could decide, Quinn grabbed his arm.

"No way," he said.

"But I know Jeremiah," Gage said.

"Stay out of this!"

Quinn and his two detectives sprinted toward an equally ugly tan slab of a building on the other side of the lawn, shadowed by two giant oaks whose leaves were in the crimson throes of fall. Four uniformed cops, weapons drawn, gathered outside the double-glass doors. People clad in Birkenstocks and blue jeans, students and faculty alike, rubbernecked from the sidewalk, another two uniformed cops keeping them at bay.

"Probably not a good idea," Karen said.

"It's never stopped me before."

"Gage—"

Without a backward glance, he hustled for the cafeteria, holding his cane like a relay baton. His creaky knee would hold. It always did. The sun, breaking through the oaks and the firs, streaked the still-damp grass like the bars of a xylophone. Pressing through the crowd of onlookers, a female cop shouted at him to get back, but he waved her off and joined Quinn and the detectives outside the front door. They all had their guns drawn. Gage didn't even have a gun. He'd left his Beretta at home.

"Gage," Quinn said, "I thought I told you—"

Before anyone could stop him, he yanked open the door and slipped into the building.

He took in the hall at a glance: a checkered black-and-white tile floor, flyers tacked to bulletin boards, an old-fashioned reader board with stick-on letters spelling out the meals for the day. Two doughy-faced male cops, both young enough that they could still have been in high school, flanked a set of swinging doors just to the left. Backs leaning against the wall, Glocks raised, they looked wide-eyed and far too trigger-happy. They turned and gaped at him with the panic of small-town cops whose training hadn't prepared them for this.

"He's inside," one of them said. "There's—there's kids in there."

Gage heard wet soles squeaking on the tiles behind him and the rustle of clothes. Before the two cops could truly realize that Gage didn't belong, he grabbed the door handles and swung them open far enough that he flitted through the crack like a snake.

No thinking. No debate. If he stopped to consider what he was doing, he knew he wouldn't do it.

It was a cavernous room with a dozen circular tables, about a third filled with students with their faces on the table and their hands cupped behind their heads. He caught a whiff of bacon and maple syrup. A girl in the corner was crying, but otherwise nobody made a sound. Jeremiah sat cross-legged on an empty table in the middle of the room, the revolver pointed directly under his own chin. The .38 Smith & Wesson. Hair messy, chin bearing a patch of beard, he looked straight at Gage without acknowledging him. A blank stare. A dead stare.

Hands raised, Gage approached. Jeremiah's Superman pajama bottoms were frayed at the knees, and his white sleeveless undershirt was so tight, Gage could see his rib cage. His shoulder blades stuck out like butter knives pressing through white sheets. At a nearby table, a big guy in a Broncos jersey whimpered. A second girl joined the girl in the corner who was crying. Ten paces away, Jeremiah finally spoke in a thick quaver.

"D-d-don't," he said.

"Jeremiah," Gage said.

"I'm going—I'm going to do it."

"Jeremiah Cooper, I just want to talk to you."

In response, Jeremiah gritted his teeth and jabbed the Smith & Wesson harder against his chin. He closed his eyes. The revolver looked enormous in his little hand, comically large, like something out of a cartoon. Up close, Gage saw the rawness of his cheeks, the pink around the eyes, the tracks on the skin where the tears had dried.

"Killing yourself won't bring him back," Gage said. "And it will make a lot of people very sad, including me. Zoe. Your parents."

"I want to die."

"Put the gun down."

"Good-bye."

*"Stop!"*

Gage's shout had the intended effect: it shocked Jeremiah out of whatever detonation sequence was programmed into his brain, prompting him to open his eyes and look at Gage. The gun was still pointed at his chin, his finger was still on the trigger, but he was *present*. He was looking at Gage, and he was actually fully in the room. It was the window Gage was waiting for.

"I didn't think you were so selfish," Gage said.

Jeremiah blinked a few times. "What?"

"You really want to do this to all these people?"

"I don't—I don't understand—"

Gage motioned to the kids cowering at the tables, and as his hand swept across them, many hunkered even lower in their seats. "Look at them, Jeremiah! You really want them to watch you blow your brains out? You want that image in their minds for the rest of their lives? Do you know how that's going to affect them?"

"This isn't … about them. I'm not—not going to hurt them."

"But you are! You're going to scar these people for the rest of their lives. Is that what you want?"

Jeremiah relaxed his grip on the revolver a tiny bit. "They don't care. They don't care about me."

"You want to kill yourself? Fine. But not here. Not like this, in front of all these innocent kids. People deserve to know the truth, Jeremiah. And you can tell us what happened. You can explain. Doesn't Connor deserve that, at least? His mother?"

Something in what he said opened the floodgates, and the tears started to roll. "I don't know if I can do it," Jeremiah said.

"You can do it."

"I didn't—didn't want this."

"I know," Gage said. "Jeremiah, just put down the gun. Put down the gun and let's talk about it."

Jeremiah blinked through his tears. They stood like that, the two of them, suspended in place and time, an unnatural stillness pervading the room until somewhere off in the kitchen, behind the stainless-steel buffet table and around a brick divider, a dish clinked. An Asian girl three tables away moaned.

Something had to give. Hands still held aloft, Gage took a step forward, a small step but big enough that Jeremiah noticed. Gage wanted him to notice. He wanted him to see.

"I—I don't know if—" Jeremiah said.

"There's a better way out of this," Gage said. He took another step.

"I need—need some time."

"You'll have all the time you need." Another step.

"Please. Please, don't."

"Jeremiah, give me the gun."

"Please."

"It's all right," Gage said, hand reaching.

"I—I—don't—"

Then Gage was there, his hand on the boy's gun hand. The skin was cool and clammy and, at Gage's touch, trembled violently. Without even touching the revolver itself, Gage eased Jeremiah's gun hand away from his chin and to the side, down, so it pointed at the center of the table.

It was as if a plug had been pulled. All that coiled-up rage and grief inside Jeremiah drained in a second. He bowed his head and sobbed, releasing the revolver into Gage's grasp.

There was a commotion behind them, the doors swinging open, the scuff and squeak of boots on the tiles, the rush of many footsteps. This triggered a second wave of pandemonium as the quivering students suddenly let loose with all their pent-up fear—shouting, screaming, crying, laughing, even some applause, people rising from their seats, chairs knocking over, the rush of many bodies.

When Jeremiah mumbled something, it would have been lost in the cacophony of noise if Gage hadn't been standing so close.

"I—I didn't shoot him," Jeremiah said.

Then the police descended, a swarm of bulletproof vests and handguns.

*Chapter 7*

The first decision out of the president's office was to cancel classes for Friday. Emails and calls went out. Flyers were placed around the BBCC campus. "This was a time to seek solace and comfort from those we loved and who loved us." That was an actual line from President Higham's letter. It was only a few hours after that email that a second went out declaring that classes would be canceled the following week as well. Not only was an investigation being conducted by the police, but the school would be doing its own internal review to make certain it was doing all it could to prevent these kinds of tragedies.

Not being equipped with phone or email, Gage heard none of this. The first he heard about it was from Zoe. Later that night, the clock on the wall edging close to midnight, the two of them hunkered down in the living room in their usual places: Gage in his leather recliner, eyelids growing heavy, both the *New York Times* and the *Wall Street Journal* in his lap; Zoe stretched out on the couch, earbuds in, eyes closed and hands folded on her stomach.

They hadn't spoken in hours, not after he'd asked, for perhaps the twentieth time, if she was okay. She'd finally snapped that if he would just stop asking, she *would* be okay. The garlic-chicken pizza and Diet Pepsi were devoured with only the conversation of the wind. He was working up to a way to ask her a twenty-first time when she lifted her phone, did a little of that magic finger swiping, and announced in a deadpan voice what the various communications from President Higham had said.

"Probably for the best," Gage said.

"Yeah, whatever," Zoe said. "Wasn't like I was going back anyway."

"What's that supposed to mean?"

Still wearing the earbuds, she closed her eyes and tapped her fingers in time to the beat of music he couldn't hear.

"Zoe," he said.

Her only response was to deepen her frown.

"Zoe," he said, "come on, let's have a conversation about this."

The frown deepened, but after a few stilted seconds, she finally removed her earbuds and raised her eyebrows at him. They were eyebrows, he noticed, that had recently been plucked to a thin line, something she had repeatedly said she would never do. She was still dressed in a black T-shirt and black jeans, but the more natural hair color, the trimmed eyebrows, and the lack of facial adornment were all subtle changes that had the overall effect of producing a Zoe who wasn't standing out from the crowd in such a bold way.

He motioned for her to sit up. With an exasperated sigh, she did, though her frown was now approaching world-record territory.

"What?" she said.

"I'd just like to have your full attention for a minute."

"Fine, you got it. What? And don't ask me if I'm all right again or I'm going to break a window."

Gage folded the newspapers and dropped them on the floor next to the recliner. "I just want to know what you meant when you said you weren't going back."

"What, was I speaking Spanish or something?" Zoe said. "Means just want I said. I'm not going back to school. *Finito.*"

"You mean, you're not going back to *that* school."

"No, I mean I'm not going back to school at all. I don't see the point."

"Zoe—"

"I'll get a job in a coffee shop or something. Or maybe I'll learn how to blow glass. That seems to really be the thing on the Oregon coast."

"I see."

"Or maybe I'll work at the movie theater."

"Okay."

"Or maybe I'll see if Alex needs some help again in his bookshop. He seemed to like having me around in the summer."

"It's possible," Gage said. "But let me ask you one thing. Do you really have to make this decision now?"

"It's made," Zoe said. "School's not for me."

"You got nearly straight A's and perfect scores on your SAT, and school's not for you?"

"That crap doesn't mean anything."

"I'm just saying, maybe you should just see how you feel in a week. You have some time to think about this. To deal with what happened."

"This has nothing—"

"Maybe talk to someone. A therapist maybe."

"No way!"

"Zoe, I'm just saying—"

"I don't need some batty bimbo with a master's degree telling me how to live my life." Her eyes quivered, and a shock of pink appeared in her cheeks. "I've been there. Done that. Never helped. I'm better off dealing with stuff on my own."

Gage sighed. "You witnessed something pretty awful. It might help to talk to someone with training in this sort of the thing."

"Oh yeah? Then why didn't you see a therapist after Janet died?"

"This isn't about me."

"You didn't answer my question."

"It was probably a mistake. I should have talked to someone."

"Liar. You just like dealing with your crap on your own."

"Hey," Gage said, "you really want to use me as a model on how to deal with tragedy? Come on, you can do better than me.

Just because I have perfected the art of screwing up my life doesn't mean you have to follow in my footsteps."

"I'm *not* going back to school," Zoe insisted, enunciating each word in a brittle voice. "Never. Never. Never."

"Fine," Gage said. "You think that would make Connor happy?"

"What?"

"Or Jeremiah? You think that's what they'd want for you?"

"I don't believe this!"

"I'm just trying to get through to you!"

"No, you're being an asshole!" She leapt to her feet, pointed a finger at him as if to say something, then marched toward her room—before spinning around violently and marching straight back. "I just saw someone I care about shot in the head! And on top of that—on top of *that*, they just arrested my best friend because they think he did it! What is some therapist going to say? These things happen? Come on!"

"Usually therapists do more listening than talking."

"Yeah, well, I got plenty of friends for that."

"Lucky you. I've never been good at making friends." She didn't laugh. He didn't really expect her to, but it would have been an encouraging sign. "Hold on a second. You said *they think* he did it. Are you telling me you don't?"

She glared at him like a bull staring down a rodeo clown who'd just jumped out of the ring. "I don't know," she said.

"You think he's innocent?"

"No. Maybe. I don't know."

"Zoe, do you know something about Jeremiah? Something you're not telling me?"

"I don't know anything. I just—I don't think Jeremiah could do that. Not to Connor. They spent all their time together."

"Did they spend much time together before they started going to BBCC?"

"What, you doing your detective thing or something?" When he didn't answer, she closed her eyes and rubbed her temples. "I'm really tired, Garrison. I just want to lie down. Sleep this off.

Maybe I'll—maybe I'll feel a little better in the morning."

"Sure," Gage said, "but I'm pretty sure you'll be talking about it to Brisbane and Trenton tomorrow. Figure you might want to talk it through with me first."

"I just told you I don't know anything."

"You probably know more about those two than anybody else, right?"

"I guess."

"Then they're going to have a lot of questions for you. I'm just saying you might want to be ready."

Groaning, Zoe plopped herself onto the couch. She trained that deep frown of hers on the floor for a few seconds before abruptly looking up at him.

"Wait a second," Zoe said. "You think he's innocent, too, don't you?"

"I didn't say I—"

"Come on, what did you see? You go all Sherlock Homes and spot a clue that proves he didn't do it?"

"Nothing like that."

"Then what?"

"He told me."

"He *what?*"

"He told me he's innocent. I kind of believe him."

"He *told* you? He just told you he's innocent and you believe him?"

"I said 'kind of.' I'm not sure either way."

Zoe shook her head. "What if it comes back that the gun he was holding was the one that shot Connor?"

"It does look like the same Smith & Wesson."

"But you still think he might be innocent?"

"Innocent until proven guilty," Gage said. "Let me ask you this. You said they spent all their time together. What did you mean?"

"I mean, they were hanging out so much I barely saw them. Watching *Star Trek*, playing those card games, Magic and whatever. PlayStation. Only time I really saw them was in the cafeteria or in astronomy class. That's the one we all had together. The rest of the time ..." She shrugged. "I was kind of sad not seeing Jeremiah much, but also kind of happy for him, I guess. He finally had a good friend."

"He seemed like he really needed that," Gage said.

"Yeah."

"Let me ask you something else. It's a bit of an awkward question, but I won't be the only one to ask. Do you have any reason to think they were lovers?"

The dozing Zoe whip-snapped to a hard glare faster than if he'd pricked her with a needle. "Why is that awkward?"

"I just meant—"

"It's not awkward for *me*. Is it awkward for *you?*"

"No."

"Are you sure? Why don't you just come out and ask if they were homosexuals? Do you have a problem with the word *homosexual?*"

"I don't have a problem with that word."

"Homosexual."

"Right."

"You don't want to say it. Come on, just say it."

"Zoe—"

"Say it, say it."

"Fine, homosexual. What's the big deal?

She grinned. "How about gay? Can you say that? Or queer?"

"Zoe—"

"Faggot? That's a nasty one, right? I bet you don't want to say that."

Her grin was more like a leer now. Gage folded his hands in his lap and waited. This wasn't about him. He could see that, even if he couldn't deny that she was at least partly right, that he *did* have a problem saying the word *homosexual*. And the other ones. It embarrassed him, not the intellectual idea of it, but his own response. There was some revulsion. He wanted to think of himself as an enlightened person—open-minded, fair, not tied down by dogma or small-mindedness. But there was some raw emotional response that betrayed his lofty ideals, and Zoe had homed in on it like a bee to honey.

"I'm not perfect," Gage said. "I may have lived in New York for years, but I'm just a Montana boy at heart. But I am trying, Zoe. Cut me some slack, okay?"

She went on leering, an expression so twisted it turned his stomach, then, abruptly, the curtain was pulled away. The play was over. She blinked rapidly. He saw something raw and exposed that she'd been doing her best to keep buried.

"Oh shit," she said.

"It's all right."

"He's dead."

"I know."

"All that ... all that blood ..."

He went to her, an awkward pivot on his awkward knee, and sat next to her on the couch, putting an arm around her and holding her close. There weren't that many tears. When she stopped, he took his arm away and they sat like that, quiet, listening to the hum of the fridge in the kitchen.

"I'm tired," she said.

"It's been a long day."

"But I don't know if I can sleep."

"Me either," Gage said. "Probably still a good idea to try, though. Tomorrow will be another long day."

"Yeah."

With a sigh, she rose languidly from the couch. She started for the hall, then stopped and turned back. It may have been his imagination, or just the slump of her shoulders, but she seemed shorter somehow. How much could life throw at this girl? After the past couple of years, it was amazing she was still standing at all.

"There *is* something you should know," she said.

"What's that?"

"I asked him once. You know, if he was gay. Jeremiah."

"And what did he tell you?"

Zoe made a face as if she'd eaten something unpleasant and

was trying to keep it down. "I probably shouldn't have done it. It's just ... he was having so many problems. With some kids at school. With his parents. I thought maybe, you know, if he just kind of got some stuff out in the open ..."

"What did he say?"

"He got real angry. He denied it. He said he liked girls. I asked him why he never asked me out, then, and he got even angrier. Like *real* angry—screaming and punching-the-wall kind of thing. It freaked me out, so I got out of there. He called me later crying and apologized and stuff. Told me he'd never asked me out because we had such a good friendship. That sort of thing. I could tell it was a lot of bullshit, but I wasn't going to push it anymore."

"So you think he *was* gay, but he was repressing it?"

"Yeah. Big-time."

"And do you think Connor was gay?"

Zoe shrugged. "I don't know. I didn't know him well enough. But maybe, yeah. Probably. And I've been thinking ... if Jeremiah got that angry just when I asked him if he was gay, what would he do if ..." She trailed off, shaking her head.

"If Connor made a pass at him?" Gage asked.

"Yeah," Zoe said. "What if Connor tried to, you know, kiss Jeremiah or something? Or told him how he felt? Do you think he ... do you think he could ...?"

"It's possible," Gage said.

"That wouldn't make him innocent."

"No, it wouldn't."

"I *want* to believe he's innocent."

"Me too."

*Chapter 8*

**F**riday morning, after restless sleep and a meager breakfast of toast and coffee, Gage and Zoe headed for the police station. It was Zoe's idea. Why wait around all day for the cops to eventually get around to swinging by the house? Gage debated calling a lawyer he knew in town but decided it was an unnecessary complication at this point. He'd wait to see the direction the questions took.

The sky over the two-lane highway was the kind of soppy, biscuits-and-gravy gray that he'd come to expect from Novembers in Barnacle Bluffs, far more the norm than the previous day's sunny weather. Tiny droplets beaded the front window, the air so thick that yellow halos surrounded the headlights of the oncoming cars. His old Volkswagen van, purchased shortly after he'd arrived in town seven years earlier, grumbled and groaned the whole way to the station, always seemingly on the verge of giving up the ghost for good but never quite doing so.

Giving up the ghost for good. It was how Gage felt most days, which was probably why he refused to get something better even though everyone insisted he should. *Especially* because everyone insisted he should. That was always the way with him. The more people wanted him to do something, the more he wanted to do the opposite.

A few minutes later, they parked outside the police station, a small building by Big Dipper Lake that looked like somebody had retrofitted a ranch house rather than built it from scratch.

"Is Jeremiah here?" Zoe asked.

"Most likely in one of the holding cells," Gage said, "until he's transferred to the county lockup in a week or so."

"You think they'd let us see him?"

"I don't think we should ask."

"He's probably scared shitless."

"Probably."

"Even just for a few—"

"No, Zoe. Not right now."

She frowned but didn't protest further. After stepping into a bustling reception area, they were ushered into a windowless questioning room where a large gray metal table had been bolted to the floor. They sat in the plastic chairs and didn't even have time to tap their thumbs before the door opened and Quinn entered, two paper cups of coffee in hand. Brisbane and Trenton followed.

"Got some bad coffee for you," Quinn said.

"My favorite," Gage said. "This must be a big deal. We're getting the big boss himself and not just his henchmen."

"Watch who you're calling henchmen," Trenton snapped.

Zoe's expression was already flat; she was somewhere else. As everyone settled into their seats, Gage noticed a red nick on Quinn's neck where he'd cut himself and saw that he'd missed a button on his plaid shirt. The bags under Brisbane's eyes, always dark, were even darker, big enough to store nuts in for the winter. Trenton, on the other hand, looked even sharper and snappier than usual—and taller, too, if that were possible, his back as straight as the wall, chin jutting out like a proud man facing a firing squad.

"I'm sorry to drag you down here, Zoe," Quinn said, and he did sound legitimately sad. Other than Gage, nobody knew more about what Zoe had gone through in the past few years than Quinn. "We just have a few questions, then we'll let you go."

She didn't answer. Quinn looked at Gage for guidance, and he could only shrug. He didn't think she was particularly nervous; there were just a lot of bad memories associated with cops. Even in her previous life, before she'd come to live in Barnacle Bluffs, she must have had some encounters with law enforcement, her parents being drug addicts. It was a small miracle she could speak at all, which was, when it came down to it, how Gage summed up what he thought about Zoe in total. A small miracle.

"Let's start with how well you know both these boys," Quinn said. "Just tell us the nature of your relationships with them."

"We were all just friends."

"I see."

She glared at the chief as if expecting a challenge. He didn't, smiling his Mr. Rogers smile. Gage tried his coffee. It was cold and bitter. After a moment's pause, Zoe started to talk, haltingly at first, then smoother, telling the cops much of what they'd discussed the previous night—minus one significant detail. She didn't say anything about Jeremiah's freak-out about possibly being gay. Quinn, however, zeroed right in on the omission like a buzzard spotting fresh roadkill.

"I appreciate the information," Quinn said. "Do you have any reason to believe the two of them exhibited homosexual tendencies?"

"Homosexual tendencies?" Zoe said.

"Do you think two of the two of them were, well, more than friends?"

"They were both members of the official *Star Trek* fan club. Is that what you mean?"

Gage couldn't help but chuckle at that, and both Brisbane and Trenton shot him a dirty look. Quinn, on the other hand, merely smiled thinly.

"Come on now," Quinn said. "Don't make this hard for us here. You know what I'm talking about."

"No, I really don't. I'm just a small-town Christian girl. I don't know about all this sexual-tendency stuff."

"Right," Trenton said, "you with the nose stud and the dark

eye shadow. You've got small-town girl written all over you."

"And you've got homosexual tendencies written all over you," Zoe shot back.

"Oh boy," Gage said.

Trenton, with his pale Irish complexion, turned red as fast as a traffic light. It may just have been wishful thinking on Gage's part, but he thought he detected the glimmerings of a smile from Quinn, who raised his arm in front of Trenton as if to restrain him.

"Hold on, we're all friends here," Quinn said.

"We're not friends," Zoe said. "When have cops *ever* been my friends? You've done nothing for me."

"Don't we all want the same thing?" Quinn said. "We just want to find out what happened that night. I'm just asking for a little cooperation, that's all."

"I *am* cooperating," Zoe said.

"Okay. How about doing it without the attitude?"

Gage had heard enough. "How about you just ask the questions and forget about lecturing Zoe, okay? Or maybe it's time for us to call a lawyer."

"There's no need for that," Quinn said.

"This whole thing is a waste of time," Trenton said. "Anybody doubt ballistics will nail that kid to the cross? We caught him with the gun in his hand!"

"Hold on," Quinn said.

"How about we ask a few questions?" Gage said. "A little tit for tat here. You have any witnesses that heard the gunshot?"

"Unfortunately not," Quinn said.

"Hard to believe."

"A lot of people playing loud music yesterday—including Connor Fleicher, apparently, while he was working on the computer. Many people used to complain about him."

"It's true," Zoe said. "Connor used to like to play movie theme songs really loud. Like *Indiana Jones*, that sort of thing."

"You nail down a time of death?" Gage asked.

Brisbane, who'd silently watched the whole conversation as

if he were tied to his chair, now shook his head and grumbled, "I don't know why we should answer any of his questions. We're just inviting trouble."

"I'm just telling him things he'll find out soon enough anyway," Quinn said to him. Then, turning back to Gage, he added, "The ME estimates the time of death at about 4 a.m. Thursday morning. The guess is that he was shot an hour earlier and basically bled to death."

"Jesus," Zoe said.

"When was the last time anybody saw Connor or Jeremiah?" Gage asked.

"We're working on that now," Quinn said.

Gage nodded his head at Brisbane and Trenton. "With who? You got Barnacle Bluffs' finest sitting in this room."

"I don't like the way he said finest," Brisbane muttered.

"Me either," Trenton said.

Quinn drummed his fingers on the table, nails tapping on the metal. He looked at Zoe. He looked at Gage again. "Either of you know anything else that could help us?"

"Not really," Zoe said.

"And where were you, again, before you found Connor?"

"I told you. I'd just come from the library. I sometimes like to study early in the morning before breakfast."

"You talk to anybody there?"

"Not really. But I did check out a book."

"Which book?"

"What?"

"Which book? What did you check out?"

Zoe shook her head. "I don't know. I don't remember. What does that have to do with anything?"

"Maybe nothing," Quinn said. "You don't remember it?"

"No. If you haven't noticed, a lot has happened since then."

"I've noticed. But would it happen to be a book called *Dealing with Loss?*"

"Hold on," Gage said. "I'm not liking the tone here. Where are you going with this?"

"Don't know," Quinn said. "I just thought that was a curious book to check out on the same day Connor Fleicher was murdered."

"You searched her room without a warrant?"

"Didn't need to," Quinn said. "The girl working the counter at the library remembered Zoe checking out the book. They even had a conversation about it. You remember the conversation, Zoe?"

"Don't answer," Gage said. And then, to Quinn, he said, "If you guys have any more questions, we'll schedule a time and have a lawyer present."

Trenton chuckled. "Looks like somebody's got something to hide."

"I have *nothing* to hide," Zoe said. "I've told you—"

Gage held up his hand, silencing Zoe. He rose, and Zoe, somewhat reluctantly, rose with him. Quinn crossed his arms and leaned back in his chair. The two detectives tried to melt Gage with their eyes.

"She's *not* a suspect," Quinn said.

"You're certainly acting like it," Gage said.

"Let's just call her a person of interest."

"We done?"

"Gage, we all want the same thing here. I know Zoe couldn't have done it because the security cameras at the library verify what she's told me. I just think she knows more about these two boys than she's letting on, that's all."

"You already have the security footage?" Gage said. "That was fast."

"The college is being *very* cooperative," Quinn said.

"What about the security cameras at the dorm?"

"Oh!" Trenton chirped in. "Now look who's asking questions again!"

"Didn't have them," Quinn said, ignoring his detective. "Apparently the student association had privacy concerns about ten years ago, so they were removed. One last question. Zoe, you can refuse to answer if that's your prerogative, but I have to ask. Is there anything you know, anything you're not telling us, that would explain why Jeremiah Cooper might shoot Connor Fleicher?"

"You don't—" Gage began.

"No," Zoe said.

"You're sure?" Quinn said.

"He's not a killer," Zoe said.

"Not the jealous type?"

"What would he have to be jealous of? They were best friends!"

"All right, we're done," Gage said, taking her arm and leading her to the door. "Any more questions, it's with an attorney present."

Zoe looked like she wanted to get a few words in, but Gage hustled her out the door. The chief and the detectives followed him, past the carpeted cubicles and the chirping phones and the faux oak end tables weighed down by stacks of two-year-old magazines. When Gage was at the front reception area, Quinn called out to him.

"One last thing," he said.

Zoe turned, but Gage prodded her through the front door. Only when there was a wall of glass between her and Quinn did Gage turn and raise his eyebrows in response. Quinn, without his detectives now, leaned with his elbows on the front counter, looking all the world like a small-town sheriff watching a couple of hooligans walk out of his favorite saloon.

"I have a minor request," Quinn said.

And that is?"

"Promise me you'll stay out of this one."

"*Promise* you?"

"Just tell me you won't go snooping around where you don't belong."

"And what fun would that be?"

Quinn sighed. "Somehow I knew you'd say that."

* * *

71

* * *

WHEN GAGE TRIED to talk to Zoe at the house, she grumbled that she needed to be alone. As she shuffled off to her room, he told her he was going to get some groceries and asked if she wanted anything. All he got in response was a slammed door, then, a few seconds later, her stereo cranked up so loud it made the Monet print on the wall vibrate. He waited a few minutes, debating whether he should really leave her alone, but decided they'd only fight if he stayed. He didn't know exactly *why* she was mad at him, but he guessed it had something to do with the way he hustled her out of the police station without giving her a chance to ask if she could see Jeremiah.

His own mental state wasn't much better. It was true that his cupboards were getting pretty bare, but that could wait. The sun, a pale dot, was like a thumbnail pushing through a hole in a gray wool sock. Books and Oddities didn't open until ten, still a half hour away, but when Gage turned the van into the gravel parking lot of Horseshoe Mall, he saw that the red neon Open sign in the front window was already aglow. Gunderson's, the antique store, was also open, but the other dozen shops in the U-shaped outdoor mall were still dark.

There were a handful of cars in the parking lot, but one caught his eye—a Honda Civic so caked with grime, it looked tan instead of white.

His heart did a little skip. He walked across the creaky covered boardwalk in front of the stores, feeling the morning breeze blow damp and cool on his cane hand. When he entered the shop, the bell over the door ringing, he didn't find anyone at the counter. The musty smell of old books greeted Gage like an old friend. Two mugs of coffee were perched on the glass countertop. He heard the murmur of voices somewhere in the stacks, tightly packed rows of pine bookshelves so tall they nearly touched the buzzing fluorescent lights. Gage leaned his cane against the counter.

"Alex?" he said.

"You bring me donuts this morning?" Alex called over the stacks.

"Sorry," Gage said.

Alex emerged from the stacks with a yellow trade paperback in hand, Karen a few steps behind. She smiled at him, her eyes possessing a glimmer they hadn't had the previous day, a spark of life that had been missing. Her tight black turtleneck shirt and hip-hugging jeans revealed an athletic figure that had been hidden by yesterday's baggy sweatshirt. This, of course, made the perpetually frumpy Alex seem even frumpier by comparison.

"I can't believe you didn't bring donuts," Alex said.

"I'm trying to watch my weight."

"Liar."

"Hey! I've gained at least ten pounds lately. Too many cheeseburgers."

"My friend," Alex said, "I doubt you've gained ten pounds since your twenties. Remember, I was *there* when you were in your twenties. You may have a bit more gray hair, but otherwise you look pretty much like you did when you walked into the FBI academy."

This got Karen to raise her eyebrows. "I didn't know Garrison was one of your students."

"In fact," Gage said, "he was the one who kicked me out."

"I did no such thing," Alex said. He took a sip from his coffee, then wrinkled his nose. "No donuts and cold coffee. If it wasn't for this lovely lady stopping by to chat, I'd probably give up and call it a day."

"If I had realized how much donuts would mean to you today, I would have brought you three dozen. Maybe even four."

"Remember that next time. Donuts *always* mean a lot to me. And anyway, to get back to the topic at hand, I distinctly remember you leaving Virginia of your own free will. Nobody kicked you out."

"But you did *ask* me to leave."

"I *asked* you to think about whether you were the type of person who could really operate effectively inside a highly structured organization like the Federal Bureau of Investigation. Your … approach to authority seemed to be at odds with what was required of a special agent."

"That's a nice way of saying I don't take orders well."

"That's a nice way of saying you work very well independently. And *furthermore*," Alex continued, raising his finger to stop Gage from interjecting, "this particular personality trait of yours was the *only* reason I asked you to consider your options. I happen to also recall that you were at the top of your class in just about everything that really mattered. Marksmanship. Defensive tactics."

"Well …"

"When you actually took a test, you usually aced it. Even in something like communication studies. I found that one a little ironic." Alex winked at Karen. "The problem with Gage was—and still is, really—if he couldn't see the reason for doing something, he just didn't do it. Always had to walk to the beat of his own drummer. Doesn't always work in the FBI, does it, Karen?"

"You leave her out of this," Gage said. "She's just an innocent bystander to all of your hectoring."

"Sometimes you've got to be a team player," Alex said.

"I *am* a team. A team of one."

"Haven't you ever heard there's no *i* in the word *team*?"

"That's true. But there *is* an *i* in the word *bullshit*. I guess I just found out back in Quantico that I don't have a high tolerance for the stuff."

"I know exactly what you mean," Karen said.

They both looked at her, waiting for her to elaborate, but she just shrugged. Alex took another sip from his coffee and dabbed at his mustache with a napkin while studiously watching both Gage and Karen with a mischievous gleam in his eye. Gage nodded toward Karen.

"Surprised you're still here," he said. "I figured you'd be on your way by now."

"Oh, I don't know," she said. "Thought I might stick around a bit. See how things turn out."

"Things?"

"You know. With the boys."

"Ah."

"Maybe even, you know, offer a helping hand—if you need one."

Her eyes, usually so steady and penetrating, wavered. He didn't know what was going on with her, what had prompted her trip or this sudden desire to dive into a local murder case, but he could see that she was struggling to maintain that well-practiced cool demeanor of hers.

"Well," he said, "the police have made it pretty clear I'm to stay well clear of this particular investigation. Besides, I've got Zoe to focus on right now."

"How's she doing?" Alex asked.

"She's taking this one pretty hard."

"She's a tough kid," Alex said. "She's been through a lot and always comes out stronger. Be no different this time."

"I hope so."

"Tell her she's welcome to hang out with me. Even stay over with us at the inn if she wants company. I think Eve is making another batch of baklava as we speak." He grinned at Karen. "No one makes baklava like Eve."

"I'll tell her," Gage said, "but I'm hoping my company is enough for her."

Alex removed his glasses and cleaned them with his sleeve. "What kind of company are you going to be when you're not around?"

"What?"

"How are you going to be there when you're out investigating Connor Fleicher's murder?"

Gage shook his head. "Didn't you just hear what I said? I said—"

"I *know* what you said. I also know what you're going to *do*. Didn't you stop by here to bounce ideas off me on who to talk to first? It certainly wasn't to bring me donuts, we've already established that."

Karen laughed a little. "Note to self. *Always* bring Alex donuts."

"I just stopped by to say hello," Gage said.

"Right. Well, hello."

"What's gotten into you, anyway? You seem even more surly than normal. You run out of bran flakes at the house?"

"Don't change the subject. I'm much older than you and have the right to be cantankerous if the whim strikes me. Let's stay focused on your new case."

"It's not a case."

"Even without the magical properties of donuts in my system, I'm happy to help you brainstorm."

"I told you—"

"And your new partner is free to chime in as well."

"My new ..." Gage began, then looked at Karen to see if this comment surprised her as much as it had surprised him, and he could see that it did. "First of all, even if I was working this case—"

"So at least we agree that it's a case."

"*Even* if I was, you know that I've never had a partner in my life. It's not my style."

"I want you to know I had nothing to do with this," Karen said.

"Oh, don't worry," Gage said, "I know my friend here well enough to know that he needs no encouragement to meddle."

"*Meddle* is such a negative word," Alex said. "Let's call it offering necessary if unwelcome advice and counsel—and for free, no less!"

"Whatever you want to call it," Gage said, "you need to stop. I'm not getting involved with this one."

"Right."

"I'm not!"

Alex took a sip of his coffee and wrinkled his nose. "Still cold. All right, so tell me this. Where are you going after this?"

"Haven't thought about it."

"The college?"

"Why would I go there?"

"To ask people questions."

Gage sighed. "You really are relentless, aren't you?"

"One of my best qualities," Alex said. "That, and I happen to be the world's greatest lover—though this fact is, sadly, unknown to most women. So you really aren't going to investigate Connor Fleicher's murder?"

Gage glanced at the stack of hardcover books on the counter, then placed his left hand on the top book and his right hand over his heart. "I swear on this slightly wrinkled Clive Cussler that no, I won't be investigating the boy's murder."

"Fine," Alex said with a sniff, then rose abruptly from his chair. "Then since you have nothing better to do, you can watch the store for me. Come on, Karen, I may not be as handsome as our boy Gage here, but at least I'm not too stupid to pass up spending an afternoon with a pretty lady. We can take my van."

"Wait a minute," Gage said. "Where are you going?"

"What if I told you *I* was taking this case?"

Gage stared, dumbfounded.

"It's not so crazy a thought, is it?" Alex said. "Before I taught at the academy, I *was* a special agent for over twenty years."

"Um …"

"I'm going to call my new outfit Books and Oddities and Private Investigation. Has a nice ring to it, don't you think?"

"You're serious?"

"No, but it still has a nice ring to it. Actually, I told this little lady here that I would show her the sights in town if you wouldn't do it. And since she won't be busy with you, then she's obviously free to be a tourist the rest of the day." He tipped his head at Karen. "Ready, my dear?"

"Now hold on a minute," Gage said.

"Just remember not to take in any old encyclopedias," Alex said.

"I never said I wouldn't show her the sights."

They both looked at him, Alex's expression by far the more smug of the two. It was the sort of smugness that Gage found endearing when it wasn't directed at him. Karen just seemed befuddled by all their banter.

"Great," Alex said. "Make sure you buy her a T-shirt."

## Chapter 9

They were in the van, headed south on Highway 101 under overcast skies, when Karen finally broached the subject that had been on Gage's mind, off and on, since the previous morning.

"About that kiss," she said.

She stared out the front windshield, hands resting lightly on her jeans. She was tidy and compact, and even dressed casually in jeans and a black turtleneck, there was an air of seriousness about her, of focused energy and relentless purpose. With her back straight and chin level, inside the rattling jalopy of his van, she made him think of a raven in a junkyard.

"About that kiss," Gage echoed.

"I know it came out of nowhere."

"Yes."

"I want to pretend it didn't happen."

"Okay."

She glanced at him. He heard it in his voice, too, and it surprised him—the slight twinge of disappointment. Now it was his turn to stare at the glistening asphalt winding along the coast ahead of them. He gripped the steering wheel, trying to remember how far it was to Devil's Punch Bowl. That's where he'd suggested he'd take her first—a strange-shaped rock configuration that caused the ocean breakers to splash high into the air with tremendous force and a popular tourist attraction located outside Newport. The idea was to start there and work their way north.

The traffic was pleasantly light for a Friday. Though it wasn't raining, the moisture in the air built up on the window until he was forced to turn on the windshield wipers. He was glad for the distraction. It gave him something to do other than look at her.

"So you're okay with that?" she said.

"Okay with what?"

"You know. Pretending it didn't ... you know ..."

"Oh, sure," he said.

"I just didn't want you to think I was, you know, after something. Even if you were interested ... I, well, I'm not in a place where I can do that, you know. Be important to somebody."

Gage nodded. He didn't know where this was coming from, and the tone of her voice didn't lead him to believe she wanted him to ask, but he knew all about letting people down. He'd been doing it his whole life. Janet, Angela, Carmen, and Zoe. And now Alex, too, it seemed, if Gage was interpreting the surliness back at the store correctly. What was all that about?

Well, he *knew* what it was about, if he was honest with himself. A year ago, standing in front of Angela's grave, he'd sworn an oath to stop hiding, to wake from his half-decade of mental stupor and get back to doing what he was good at: private investigation. Helping people. Solving problems. Making a difference in his own way, when and where he could. And yet other than a few minor cases, ones that could hardly even be called cases, what had he done but go on pretending that nothing had changed?

Yes, maybe there was no paying client here, but that was just a technicality, wasn't it? There'd been several dozen inquiries over the past year about whether he was for hire again and he'd found a technicality to disqualify most of them—legitimately, of course. That case wasn't in his area of specialty. This case was a little too shady on the legal side. Only now, thinking about them in the context of letting people down, did Gage fully realize what he had done. Officially, he may have been working again, but unofficially he'd been doing everything in his power to avoid making any real difference in people's lives. It was enough to make him want to break his cane in half.

"Did I say something wrong?" Karen asked.

"Hmm?" Gage said.

"You seem … disturbed. Look, if you want to talk about what happened—"

"It's not about that. I've just been realizing that I'm really not all that interested in doing a bunch of sightseeing today."

"You're not?"

Gage shook his head slowly, unsure what her reaction would be, and was surprised when she sighed with relief.

"Thank God," she said.

"You're not disappointed?"

"No way. Does this mean …?"

"It means maybe we should get back to doing what we should have been doing in the first place."

"Looking into Connor Fleicher's death?"

"Yep. If you want to join me, it's the least I can do for jerking you around today."

She smiled a big, radiant smile. "Are you kidding? You're right on schedule. Alex told me you'd come around before we'd even been in the car ten minutes. He said if we ever stepped foot in a souvenir shop, he'd give me a hundred dollars."

Gage shook his head. "I'm glad I'm so predictable."

"Only in the best way."

"I'm not sure what that means."

"Me either. But he cares about you a lot, you know?"

"Alex? Yeah. I know. He can be a bit of a pain in the ass, but I don't know what I'd do without him."

She chuckled.

"What?" Gage said.

"Well, that's exactly what he said about you."

\* \* \*

SINCE THEY'D ONLY driven a few miles past the city limits, it was

81

a quick jaunt back to Barnacle Bluffs Community College. It was the logical place to start, but he wasn't sure if any good would come of it with the school officially closed. He was therefore surprised when the van, cresting the hill and emerging through the thicket of Douglas firs, came upon the person he would have put at the top of his list.

"Berry?" Gage said aloud.

Connor Fleicher's mother was walking in the middle of the road, straight toward them, head down and hugging herself tightly. If he'd been barreling up the road like some of the kids did, he may very well have hit her—even dressed as she was, in garish pink jeans and a tight orange T-shirt so bright it probably would have glowed in the dark. As it was, he still barely managed to slam on the brakes and skid to a halt.

Even then, with the Volkswagen's engine still ticking, it was a long time before Berry looked up. With the light slanting from behind her and the air within the trees hazy and thick, it was difficult to read her expression through the Volkswagen's dirty windshield. But Gage could see enough to know that the pixie-ish woman clinging desperately to her youth that he'd met two months earlier was nowhere to be found. Her teenybopper clothes only made the contrast with the person wearing them that much starker. This frail thing was a zombie, her eyes flat, her skin pale and drawn tight over her thin face so that her cheekbones looked as sharp as razor blades.

"Jesus," Karen said.

Gage turned on his hazard lights. Slowly, as if Berry were a doe they were afraid of spooking, they both got out of the car. They didn't have to worry. Her only sign of movement was to sway slightly. Her short chestnut hair, styled with the candlestick swirl the last time he'd seen her, now lay flat and lifeless, her bangs clumped and plastered to her forehead.

A breeze of wet earth and fir shushed its way through the trees. Gage saw no cars in either direction. Using his cane, taking his time, he approached her straight-on. He tried a smile and got nothing in return. A few birds tweeted from the treetops, and down the road behind them he heard a muffled buzz of traffic on the highway, but otherwise it was quiet.

"Ms. Fleicher?" he said.

When she didn't answer, Karen touched her arm. It was only then that some amount of focus came into her eyes, a slow return to life, a few blinks.

"He's gone," she said.

Her voice was a hair above a whisper. Up close now, Gage saw she wore no makeup, all the little creases and wrinkles on her pale face exposed in the misty air, like hairline fissures in a white marble table. Her lips bore a few traces of red lipstick, patches of it like skin grafts.

"I'm sorry," Gage said.

She looked at him as if seeing him for the first time. "He's gone," she said again.

"I know," Gage said. "I'm truly sorry for your loss, Ms. Fleicher. Can we take you back to your car?"

"My car?" she said.

"Is it parked by the dorm?"

Her eyes welled up. "I can't go there," she said.

"You don't have to," Gage said.

"Came—came to get his things …"

"Ms. Fleicher—"

"He's gone … he's really gone …"

The tears hanging around the rims of her eyes finally spilled down her cheeks. Gage heard the low rumble of a truck coming up the road behind them. Taking Berry firmly by the arm, he guided her to the van, where Karen helped her into the backseat.

Gage climbed in the front and waited, hand on the ignition, for the truck coming up the road. It was actually an SUV, a black Ford Expedition—and when it passed them on the left, he saw the bald, broad-shouldered Arne Cooper glaring at him.

"Oh, this gets better and better," Gage said.

"Who was that?" Karen asked.

Gage started to answer, then remembered his passenger. He glanced in the rearview mirror. Berry slumped against her seatbelt as if it was the only thing keeping her upright, her face downcast. If she'd seen Arne, she certainly wasn't acting like it. He didn't know how she'd react if she came face to face with the father of the boy who was suspected of killing her son, but he didn't think it would go well.

"Ms. Fleicher?" he said.

She stared unblinking at the floor. He turned in his seat, speaking louder this time.

"Berry?"

She looked at him.

"You don't have to go there right now."

"Okay."

"How would you like to go somewhere and talk for a little while? Get some coffee?"

"Coffee?"

"Or something else. We could take you home, too, if you'd like."

"No. No, I don't want to go back there either. I *can't* go back there."

"All right."

"Not right now."

"You don't have to. Coffee, then?"

She looked at the floor. He was going to ask her again when she finally responded with a barely perceptible tip of the head. It wasn't exactly unbridled enthusiasm, but he'd take it. When he started the van, Karen was still staring at him, her face questioning, and he mouthed the words *Arne Cooper,* to which she responded with a silent *Ah.*

TEN MINUTES LATER they were seated in a corner booth at the Diner, a hole-in-the-wall affair a couple of blocks off Highway 101 that was Gage's favorite restaurant. Its actual name was McAllister's Family Diner, but it had possessed that name less than a year, the next in a long series of names as the diner had been sold from one owner to another, always limping along, never making enough to justify someone putting their heart and soul into it but always turning enough profit that some eager-eyed Portlander suffering a midlife crisis thought this was their ticket to a good life on the beach. So the locals pretty much just called it the Diner. Some of the old-timers called it Ed's Diner, after the original owner, Ed Boone, but he'd been gone over two decades and there weren't many locals still around who remembered him.

Someone had dropped a quarter in the jukebox, and Otis Redding's smooth baritone echoed off the black-and-white tile floor and the plain white walls, competing for attention with the loud sizzle of the griddle. The scent of bacon was in the air. Two old guys in wrinkled plaid shirts and grease-stained baseball caps, regulars Gage recognized, occupied a booth three away from them, and a UPS driver in uniform sat at the counter intently looking at an iPad, but otherwise the place was empty. Gage and Karen sat on one side of the red vinyl booth, Berry on the other. Three white porcelain mugs of coffee steamed the air between them.

"I don't—I don't know," Berry said. "I mean, I don't think ... I can't remember if ... well ..."

She worried the edge of her napkin with her right hand, eyes glistening as if she might cry at any moment, the stencil letters of the word *Diner* in the window casting their shadow on her wan face. Gage had asked her, as delicately as he could, whether Connor had ever given the impression that he was in danger.

"I know it's really soon," Gage said.

She nodded as if he had said something quite sage. "I don't know what I'm going to do with—with the body. Ted says we should cremate him, but I don't know. I kind of want a funeral. I'd ... I'd kind of like to look at his face one more time, but the bullet came in ... came in the back ... well, you know."

Karen reached over and placed her hand on top of Berry's, who smiled weakly in appreciation.

"Is Ted your husband?"

"Ex," she said.

"Is he from Waldport too?"

Berry started to answer, then, blinking a few times, looked at him with more awareness. "I read about you, you know. On the Internet."

"Oh no," Gage said.

"You're kind of a famous detective."

"I wouldn't say that."

"That thing a year ago with the scientist guy. I Googled you, and stuff about it even came up on CNN. I'm not really a reading-the-news sort of person, but it seemed like a pretty big deal."

Gage shrugged. "It involved an old friend. I kind of got sucked into it."

"Is that what's happening here? You're getting sucked into this?"

"Something like that."

"But I don't understand. Jeremiah is locked up. He had the gun in his hand."

"I know."

"But you don't think he did it?"

"I just want to know for certain."

"The police seem certain."

"Yeah, well."

Berry folded the napkin in half, creasing the edge. "I don't think he did it either."

"You don't?"

Berry shook her head. "I have feelings about these sorts of things. I'm not a psychic or anything—well, maybe I am, but only a little. Just strong feelings. And I just don't think Jeremiah did it. But I haven't said anything, because everyone just seems so sure he did do it and maybe, I thought, maybe I'm just all mixed up because of what happened so my feelings aren't straight. But no. No, I don't think he did."

"Do you have any idea who might want to hurt him?" Gage asked.

"I could hire you," Berry said. "Officially. So you get paid."

"That's not necessary."

"I don't have a lot of money, but Ted does. He's a dentist. In Bend. Lots of rich retirees there with bad teeth, so he does pretty good. He could pay you."

"Please, Berry. I'm not doing this for money."

"Then why are you doing it?"

"Peace of mind. For Zoe. Because it's what I do." He shrugged.

"Oh."

They sat quietly. Otis Redding finished his song, leaving the sizzle of the griddle and the clink of silverware from the two old-timers in the corner. Gage took a sip of his coffee. Berry reached for hers, toying with the handle. From what he could tell, she hadn't taken a single sip. Outside the window, an ocean breeze sent a plastic bag from Jaybee's grocery skittering up the road.

"I don't know," Berry said. "I wish I ... I wish I knew something."

"Did you talk to Connor much the past few months?" Gage asked.

Berry shook her head.

"At all?" Gage pressed.

"A couple times. On the phone. But only for a minute."

"Did he say anything that made you worry? Anything strange?"

"No. Not that I ... well, that was the strange part."

"What's that?"

"Him not calling. Or not answering my calls." She rotated her cup around a few times, staring intently at the rising steam. "We used to be so close. Or I thought we were. We talked about everything. My crazy clients. His troubles at school. But once he was at BBCC, there was just nothing. It was like he didn't want anything to do with me."

"I doubt it was that," Karen said.

"I'm not sure what I did wrong."

"You didn't do anything wrong," Karen said.

"Did he ever say anything about Jeremiah?" Gage asked.

"Only that they were hanging out a lot."

"How long ago did they meet? Didn't you say something

about it being at a *Star Trek* convention?"

Berry nodded and finally took a sip from her coffee. "It was this summer. Not that long ago. July, I guess. Yeah, a week after the Fourth. It was in Portland. I dropped him off at the convention center in the morning, then went shopping downtown. When I picked him up, he was hanging out with a group of kids. One was Jeremiah."

"How did Jeremiah get there?"

"Oh, I don't know. His mom maybe. I think he said something about his mom picking him up."

Gage tried to imagine the type of woman who would marry Arne Cooper and failed. "You mentioned trouble at school. What kind of trouble?"

"Oh, you know," Berry said, "the normal kind for a high school kid."

"Bad grades? Alcohol? Drugs?"

"No, no. Nothing like that." She sounded offended that Gage would even suggest such a possibility. "He always got straight A's. And his SATs were great. He didn't like the taste of alcohol, and he always said kids who smoked weed were losers. No, it was more just that he was depressed all the time. And some kids at school were always teasing him. He didn't fit in. He said he didn't care, but ..."

She shrugged. The walls of her mental tent looked ready to collapse, and he debated about the next question. He'd been holding off, trying to get a sense of how Berry would take it, but he could tell that what little energy she had was almost spent. It wouldn't be long and she'd be back in her emotional cocoon.

"Berry, I need to ask you something," Gage said. "It might be important. Do you think your son was gay?"

There was a moment, a hesitation or a pause, before the reaction came, that Gage would dwell on later—a flicker of doubt before a curtain of indignation closed over her features. She blinked a few times, resetting. A flush of red spread across her cheeks.

"No," she said. "No, definitely not."

"I didn't mean to cause offense."

"Why would it cause offense? There's nothing wrong with it. Lots of people are gay. Elton John is gay. And, um, that talk-show host. Ellen … Ellen something or other."

"DeGeneres," Karen said.

"Right. That one. And Jodie Foster. There's more gay people than ever these days."

"They were probably always gay," Gage said.

"What?"

"Nothing."

Berry shook her head. "Connor wasn't gay. I would have known. I'm his mother, after all. And he would have told me anyway. We were very close. We talked about everything."

Her voice had gotten louder, more brittle. Gage wanted to press a little more, find out exactly what sorts of things they *did* talk about, but he could see the ice beginning to crack. It wouldn't take much, a little nudge, and she'd end up having a breakdown right there in the diner. The old-timers in the corner glanced their way.

"You feel ready to go back to the college?" Gage asked.

She nodded, though it was more like bowing her head in resignation than an answer.

*Chapter 10*

**W**hen they reached the campus, Gage expected to find a bevy of police cars, press vehicles, and other signs that something terrible had occurred in this place only a couple of days previously. He was surprised to find only one police cruiser parked near the building, the entrance cordoned off with yellow tape. There were a few cars packed outside the monolithic dormitory: a dented old station wagon, two small Hondas, and Berry's blue Suburban. Arne Cooper's Expedition was nowhere to be found.

"I don't want to go in there," Berry said.

"You don't have to," Karen said.

"I just want to get his things and go home."

"We'll do it for you," Karen said.

"I have to warn you, though," Gage said, "that his room is probably locked down as a crime scene. They're not going to be too keen on us taking your son's things."

"I don't need all of his things," Berry said. "Not now. I just want—I just want his pad."

"His iPad?" Karen asked.

"No, his drawing pad," she said. "He likes to doodle things in it. Mostly science-fictiony things, but it's important to him. I used to … um, put his drawings on the refrigerator when he was little. I still do sometimes. I just—I just didn't want it lost. I can get the other things later. Or never. I don't care, I guess. I just want his drawings."

"We'll see what we can do," Gage said.

The campus sidewalks, woven with shadows from the pines and slices of sunlight, were eerily vacant. He'd no sooner pulled the van into the spot next to the Suburban, however, when two young men appeared at his window. Their gray-and-blue uniforms looked remarkably like standard-issue police uniforms, except that they had only batons attached to their belts and the words *BBCC Security* emblazoned on their silver badges. One of them tapped on Gage's window with his baton even as Gage had already started to roll it down.

"Don't do that," Gage said.

"Campus closed today, sir," the kid said, a redhead with a crooked nose. He was young enough that he had only acne on his forehead rather than the divots and discoloration that were acne's scars.

"Even my pottery class?" Gage asked.

"What?"

"I have Berry Fleicher with me. She just wants us to get her son's drawing pad. It's important to her."

The kid stared. The one behind him, who was much like his counterpart other than his dirty-blond hair, stood as still as a coin meter. It took so long for the redhead to react that Gage was starting to wonder if he'd even heard him, before he finally glanced in the backseat. He stood there staring for a long time before he looked at Gage again.

"I'll have to radio this in, sir," the kid said. "This is a secure crime scene."

"You do that. In the meantime, we're going in."

"Sir—"

Gage opened the door swiftly enough that the kid was forced to jump back a step. He ripped a radio off his belt with such fervor that for a moment Gage thought maybe the kid was going for some kind of weapon. By the time Karen was out of the car, he was already squawking into the receiver that they had a situation here, he needed authorization, roger roger, lots of other macho nonsense. Gage leaned in to check one more time with Berry to see if she was all right by herself, but she looked so forlorn, so collapsed and folded into herself, that he didn't want to take a chance that he'd cause her to disintegrate if he said even a word to her. He grabbed his cane and shut the door.

Heading for the building, cane clicking on the sidewalk, Gage glanced over his shoulder to see that the two guards followed them. The dormitory's front door opened and a square-faced man in a similar gray-and-blue uniform, his blocky gray hair looking two-dimensional, stepped out to greet them, still talking on his radio.

"Stand down," he said, his voice reaching Gage's ears from both the radio behind him and the man himself.

"Really?" Gage said.

The man slipped the radio back on his belt. He had the kind of saggy, flush complexion of someone who'd spent most of his life trying to find the bottom of a shot glass. "We need authorization for this, sir," he said. Even his breath smelled of booze.

Gage pointed at his van. "Do you know who's sitting in that Volkswagen over there?"

"Sir—"

"It's Berry Fleicher, the victim's mother. She just wants us to get his drawing pad. I doubt the police will miss all his renderings of Klingons."

Gage started for the door. Unfortunately, the older security guard stepped in the way and placed a hand on Gage's chest. Gage slapped it away, and all three of the security guards scurried into motion, jumping into his path and barking orders at him, a jumble of movement and noise.

"Don't put your hand on me again," Gage said.

"Stand back, sir," the older man said, his knuckles bone-white as he gripped the baton still strapped to his side.

"Oh, for Christ's sake," Gage said.

"We have our orders, sir. No one goes in or out of the dorm without authorization."

"Whose authorization? The police?"

The man shook his head. "No, sir. From the vice president of academic affairs, Provost MacDonald."

"And he gave the order?"

"Yes, sir."

"At the request of the police?"

"I don't know, sir. I'd really appreciate it if you stand back a few steps, sir. You're making us all a bit nervous, sir."

"Stop calling me sir," Gage said. "It's making me edgy, and when I get edgy, I start hitting people with my cane. The name's Garrison Gage. I'm a private investigator working for Berry Fleicher."

"I know who you are, sir," the man said.

The way he said it, so pointedly, it was almost as if he were issuing a threat—as if there was some kind of conspiracy afoot, everybody talking about Gage, warning each other, keeping tabs, following his every move. It made Gage think of Percy's warning not to stir things up in town, how they could turn on him if he pushed too hard in the wrong ways.

"Uh-huh," Gage said. "What's your name?"

"Officer Jantz, sir—Mr. Garrison, sir."

"Officer's your first name?"

"Sir—"

"Are you a football fan, Officer?"

"What?"

"Specifically our local high school heroes, the Bobcats?"

"I'm not sure I follow," Jantz said, though his narrowing eyes said the opposite.

"I just want to know whose side you're on."

Jantz took a moment to respond, and when he did, his voice had gone from cool to subzero in friendliness. "Just doing my job ... *sir.*"

"Right. Is Provost MacDonald in today?"

Officer Jantz's eyes told Gage the answer was yes before the man even started to speak. "Sir—"

"Where's his office? Is it on the other side of the cafeteria there?"

When Jantz didn't answer, Gage turned abruptly and headed for the sidewalk that led to the cafeteria building and beyond, leaving the three security guards to squabble among themselves. He heard the squawk of the radio, Jantz delivering a warning to someone about Gage, but then Gage was beyond earshot. Karen hurried to keep up. Pine needles and crumpled oak leaves littered the lawn on both sides of the sidewalk. A rake lay by a pile of leaves near an idle John Deere riding mower, but there were no grounds crew to be seen.

"Are you always that … friendly?" Karen asked him.

"Only on my best days," he said.

"You don't care for people in positions of authority much, do you?"

"That's not true. I like Santa Claus. He's in a position of authority. He decides who's naughty and nice. Plus, he also has employees who wear uniforms."

"So your one exception is a fictional character who doles out gifts to children based on an arbitrary system of merit?"

Gage gaped at her. "He's fictional?"

"I stand corrected."

"If he's fictional, why do I still find coal in my stocking every Christmas?"

Reaching the cafeteria, they veered to the right, swinging their way around it, passing empty benches and bike racks with bikes still chained to them, not a single student to be seen anywhere. A few other buildings, nestled among the firs, came into view, three of them, just as brown and squat and deserted as the others. The campus could have been the scene of a *Twilight Zone* episode. Gage glanced over his shoulder and saw that one of the security officers, the dark-haired kid who hadn't said a word, was following them. When the kid saw that Gage was looking, he whispered into his radio with one hand and reached for his baton with the other.

Every time Gage saw them reach for their batons, he was momentarily filled with the desire to challenge them to a duel. They had their batons. He had his cane.

The administration building was the farthest from the others, helpfully named Administration Building, tucked so close to the towering fir trees behind it that the long slender trunks seemed at first glance to be spires attached to the building. An atrium in the front, with slightly opaque smoked glass, was the building's one gesture toward aesthetics and modernity, though in reality it only served to give the place an air of phony pretentiousness.

"What are you going to do?" Karen asked.

"Ask him why we can't have Connor's drawing pad," Gage said.

"And if that doesn't work?"

"I haven't thought that far head."

Inside the atrium, they found an obnoxiously large reception desk made of the same smoked glass. Nobody sat behind it. Before the security guard reached the door, Gage and Karen headed down a hall with blue carpet so thin and smooth, it reflected the overhead fluorescent lights like it was water. The registrar's glass window was closed and a black curtain drawn behind it. They followed the reader board and took a right at the end of the hall. Gage heard the guard call out to them, but he rounded the corner without a glance back.

The buzzing lights and the hum of a drinking fountain were all that greeted them. Except for the door at the end of the hall, the one they needed, the dozen or so other doors were closed. They stepped through the open door into an area as soothing as a dentist's waiting room, oak end tables, cushioned chairs, watercolor paintings lining the walls. A young blond woman—hardly more than a girl, she couldn't have been more than twenty—came out from behind a cherrywood desk. Her stylish outfit, a charcoal gray pantsuit adorned with a sparkling Bearcat pendant on the lapel, would have been the envy even of women on Madison Avenue, but her awkward walk and nervous mannerisms gave off the whiff of someone playing a role.

"Can I help you, sir?" she said, her voice cracking a little at the end.

"I guess you're considered essential personnel, huh?" Gage said.

"What?"

There were three doors off the reception area, all of them conveniently labeled: Vice President of Academic Affairs Dan MacDonald, Vice President of Finance Ed Leiber, and Executive Assistant Janet O'Dell. Dan's door was cracked open, the others closed. "Is Dan in?" Gage asked.

"Sir," the girl said, "if you don't have an appointment—"

"Really?" Gage said. "You're going to dust off that one with what's going on right now?"

This, apparently, was too complex an interaction for the poor girl, because she merely blinked at them. Judging by the way her curves fit into that pantsuit of hers, he guessed that she hadn't been hired because of her mental fortitude. Before Gage could explain, Dan MacDonald appeared in his doorway. Mid-fifties and still lean, tall enough that he could have once played basketball for the school, he was dressed in tan chinos and a powder-blue polo with the Bearcat logo over the right breast. The shirt was tight enough to show the world how much time he spent at the gym, which must have been plenty considering the wide swath of his chest and the way his biceps bulged in his short sleeves. His black hair, slicked straight back, was thin enough that Gage saw bits of gleaming scalp. His nose was a bit crooked, his face blocky and rumpled, weathered by the sun and the scuffles of his youth.

The door behind them opened and the security guard came through, still gripping the baton, locked and loaded. MacDonald held up his hand with the swiftness of a cop stopping traffic.

"It's okay," MacDonald said, "I'll see them."

He could have pricked the guard with a balloon, the way the kid deflated. MacDonald gestured to his office, and Gage and Karen stepped through the doorway. Walking by him, Gage got a whiff of the man's cologne, like a tropical breeze with a hint of mango.

The room was small but meticulously decorated—an oak desk, oak paneling, lots of pictures on the walls, a few ferns strategically arranged. The whole back was a window to the forest. The pictures, in oak frames that matched the desk, all showed MacDonald in various exotic locales, in front of pyramids and mountain ranges, castles and canyons. MacDonald crossed behind his desk, and Gage and Karen stood behind the two chairs, but none of them sat. The laptop on his desk purred like a cat. They shook hands and made introductions. MacDonald had big hands and a grip that matched them.

"The great detective at last," he said.

"Excuse me?" Gage said.

"I've read all about you—kind of been a fan since you found that girl on the beach a couple years ago."

"Abby Heddle," Gage said.

"Right. Very impressive, the way you found the killers. Really shook up the town."

"Yeah."

"And the woman last year, your friend. That was a tough business too."

"Uh-huh."

MacDonald shook his head, glancing down at his laptop. "And now this. I was just reading the *Oregonian*. Our little town keeps getting in the news for all the wrong reasons. And you're always in the middle of it."

"Believe me," Gage said, "it's not my intention."

"Oh, I know. You came here to retire, didn't you?"

"No, I came here to quit. I'm too young to retire."

MacDonald closed his laptop and ran a hand through his hair. There was enough product in it that the gesture hardly made a dent. "Maybe it's time to quit somewhere else."

"I'm sorry?"

"Maybe you should pick another town. One that fits you better."

"Wow. Thank you for that unsolicited travel advice."

"It's not me," MacDonald said. "Like I said, I'm a fan."

"Like you said."

"But your name gets mentioned a lot. Some of the parents weren't all that comfortable with Zoe in the dorm. People were concerned."

"Oh, they were, were they?"

"Please," MacDonald said, raising his hands in a gesture of helplessness, "this isn't personal."

"Sounds pretty personal to me."

"I'm just trying to give you a sense of the mood. Around this campus and this town. When you start poking around, well, people are just expecting things to go from bad to worse."

"I see."

"And when you bring an FBI agent along for the ride, it doesn't help." He nodded to Karen. "No offense."

"I'm not on duty," Karen said.

"Doesn't matter. People just see dark clouds and expect rain."

"They should bring umbrellas," Gage said.

"What? Oh, a joke. Right."

"Apparently not, based on your reaction. Listen, Dan—can I call you Dan? Or do you prefer Danny? Right now I'm just concerned with Berry Fleicher. She wants to retrieve the boy's drawing pad from his room. How can we make that happen?"

MacDonald nodded solemnly. "A drawing pad?"

"That's right."

"Why does she want it?"

"It has sentimental value."

"I see."

He clasped his hands and rested his chin upon the point of his fingers, appraising Gage and Karen the way he must have looked at a flunking undergrad. Gage imagined that most students would have melted right there, admitting that their excuses were unjustified, begging for forgiveness and departing meekly. Outside, from the reception area, came the clicking of a keyboard and the squeak of a swivel chair.

"Well," MacDonald said, as if that word and the wide, what-can-I-do sweep of hands that accompanied it were all the answer they needed.

"You're saying no?" Gage said.

"I'm saying it's out of my hands. Nobody goes in and out of that building except the police."

"And apparently campus security."

"Well, yes, of course them. Though not inside the room."

"So that's really a no?"

"I'm afraid so."

"Is there a forensics expert in there now?"

"I have no idea. It's not my concern."

"But it *is* your concern that no one else go inside."

"Yes."

Now it was Gage's turn to play the part of the thoughtful administrator, nodding and rubbing his chin. "So here's a hypothetical. What do you think one of the Portland TV stations would think if they found out that you wouldn't give the victim's mother a drawing pad filled with doodles of spaceships? What do you think they would say when they found out that the victim used to give these doodles to his mother as tokens of his affection?"

MacDonald was impressively restrained in how much of his reaction he allowed to slip through his defenses—only the slightest, barest hint of a smile, the tiniest upturn at the corners of his mouth, all lips and no teeth. This was a cobra's smile. The only thing lacking was the flick of a forked tongue.

"That," MacDonald began, drawing out the word in the most measured fashion, "would *not* be in the school's best interest."

"No," Gage said, "I imagine not. Karen, what do you think? Do you think news like that would put BBCC in a positive light?"

"I don't think that would help enrollment," she said.

"No, not at all," Gage said.

"Might hurt the bottom line."

"Yep."

"All right, all right," MacDonald said, "you made your point." He still offered them his best stoic face, but he slumped into his chair. Unable to look down on them from on high, he seemed so much less intimidating, the big desk overwhelming him. He reached for his phone. "I'll have to get permission, of course."

"Of course," Gage said.

"There's no guarantees."

"Well," Gage said, "I'm pretty confident that you can convince Chief Quinn if you use the same scintillating logic I did. I do have a couple questions first, though."

MacDonald put the phone back in its cradle. "Oh? The fun continues?"

"I want to know if you can tell me anything about these two boys that might be helpful."

"I've already told the police everything I know. Which unfortunately isn't all that much."

"Yes, but see, I'm not the police."

"Believe me," MacDonald said, "you've made that abundantly clear."

"Were they both good students? Were there any complaints about them? Anything unusual?"

MacDonald sighed. "Mr. Gage, I *really* am a fan. I meant what I said. But you've got to understand my position. My hands are tied. You can threaten me with the press again, but it won't make a difference. I have been instructed to only divulge information to the police on these matters."

"You mean you've been specifically instructed not to cooperate with me."

"It comes out that way, yes."

"By whom?"

"I'm not at liberty to discuss."

"You know," Gage said, "I'm really just trying to help here."

"I know you see it that way."

"And I suppose the same would go for other people on this campus? I'll find a lot of doors closing in my face?"

"I imagine so."

"So much for being a fan—"

"Mr. Gage—"

"All right. Well, at least we know where we stand." Gage looked at Karen. "You ready? Or are there questions you'd like to ask and not get the answers to?"

"Lots," Karen said, "but I'll keep them to myself for now."

"Probably for the best," Gage said. "I do have one more question, though. Who took the pictures?"

It took MacDonald a moment to realize that the question was directed at him. "What?"

Gage pointed at the walls. "Somebody had to take them. Who was with you? The same girlfriend, or a different one each time?"

"Oh. Various friends."

"Friends."

"Sure. I like to travel. I invited different companions to come with me."

"And yet you never put *their* pictures on the wall. Only yours."

For the first time, MacDonald showed signs of being flustered, a bit of pink in his face, a bit of a stutter in his voice. "I have pictures of my friends at home. My office is more of a public space, so I take more precautions."

"They're all of legal age, right?" Gage said.

"Excuse me?"

"The girls?"

MacDonald stared at Gage a few beats, then shook his head slightly. "I think it's time for you to go, sir."

"Do you think their parents would approve?"

MacDonald reached for his phone, and when he spoke, his voice was clipped and icy. "Should I call campus security?"

"Sure, I could use the protection. This is a rough neighborhood."

He left abruptly. MacDonald called after them, insisting there was no guarantee he could get approval from the police immediately, but Gage and Karen were down the hall before MacDonald finished his sentence. As they passed, the girl at the reception desk kept her gaze fixed on her computer monitor, like a student nervous that her hands were going to get slapped by the teacher's ruler.

While they'd been inside, the sun had climbed higher, shining down from far overhead. Steam rose off the grass, the warmth of the rays giving the tan and brick buildings more color and vibrancy. If not for the total lack of students, it would have been a good time for a promotional photo. In their absence, two more police cars had parked out front, one a standard cruiser, the other an unmarked black Crown Victoria. Gage was pretty sure who drove the unmarked one. The gray-haired supervisor emerged from the dorm, and sure enough, who should join him but two of his favorite people in the world.

"Trenton and Brisbane," Gage said. He pointed his cane at them, an innocent gesture, and all three of them flinched. "Tell me where I can buy one of those trench coats. They really are dashing."

The two detectives, grim-faced as always, only shook their heads. Standing side by side, rather than sitting as they had been back at the station, they came off even more as an odd couple: Trenton tall, pale, and lanky, with short but thick red hair; Brisbane short, weathered, and frumpy, with only a few strands of gray hair as reminders of what had once been. The knee-length trench coats were all that tied them together—except, of course, for the sour way they regarded Gage. Trenton, giving Gage his best Irish glare, thrust a spiral drawing pad at him.

"Here," he said.

"Oh, you shouldn't have," Gage said.

"Just take it, will you?"

Gage took it. It was smaller than he'd expected, the edges of the pages well worn, the white cover filled side to side with pen and ink doodles of trolls, dragons, and Conan the Barbarian-type warriors brandishing bloody swords. He flipped through it and saw more of the same inside—except for one of the last drawings. It was of a bunch of animals—elephants, giraffes, tigers—surrounding the letters *DWR*. He wondered what it meant.

"Are you sure this is the right one?" Gage asked

"Give me a break," Trenton said.

"I'd like to take a look inside the room myself."

Brisbane groaned. "Not going to happen."

"How about seeing his phone?"

"The kid's iPhone is missing," Brisbane said. "Either it was lost or the murderer took it."

"Don't tell him anything else," Trenton snapped.

"How about this?" Gage said. "You let me inside, and I'll buy you both a dozen donuts."

"How about this?" Trenton said. "You leave now, and we won't arrest you for trespassing."

"Touchy, touchy," Gage said. "You think Chief Quinn would approve that?"

"Gage," Brisbane growled, "Quinn *told* us to tell you that."

"Ah." Gage winked at Karen. "Wearing out my welcome quickly, aren't I?"

"You seem to have a knack for that," Karen said.

"Still, it seems a bit of a stretch. After all, my daughter *is* a student at this school."

"Not anymore," Brisbane said.

"What?"

Brisbane and Trenton looked at officer Jantz, who responded with a perfunctory nod. "I was just told a few minutes ago. She called in this morning. Dropped out."

This, though not exactly surprising, considering the conversation Gage had with Zoe earlier, still twisted in his stomach. What the hell was the rush? She couldn't wait a day or two to make this decision, allow him one more chance to talk her out of it? Of course that was the point, wasn't it? She didn't want to be talked out of it.

"Isn't it interesting," Gage said. "Hardly anybody working here today and yet they're still able to process her request."

"Maybe if you'd been with her instead of here," Brisbane said, "it would have been a moot point."

"What's that supposed to mean?" Gage asked.

"It means you're focusing on the wrong problem."

"I am, am I? Maybe I should focus this cane on your head."

Brisbane smiled, and it was so rare and disturbing, like seeing a turtle smile, that it momentarily took Gage aback. Brisbane was not a man who had a face for smiling. He was not a man who had a face for anything, really, but the glare and the grimace.

"Now *that* would certainly create a new problem for you," Brisbane said. "Anything else, or do you want to vent some more?"

Karen, touching his elbow, directed Gage away from the others. Rather than give in to the frustration, Gage allowed himself to be directed. He felt them staring after him all the way back to the van and, sure enough, when he reached the driver's side and afforded himself a glance over his shoulder, they were still gaping at him like a bunch of kibitzing women after the Sunday service.

"Don't," Karen said.

"I wasn't going to say anything."

"Yes, you were. I could tell."

They got into the van. Gage would have considered the whole episode a frustrating failure if not for the look on Berry's face when he handed the drawing pad to her. A face that had been flat and drained, a pale emotionless wall, flared to life. There was a flicker of hope in the way the eyes crinkled, the lips turned up, ever so slightly, in the briefest hint of a smile.

It was enough.

## Chapter 11

**B**erry Fleicher decided to drive back to Waldport on her own. She was still shaky on her feet, but it wasn't like Gage could do anything to stop her. Before he'd watched the shiny chrome fender of her Suburban disappear through the firs, Gage had asked if he could take a quick look at the drawing pad. He'd been hoping for some obvious clue, but there hadn't been much on the inside that wasn't on the outside: fire-breathing dragons, bug-eyed aliens, and one particularly detailed castle dungeon. The one with the letters *DWR* surrounded by a bunch of animals didn't make much sense, but it wasn't like Gage could make sense of the rest of the drawings. Berry, more familiar with Connor's artwork, promised she'd call if she noticed anything out of the ordinary—with the drawings or anything else.

The afternoon sun, always fickle on the coast, turned wan and flat. Gray skies gathered on the western horizon like an approaching army. Another storm coming. After a quick bowl of chowder at Pelican Pete's, Gage dropped Karen off back at her Honda, then quickly checked with Alex to make sure Zoe hadn't shown up at the store (she hadn't) before hightailing it back to the house. The investigation could wait. He had a bone to pick with a certain impetuous teenage girl.

The house was empty, but her black leather purse was on her nightstand and her tennis shoes, the ones she only wore to the beach, for hiking, or for other outdoor activities, were missing. Gage headed for the beach, hoping that's where she'd gone and not on a hike to Diamond Head or around Big Dipper Lake.

Fortunately, he hadn't even descended the stone steps that led from the bluff down to the sand when he spotted her.

She sat a few feet from the edge of the surf, hugging her knees, the white cord of her iPod earbuds disappearing into the neck of her black hoodie. A flock of seagulls strutted around the sand not far away, cawing occasionally, and an elderly couple in matching green windbreakers and floppy wide-brimmed hats walked hand in hand, but otherwise the beach was deserted. Wind ruffling his hair, he stood gripping the iron rail and watched her. She didn't move.

There was something about her sitting like that, so trance-like, that made him hesitate. Or maybe it was just the salty air clearing away the fog in his own mind. What was he hoping to accomplish here? He may have thought she was making a mistake by dropping out of school, but he had to admit to himself that this was her decision to make. She was eighteen. More important than the number, or even how she was viewed in the eyes of the law, was a simple immutable fact he'd learned in the two years she'd been in his care: the more he pushed Zoe to do something, or *not* to do something, the more likely she was to do the opposite.

Cause and effect. Stimulus and response. Maybe he'd seen it as his duty to intervene in the past, but this time he had to let her find her own way. If that way didn't include him, he had to be all right with that.

After giving himself another minute to absorb the wind on his face, really feeling the cold bite of it, he headed back to the house.

\* \* \*

HIS BRAIN CHURNING like the sea, his thoughts as blustery as the wind, Gage turned to the one activity that never failed to settle his mind: a crossword puzzle.

Back at the house, he made a pot of coffee and settled into his recliner, the *New York Times* crossword folded neatly on his lap. A touch of Irish cream in his coffee never failed to act as a balm for frazzled nerves. It was going on three o'clock. By four o'clock, he'd consumed half the pot of coffee and finished half the crossword puzzle. He was stuck on a ten-letter word that ended in *n* with "Restraining impulses" as the clue. By five o'clock, the big A-frame windows were painted black and still no teenage girl had showed up in his house.

Restraining impulses. He felt the impulse to go back to the beach, and he restrained himself. He also felt the impulse to fix himself a bourbon. He figured there was still a chance Zoe would want to talk to him, and a clear head would be better if that were the case.

The case. Without the bourbon to subdue his thoughts, his mind naturally drifted to the case. He felt as if he were flailing around in the dark with no purpose. What was he really trying to accomplish here? Connor Fleicher was dead. Jeremiah Cooper, caught with a gun in his hand, was in jail. If anybody should believe the kid was guilty, it would be Gage, who was privy to information that most people weren't. After all, he'd found Jeremiah in the rain on the beach shooting bullets into the sand, claiming that some people deserved to die. That alone would have sealed his fate with any jury. There was no logical reason to believe the kid was anything but guilty.

But Gage, a rational man by disposition, driven more by reason than fiery passion, knew that logic was not his motivator here. It was some other deep part of his brain, call it intuition or instinct, that knew, despite the evidence, that there was no way this kid could actually kill another human being. He just didn't have the capacity.

And somehow Gage would prove it.

It was then that the front door finally creaked open, a draft of cool air curling through the room. Gage peered over his cross-word and saw Zoe standing there in her hoodie, her face glisten-ing. The word came to him.

"Inhibition," he said.

"What?"

Gage wrote down the word. "Inhibition. Restraining impuls-es. Ten letters."

"Oh."

She dropped the hood, slipped off her tennis shoes and start-ed for the bedroom.

"I'd like to talk," he said.

"Not really in the mood right now."

"Me either. But it's important."

He put a little more oomph in his voice, and it caught her attention. She stopped, hand on the wall, and looked at him over her shoulder. Flecks of sand glittered in her black hair like tiny bits of confetti. Except for a tiny sapphire stud in her nose, she wore no other jewelry. Her face, shocked pink from the cold, gave her a more youthful look. If not for her eyes, which betrayed that haunted part of her that would never be innocent again, she could have been a kid coming in from making sand castles. He wished she'd gotten a chance to be that kid. Even before coming to Barnacle Bluffs, he doubted she'd been allowed to ever be in-nocent. Having parents who were meth heads generally robbed a kid of any chance at a normal childhood.

She sighed. "I know what you're going to say."

"You might be surprised."

"You think I'm making a mistake dropping out of school."

"Yep. But that's not what I was going to say."

She raised an eyebrow. He gestured to the couch. It took her a few seconds to relent, a bit of passive-aggressive slouching and sighing thrown in for dramatic effect, but she made her way there.

"You want some hot chocolate?" Gage asked.

"What?"

"Thought it might make you feel better."

"I'm fine," she said.

"Dinner?"

"Not hungry."

"I could order a pizza."

She shrugged.

"Chinese?" he said.

"Garrison."

"Okay. Clumsy attempt at connecting not working so well. I'll get to the point. I'll be honest with you. At first, I was going to tell you I thought you were making a mistake dropping out of college. I was going to try to convince you to stay."

She sighed.

"Hear me out," he said. "I *was* going to tell you that, but I realized that it really doesn't matter what I think. You're an adult now, it's your life, and you have to make the choices you have to live with."

"Thank you."

Her tone had turned icy. Best intentions aside, he was still letting his anger get in the way. Instead of sending the message that he accepted her as an adult, he was somehow doing the opposite.

"Okay, look," he said, "I'm not going to lie. I think you're being rash. I wish you'd wait, even a couple of days. But what I'm saying here is, I know it's not my call. I think you're smart—even smarter than you think you are, which is pretty smart as it is." Seeing her mouth curl up in a smile encouraged him. "I trust you're going to figure this out. I just want you to know that I'm here. I'm not going anywhere. You want someone to talk to, I'm here to listen. And unless you want my advice, I'll try to keep it to myself."

The shadow of a smile turned into a full-bore grin. "Careful not to make promises you can't keep," she said.

"Well, I said I'd *try*," Gage said.

"Good enough for me."

"So you want to talk?"

"Not really."

"Okay."

She looked down at her hands folded in her lap, still pale from the cold. "Tomorrow maybe."

"Good enough for me. Can I ask you something else?"

"Okay," she said, still wary.

"What are you going to do? If you're not in school. I'm not challenging you, just curious if you know."

"Not really. Not beyond next week." She started to say something else, then clammed up. "I'm kind of tired. Think I'll go, um, lie down."

"What a minute," Gage said. "What are you doing next week?"

"Nothing. Just, you know, helping out Alex."

"What?"

"You know, helping him at the store."

"Oh. He make a big buy lately that he needs help sorting and pricing?"

"Yeah."

She got up and headed for the hall.

"Zoe, come on," Gage said. "You're not telling me something."

"There's nothing."

"Zoe—"

"Okay, look, he *asked* me not to say anything, okay? I'm covering him at the store for a week."

"What?"

Zoe shook her head, then dropped her shoulders in defeat. "When I told him I wasn't going back to school for a while, he asked if I wanted to work at the store. He said he needed to be gone for a week."

"Gone? On vacation?"

"I asked him that. He said it was personal."

"Personal."

"Right."

Zoe shrugged and disappeared down the hall, leaving Gage in his armchair mulling over what this was all about. Gone for a week. If it had been a vacation, Gage would have heard about it, mostly because Alex would have spent the previous month complaining that Eve was forcing him to leave his perfect life, with the bookstore and the B&B, to shuffle around in flip-flops on some godforsaken beach ten thousand miles away. (Of course, coming home was another matter, when he'd proudly show off the thousands of pictures he took of sea turtles and starfish and those very same godforsaken beaches he'd been complaining about.) It worried Gage. It wasn't like Alex to keep secrets from him.

Gage briefly considered hopping over to the Turret House immediately to shake the truth out of his friend but decided it could wait until Saturday morning. He'd make a quick stop at the store on his way to visit with everybody's favorite football coach.

Seeing Arne Cooper wasn't going to be pleasant, Gage could just about guarantee that, but it had to be done. First, because it was the next logical person who might be able to help him understand Jeremiah. And second, because Gage very much wanted to talk to Jeremiah himself, but because the kid was a minor and Quinn had turned even more unhelpful than usual, Gage knew there was little chance of it happening without Arne Cooper's approval. No chance, really.

Somewhere in there he'd also have to figure out what to make of Karen Pantelli.

He told himself there was no room in his life right now for a woman—not with this Jeremiah business, and Zoe, and whatever the hell was happening with Alex. The tangle of complications only seemed to be getting more tangled by the day. Plus Karen had all kinds of complications of her own, ones she'd so far kept to herself. He told himself this, but while he made vegetable-beef soup for dinner, while he tried to settle his mind by reading the *Economist*, while he lay in his bed, his mind on an endless spin cycle, his thoughts kept returning against his will to a single image.

Karen's lips.

*Chapter 12*

The rain was back Saturday morning, though it was such a pitiful drizzle, just a half grade above a mist, that it could hardly even be called rain. On his way to Books and Oddities, Gage only had to turn on the van's windshield wipers twice. Gray clouds lay thick and low on the ocean, hiding all but a tiny stretch of dappled black-blue water from view. The moisture in the air seeped into everything—his cotton polo shirt, the ripped seat cushion, his bare fingers. Even after five minutes of gripping the steering wheel, the leather still felt cold. His knee, of course, was like a bag of ball bearings and brackets, held together by nothing but habit. This was how his knee always felt, but when the air was cold and wet, he was never allowed to forget it for even a moment.

The store opened at ten. Gage was there at five after. He found Alex, rumpled and wrinkled as always, bent over a ledger. Harry Connick Jr. was singing from the small CD player behind the counter.

"What's this business about leaving for a week?" Gage said.

Alex looked at him over the top of his reading glasses. It may have been the languid morning light, but his friend's face appeared even more worn than usual: the bags under his eyes as big as trenches, the wrinkles like deep gouges, the skin even more gray and patchy. Had Alex looked like this yesterday? It seemed hard to believe that the transformation had happened overnight, which only made Gage feel more like an ass. Something was going on with his friend, and he hadn't even noticed.

"Well, hello to you too," Alex said.

"Out with it," Gage said.

"That girl really needs to learn how to keep a secret."

"Don't blame it on Zoe. And if she knows what your secret is, she wouldn't say."

Alex turned back to his ledger, jotting a note with the ballpoint pen. Steam rose from the paper cup on the glass counter and Gage caught a whiff of it—chocolate and cinnamon, some kind of specialty mocha.

"Now I know something's wrong," Gage said. "You stopped at Bean House."

"I was just in the mood for something different."

"Exactly."

"How about an update on Jeremiah Cooper? Learn anything new?"

Gage leaned his cane against the counter. "Oh no. You're not pulling that move on me. I want to know what's going on next week. What's the secret?"

"There is no secret."

"Bullshit."

"I need to finish updating my books. Where's Karen? She get sick of you already?"

"I'm giving her a break from my winning personality. Alex, do I need to beat it out of you with my cane?"

Outside, a tanker truck rumbled by on Highway 101. After it passed, Harry Connick Jr. was in between songs, so the only sound in the store was the scratch of Alex's pen. Gage waited. If he spoke, he'd only give his friend another chance to dodge the subject, so he had to let Alex get to it in his own time. His own time took another minute, one note jotted in the ledger book after another, before he finally sighed and set the pen down in the fold of the spine. He took off his glasses, letting them hang by their strap, and rubbed his eyes.

"I'm taking Eve to OHSU on Monday," he said.

"What?"

Alex stared blankly into the stacks of his store rather than at Gage. There was such a profound sadness to him that it stopped Gage from saying anything. When somebody in Barnacle Bluffs was willing to make the two-and-a-half-hour drive to Portland for an appointment at Oregon Health & Science University, it was almost always serious. Harry Connick Jr. started up again, something about love and loss and all that jazz. Looking at his friend, and seeing the obvious anguish there, Gage felt a sinkhole open at the pit of his stomach, draining all the warmth out of him.

"They found a mass," Alex said, and his voice caught on the last word.

"Oh Jesus."

"It's only one, very small. Hasn't—hasn't spread, that we can tell from the MRI. Left breast. We're going to OHSU to have a double mastectomy. It's the best option."

"Alex, I'm so sorry. How's Eve holding up?"

"A lot better than me, I'll tell you that."

"How long have you known? I really wish you would have told me sooner."

"Yeah, well," Alex said, "it wasn't my call, buddy. I'm not even supposed to be telling you now."

"Why?"

"You know Eve. She never wants to be the center of attention, especially if she thinks it will bring people down. I told her it's not fair to her friends and family to keep it secret, but she won't really discuss it. So you can't tell her you know, okay?"

"You know I can't keep that promise," Gage said.

"Damn it, Garrison—"

"I'll tell her I got it out of you at gunpoint."

"It won't make a damn bit of difference. I'll still be sleeping on the couch."

"Then I'll buy you an extra pillow."

*"I don't need another damn pillow! I just need my wife!"*

The outburst shocked them both. Alex's eyes flared wide and dark, and his hand, gripping the pen, trembled. Pinpricks of pink dotted his face. Then, just as fast as it had arrived, the moment was gone, the flush fading, the shoulders and chin dropping.

"Sorry," Alex said.

"Forget about it."

"It's just really got to me."

"I'd think less of you if it didn't."

"I just—I don't know what I'd do without her, you know? It never crossed my mind that I'd ever have to worry about it. I'm ten years older than her. And, well, just look at me. My body looks like it's held together with duct tape and Elmer's glue."

"You do look like shit, that's for sure."

That got at least a tiny wry smile from Alex. "I love how you keep my spirits bolstered."

"I'm sorry, was that in my job description? I thought it was just to provide you with a never-ending supply of donuts."

"Yeah, well, you're pretty much failing on that front too."

"Failure is my middle name."

"I thought it was Winston."

"See?" Gage said. "Even at birth, I was already failing. Anybody with Winston as a middle name is destined to go through life as a perpetual loser."

"Well, you could blame that failure on your mother, at least."

"Hey, no comments about my mother. I could still beat you on the head with my cane."

They both laughed. It was a weak attempt at levity, but it still did the trick, even if it only lasted a moment.

"Seriously," Gage said, "if you need anything …"

"You'll be the first person I call," Alex said. "Or not call, I guess, since you don't have a phone."

"Pal, if having a phone meant you and Eve wouldn't have to deal with this crap, you know I'd have one put in tomorrow."

"I know. You okay with Zoe running the store? We should be back in a couple of days, but I want to be home with Eve as much as possible while she recuperates."

"Sure. Better to have Zoe here, where I know where she is, than running around who knows where. You going up there tonight?"

"Yeah. Staying at Hotel Monaco. Treat ourselves to a night on the town, you know. Surgery's early Monday morning, so it makes it a lot easier just being up there."

"Have a blast," Gage said. "You guys deserve it."

They shook hands, and then, surprising Gage, Alex pulled him into a hug across the counter. Not being the sort of guys who hugged, it was the kind of awkward, back-patting flicker of human contact that would hardly be called a hug by the sorts of people who knew what hugs were. Even so, Gage was surprised by how bony Alex's shoulders were, how frail he was under his baggy shirt with the ballpoint pens. When had his friend gotten so thin? The frumpy clothes had acted as a costume, hiding this transformation from view, the person inside the clothes who was shrinking by the day.

"Good luck," Gage said.

Alex returned with a halfhearted attempt at a smile, his eyes watery, before quickly turning to his ledger.


It being a Saturday in November, the heart of football season, Gage had a pretty good idea where Arne Cooper would be.

Still, when Gage parked his van next to the chain-link fence that separated the Barnacle Bluffs High School parking lot from the sunken football field, he was still somewhat surprised to spot the coach standing on the sidelines, his green windbreaker and bald head shiny from the rain, barking orders at the kids scrimmaging on the soggy field. If it had been Gage's son locked up in the Barnacle Bluffs city jail on suspicion of murder, he'd like to think he might take at least one day off from the serious business of chasing a pigskin ball around a hundred yards of grass and dirt.

The rain was really coming down, great big buckets of rain, rain so furious that it exploded in white mist on the grass, the helmets, the muddy jerseys. Gage remained in his van, hoping it would subside a bit and watching the kids below sloshing and sliding around while the coach appraised them with folded arms and a hard stare. The stadium itself, which rose a good ten feet above street level, the rest of it below, blocked all but this one view onto the field. With the windshield wipers off, it was only a few seconds before the scene disappeared behind a watery veil, just long enough that Gage was sure he saw Arne Cooper turn and spot him.

When it became obvious that the rain wasn't going to let up anytime soon, Gage sighed and put on his fedora, clambering into the storm.

He hated to bring his cane, but the danger of slipping on the concrete steps was too great to chance leaving it behind. The deluge pounded him the moment he stepped outside, raindrops pelting the top of his fedora like bullets, crackling against his leather jacket, gluing his jeans to his legs. When he stepped through the open gates of the stadium and started down the steps, one hand on the rail, the other on his cane, there was some relief from the storm, but it was gone the moment he passed out of the protection of the overhang.

Popcorn bags, paper cups, and ticket stubs littered the wooden seating and slate-gray concrete rows. Arne didn't look at him once the whole way down, nor did he look at him when Gage stopped next to him. Two other men, also dressed in green windbreakers, were out on the field acting as referees, chirping their whistles now and then. The coach was such an enormous presence, like a tent himself, that Gage was tempted to stand closer to see if he could get a little shelter from the relentless downpour.

"Not even a day off, huh?" Gage said.

Arne didn't answer. Gage glanced at him and marveled at the way the coach didn't so much as twitch as the water pounded off his forehead, ran into his eyes, streaked across his face. A stoic performance. The part of the statue will be played by Arne Cooper. Gage was about to comment on this when Arne suddenly shouted at a kid who fumbled a pass, telling him to get his legs moving. It was said with such authority that Gage had to suppress the desire to get his own legs moving right onto the field himself.

Another minute passed without a word before Arne finally spoke.

"Kids need the work," Arne said. "They were sloppy yesterday."

"I wasn't talking about the kids," Gage said.

"I don't see no point in sitting around moping."

"Your son is in jail."

"Where he deserves to be."

"So you think he's guilty?"

"He *is* guilty. Everybody knows it."

"I don't," Gage said.

"Then you're an idiot."

"Tell me something I don't know. But I'm still kind of surprised you're so sure about this. He *is* your son. Do you know something everybody else doesn't?"

Finally, Arne looked at him, and it was a scowling mean-ass sort of stare that Gage could see turning even the most hardened of Arne's teenage athletes to jelly. Even Gage had to admit it affected him a bit, a sort of rumble in his gut. Of course, that also might have just been his body's way of saying he needed a sandwich. It was hard to tell.

"Very nice," Gage said. "Just need to get a little more sneer into it."

"What?"

"That expression. I can see you've had a lot of practice with it."

"Man, I'm really tired of your sorry ass. What the hell do you want, anyway? You want my gun again?"

Gage suppressed a desire to pat the place on his jacket where, underneath, his own Beretta lay in its holster. While he hadn't expected Arne to do anything stupid, Gage still thought it was better to play it safe. "Should I?" he asked.

"Well, it's a little late now, isn't it? Police got it."

"We still don't know if that was the revolver that was actually used to kill Connor."

"Are you kidding me? Jerry was caught with it red-handed!"

"Yes, that's true. But *Jeremiah* was pointing it at his own head at the time."

"Because he was ashamed of what he done!"

"Maybe. But if I was Jeremiah's father, I'd think I'd like to wait until the ballistics report definitively proved that was the gun before assuming it was. In my line of work, I've found that things are not always what they first seem."

Arne, eyes flaring through the watery sheen, stared at Gage another few seconds before turning his attention back to the field. "Never thought the kid could do something like this. I kill an ant in the house and Jerry would practically pass out. And he's got more strange phobias than anybody I know. I mean, he wouldn't eat peanuts because he might choke on one! Peanuts, for God's sake! We live on the ocean, but he won't swim because a shark might get him. A shark! When's the last time we had a shark attack in Barnacle Bluffs? Eighteen hundreds?"

Gage waited patiently, letting Arne burn this anger from his system. But it wasn't quite anger, was it? No, it had all the appearances of anger, but this was something else altogether. This cataloging of his son's flaws was a kind of grief, an expression of loss that might have been all that a man like Arne Cooper was capable of showing.

Through all this, the rain persisted. Even though his fedora was thick leather, Gage could already feel his hair dampening just from the moisture in the air. His fingers, gripping his cane, felt cold and numb.

"I'd like to talk to him," Gage said.

"What?" Arne looked at him, as if searching for the joke.

"Your son. I'll need your permission."

"No way."

"Don't you want to know his side of the story?"

"I already saw," Arne said. "I know his side of the story. He walked in there and shot the other kid in the back of the head with my gun."

"He told you this?"

"I said I saw him, didn't I?"

"Saw and talked are not the same thing."

"He didn't need to tell me. He didn't tell me he didn't do it either. That's enough. He's ashamed. He—" Arne caught on whatever word he was going to say, blinking rapidly, then shaking it off. "Don't matter. It's over. I just want him to confess so we don't have to go through the whole trial stuff. Then the town can move on. We can move on. Jeanie and I. Everybody. That's what's got to happen. He knows it too. I told him, but he already knows it."

"You told him to confess?" Gage said.

"It's the right thing to do."

"You told your own son to confess to murder when there's still no definitive proof he really did it?"

"All right," Arne said, "we're done here."

"I need your permission to talk to him."

"Go screw yourself."

"Is your son gay?"

"What?"

This got the bull to turn. Gage didn't think Arne Cooper could tower over him any more, but he was wrong. He might not have gotten any taller, but there was something about how he leaned in, something about the way he filled the space between them, that made Arne enormous, more beast than man. Nostrils flaring. A bit of teeth showing in the sneer. Gage couldn't even imagine being a kid of Jeremiah's size and trying to stand up to a man like his father.

"Who told you that?" Arne said.

"You're not denying it?"

"Of course I'm denying it! My son isn't no homo."

"Did he date girls?"

"What's that got to do with anything? So he was shy. Big deal."

"Did he do anything that made you think he was even interested in the opposite sex?"

"Okay. Okay, you got to go right now."

It hadn't escaped Gage's attention that Arne had balled his

hands into fists—if they could even be called fists. To get hit by one of those fists would be like getting hit by a truck. A train. A mountain. Two mountains. Gage may have gotten the better of Arne Cooper once, but he'd had the element of surprise, plus the advantage of working in the confined space of his doorway. Out in the open, with the relentless rain making things even more difficult, the odds would probably tilt a little in Arne's favor. Maybe even more than a little.

"You're not going to give me permission, then?" Gage said.

"Get the fuck out of here!"

Gage glanced at the field. This was shouted loud enough that even in the downpour, it attracted an audience. Or maybe they'd already had one, the threat of violence in their posture enough to get people's attention. The players, the assistant coaches, all of them had abandoned what they were doing to stare. Oh, how the coach wanted to plant that fist in the middle of Gage's face. Nothing was more plainly obvious. And Gage, tightening his numb fingers on the handle of his cane, was tempted to give the coach his shot.

But this wouldn't help Jeremiah. And it certainly wouldn't endear him to his fellow Barnacle Bluffians. There was no doubt who was the more liked of the two men about to come to blows.

"Thanks for your time," Gage said.

*Chapter 13*

**B**ack in the van, the monsoon continuing unabated, Gage gripped the steering wheel for a good ten minutes before he felt his pulse begin to slow. His fingers were so numb they ached. The world outside his windows was hidden behind endless curtains of water. A cannon could have gone off on the football field and he wouldn't have heard it, the roar was so loud. His jacket and fedora had done little to protect him from the onslaught; he felt as if he were sloshing around in a half-filled washing machine.

Still, it was all he could do to keep himself from going right back out there. It would feel so good to whack Arne Cooper in the head.

Instead, he started the ignition and headed back to Highway 101, where he stopped at the nearest Chevron. While some kid wearing too much cologne filled his tank, Gage rifled through what was left of the phone book in the booth outside. Bingo. The address of Arne and Jeanie Cooper was listed. Why wouldn't the head coach want his address public? Small-town mentality won out again.

They lived in one of the newer subdivisions, behind the BB-5 Cineplex and only six blocks from the high school, a nice but cookie-cutter two-level whose most prominent feature was the garage that took up the entire first floor. It differed from the other houses on the street only in how much gray brick trim decorated the outside. Like most people who actually lived and worked in Barnacle Bluffs, rather than simply occupied it on the weekends, they had no view of the ocean. They did, however, have a wonderful view of the back of the theater.

The house was actually quite small, but the way it was designed, it was as if it was trying to puff itself up, like a man sucking in his gut and standing on the balls of his feet to impress a woman. An American flag flapped in the wind. There was no net in the portable basketball hoop, which was really the only sign of neglect. The house was immaculate otherwise.

No cars out front. When he got out of the van, he saw an old woman peering at him through a kitchen window across the street. He waved at her and she snapped her blinds closed.

The massive deluge had slowed to a minor deluge, but as soaked as Gage was, it really made no difference whether it was raining at all. Regardless, he was glad for the arch over the front door. He rang the doorbell and no one answered. He knocked and got the same result. He sensed the old woman watching him from her perch behind her blinds. Making notes. If he knocked again, he was pretty sure she'd call the police. Why not? Only people up to no good knocked a second time.

Fortunately, he didn't need to take this chance. A white Ford Escort turned into the cul-de-sac, stopped at the driveway, and, after a moment's pause when he was sure the person behind the whirling windshield wipers was studying him, finally turned into the driveway. The garage opened. The car rolled inside. The garage closed. In between, he caught a glimpse of a stout woman wearing a red scarf over curly chestnut hair.

He waited a few minutes and tried the doorbell again. No answer. He knocked, then knocked again a little harder.

Finally, the door opened, catching on the chain. Jeanie Cooper, no longer wearing her scarf, peered at him with wide, fearful eyes.

"I'm afraid I'll have to ask you to leave," she said with a tremulous voice.

"Without buying any magazines?" Gage said.

She blinked a few times, her lashes long and dark. She wore enough makeup that it clung to her face like a plate of armor. For somebody who'd just been out in a hell of a storm, the makeup looked awfully fresh. Had she actually touched herself up? He couldn't see much of her through the tiny crack in the door, but what he could see was a short woman in a floral print dress, her pearl necklace too big to be anything but fake. She had a small mouth and a slight double chin. It was hard to pinpoint her age because of the makeup, but he guessed late forties, like Arne.

"I'm sorry?" she said.

"I'm not selling anything."

"I know who you are. I'm not supposed to talk to you."

"Who told you that? Arne?"

"Please leave. I don't want any trouble." She started to close the door.

"I think your son's innocent, Mrs. Cooper," Gage said.

That got her attention. She blinked those long lashes of hers a few more times, searching his eyes. The door was only open a few inches. Gage felt the heat within the house streaming out, brushing past his face.

"I just want to help your son, ma'am," Gage said. "That's the only reason I'm here. If you think there's any chance that your son didn't do this, you really should talk to me."

She hesitated. "I really have to go."

"Mrs. Cooper, please. I just want to talk. Give me five minutes. You can kick me out at any time. I like your son. He's a good kid, and I'd hate for him to spend the rest of his life in prison for something he didn't do."

This got her to tear up, though she gamely kept the waterworks at bay. They were hanging on the edge. Any more pushing and he knew he'd lose her, so all he could do was wait.

"I don't know," she said.

"Just a few minutes."

"Arne—"

"He doesn't have to know."

Then, as if they were conducting some clandestine exchange, she unlatched the chain, leaned out a little farther, and glanced around the neighborhood. Satisfied, she stepped back and allowed Gage into the house, closing the door quickly behind him. Standing there on the red brick foyer, dripping on the tiles, Gage felt as if he'd just surfaced from a deep dive.

The first thing he encountered—it was impossible not to, since it was a huge and positioned right in front of the door—was a massive picture of Jesus, set behind glass and framed in oak. Thomas Kinkade prints of glowing cottages filled the rest of the walls. A staircase led off to the left, an alcove to a kitchen to the right, and straight ahead, beyond the foyer, he saw a tidy living room with a leather couch, two matching wingback chairs, and a flat-screen television that took up nearly an entire wall. He spotted more Thomas Kinkade prints and dozens of little white porcelain angels.

"It's a very nice living room," he said.

"Thank you," she said, wringing her hands together.

"You really like angels, I see." Gage was trying to make conversation, loosen her up a little. If someone touched her on the shoulder from behind right now, he was pretty sure she'd scream.

"Yes," she said. "They—they remind me to walk God's path."

"It's good to have those reminders."

"And they also—also remind me that none of us are beyond redemption."

"Even Jeremiah?" he asked.

Tears sprang up in her eyes, so fast it was as if he'd hit a button, and she blinked them away. "All of us. Otherwise—otherwise there would be no reason to go on living. You just need to read the Bible. If more people read the Bible and stayed true to it, the world would be a better place. There's so much wickedness out there."

Gage, whose own opinion about religion was a bit more complicated, decided that now was not the time to engage in a philosophical discussion. "I want to help your son, Mrs. Cooper."

"I don't see how. There's so much evidence … everyone seems so sure. I don't—I don't know what can change things. I've prayed and prayed. Arne says we just have to hope the lawyer can get a lighter sentence. Insanity plea. I don't know."

"Do you have a lawyer yet?"

"No. No, Arne is working on it."

Water dribbled onto Gage's face, and he wiped it away with the back of his hand, which didn't do a whole lot of good since the back of his hand was like a wet sponge. He was conscious of how fragile she was. She was like one of her figurines. It wouldn't take much to shatter her. "Well, I'd like to start with the assumption he's innocent. It can't hurt, right? Let's just assume he didn't do it and go from there. Can I ask you a few questions?"

"I don't know. I have to start working on dinner. Arne will be home soon."

Gage decided to take a bit of a chance. "Ma'am … Jeanie … Can I call you Jeanie? Your son's life hangs in the balance. Don't you think dinner can wait?"

For a moment, Gage thought he'd gone too far. All over her face, around her eyes and her mouth, there was lots of quivering and twitching. A watery veil fell over her eyes.

"Yes," she said, as if she'd made a very important decision.

"Did you know about your son's friendship with Connor Fleicher?"

"Just a little. I took Jeremiah to lunch once. I asked—I asked him if he had made any friends. He mentioned Connor."

"Was there anything unusual about their friendship?"

"Like what?"

Gage didn't know how far he could go. Judging from Arne's reaction, he was guessing that if Jeremiah was gay and admitted it to himself, it was doubtful he would have admitted it to his parents. "Did his feelings toward Connor seem … more intense than a usual friendship?"

"I don't know," she said. "I didn't … I didn't see him much. He stopped coming to church. Said he had his own chapel there.

He stopped by the house a couple times to get some things, usually when Arne was at a game." The blinking came in rapid-fire sequence. The hands were wringing with such force that Gage was afraid she might break her fingers.

"I take it the two of them didn't get along?" Gage asked. "Your husband and Jeremiah?"

Jeanie shook her head, though it wasn't so much a no as if she were trying to shake off an unpleasant thought. "Arne loves him," she said.

"Did they fight a lot?"

"Not recently."

"But they did? Before?"

She nodded. "They're very different. Arne loves sports. It's his life. Jeremiah, he's a quiet boy. Reading. *Star Trek.* He loves *Star Trek. Doctor Who.* All those science-fiction shows. Some others. *Battlestar Galactica.* Arne didn't understand. I told him—told him …"

"It's all right," Gage said.

"I told him that Jeremiah's just different. He's not going to be into sports, but Arne never gave up. Kept making Jeremiah go to all those camps. Football. Basketball. Soccer. Even tennis. He just wanted Jeremiah to like a sport, any sport. But it just wasn't to be. But a couple years ago he just sort of gave up. And that's when the fights stopped. They didn't really talk much. I prayed a lot, hoping they'd find their way back together, but … It's too late now."

"Jeanie, this is a tough question to ask, but … Did you think he might ever be suicidal?"

"Arne? No. He'd never do anything like that."

Gage thought it was strange that she should immediately assume he was talking about her husband. "Jeremiah. Did you ever think your son might think of his taking his own life?"

"What? No, not Jeremiah. No, he wouldn't do that to me."

"Did you know that I caught him with your husband's gun?"

"He what?"

"Your husband's revolver. I caught him with it on the beach about a month before he started at the college, during a big storm.

He was shooting into the sand. He kept saying he was a coward. Why would he say that?"

She shook her head. "I don't—I don't understand. I never knew. I didn't know."

"Did you know that Arne had a gun?"

"Yes. For protection."

"But you never knew that Jeremiah took it?"

"Not before. Just that they, they caught him with it. At the college."

"Did you ever catch him with it before?"

"No. No, he didn't like guns. Arne took him to the shooting range once when he was, oh, maybe ten. Another one of those things. Jeremiah, he came home crying."

"Jeremiah," Gage said.

"What?"

"I just noticed that you haven't been calling him Jerry."

She nodded, not so much in agreement than as if he had made an observation she needed to consider. "He goes by both. He goes by both Jerry and Jeremiah."

"He told me he prefers Jeremiah."

"Oh?"

"Jeanie, did your son have many other friends? Especially recently? Anyone else he talked about other than Connor?"

"Well … your daughter. Zoe. He mentioned her a few times."

"Anyone else?"

"Not really."

"Not really?"

She chewed at her bottom lip. He could see that her tank was running low. Any minute he was going to lose her. The rain, in a rhythmic beat, swished against the roof like the bristles of a broom. Inside, safely ensconced with her figurines and her figurative paintings, they were safe and dry and isolated from the harsh realities of the world. Gage got the sense that this was the only place Jeanie Cooper felt even remotely comfortable, and that wasn't saying much.

"I mean, not real people," she said finally. "Maybe people on the computer. He spent a lot of time on the Internet, especially the last few years."

"What did he do on there?"

"I don't know. I don't really know."

"But you said you thought he was interacting with people on the Internet. What makes you think that?"

"I don't know."

"Jeanie ... Mrs. Cooper, please. This could be important."

She shrugged. "He just ... a couple times, he talked about some of the, what do you call them, places he talked to people on the Internet. Hangouts."

"Facebook?"

"No, he hates Facebook. He says it's a popularity contest. He likes to go to places around his shows."

"Message boards? Fan forums?"

Her eyes brightened. "Yes, that's it. Fan forums. For his shows. If he has any other friends, that's where they'd be. There was one called SpacedOut. I think that was the one he went to the most. Sometimes, when he'd be sitting with his laptop, I'd see over his shoulder that he was typing a message in one of those places. And he'd be smiling. Happy. I didn't bother him about it, because it was one of the few things that made him happy. *Makes* him happy."

Gage had noticed that she'd been drifting between the present and past tense when referring to her son, but it wasn't unusual. Back in New York, he'd run into this before, people with a loved one facing life in prison or worse, trying to cope, trying to come to terms that the person they'd cared so much about may not be playing a meaningful part of their life in the years ahead. It was part of the grieving process, of letting go, and it said something about Jeanie Cooper that she was already engaged in it.

"Did the police take his laptop?" Gage asked.

"I guess so. He took it with him to school."

"Did he have anything else he used to get on the Internet? A home computer? An iPad?"

"No. No, just the laptop." She squeezed her hands together a little more. Her left eye was visibly twitching. "I think, I think you should go now."

"I'd like to see his room," Gage said.

"Um, no. I don't think so. Not right now."

"It might help."

"How?"

"*Anything* could help at this point. I'm just trying to get a better picture of Jeremiah as a person."

"There's not a lot there. Some science-fiction models. Some posters. A year or so ago, he got rid of almost everything from his childhood. Toys, stuffed animals—he said it was time to leave it behind. He did it when I wasn't here, or I would have stopped him. Have him box it up and keep it. Maybe, maybe give some of those things to his own kids someday. If he had them. You know." Her voice fell off sharply, to a whisper, then silence, as if someone abruptly turned down the volume.

"Did something happen at the time?"

"No. Maybe. I don't know. It was after he came back from one of those conventions he liked to go to. A *Star Trek* thing."

"In Portland?"

"Yes. Yes, I think so."

"Aren't you the one who took him?"

"No, Arne did." There must have been a surprised look on Gage's face, because Jeanie continued a bit defensively. "He does love Jeremiah. He may wish that Jeremiah was more like him, but that doesn't mean he doesn't love him. He wants him to be happy. We both want him to be happy."

"I just can't imagine your husband hanging out with Klingons."

"Oh, he didn't stay. He went to visit a friend of his who coaches at Portland State. I think you better go now. He should be home soon. He won't be happy you're here."

"One last thing," Gage said, though there were actually lots more questions he'd like to ask her. "I'd like your permission to talk to Jeremiah."

"What?"

"I'm afraid the police won't allow me to talk to him without parental approval."

"Oh, I don't know."

Gage stepped a little closer, lowering his voice. "Jeanie, if I don't talk to him, I'll never be able to prove he's innocent. I don't think Jeremiah did this. I can't explain why yet. But I bet your son can. I bet he knows a lot more than he's telling us."

"Arne—"

"It's not just up to him. Jeremiah is your son too."

"He'd be very upset."

"If he finds out, probably," Gage acknowledged.

"He'll find out."

"I'm not going to lie to you. He probably will."

Her eyes grew wide as the rest of her appeared to shrink, like a mouse huddling in the corner. "He gets *so* angry."

"Does he get violent when he's angry?"

"What?"

"I mean, does he hit you? I don't want to put you in danger."

"No! He's never touched me or Jeremiah. He just … yells a lot. Sometimes he breaks things. But he's never hurt me."

"All right," Gage said, "I know I'm still asking you to take a risk. But it's for Jeremiah. I can help him. I might be the only person who can right now. I just want you to make one phone call. Tell them who you are. Ask to speak to the chief or one of the detectives. Tell them you're giving your permission for Garrison Gage to talk to your son. Can you do that for me, Jeanie? It could make all the difference."

"I don't—"

*"Please."*

He put his whole weight into the word, really leaning into it. The extra emphasis seemed to work, breaking her briefly out of her funk. She looked at him, searching, as if what she was supposed to do was written on his face.

"Okay," she said.

"You'll do it?"

"Yes."

Gage looked at her, waiting. She looked back, not seeming to comprehend.

"Do you have a phone in the living room?" he asked.

"Oh," she said, "you mean *now*."

"No better time than the present."

THE RAIN WAS still pounding—if anything, it was raining *harder*—when Gage parked the van in front of the police station.

The light was poor. Even at midday, it felt like dusk, the coiled gray clouds choking off the sun. Gage, pride getting the better of him, left his cane in the car and paid for it by slipping on the wet sidewalk by the door and nearly going down, only saving himself by grabbing the handle of the glass door. And who should be waiting for him, leaning on the front counter, but Detective Brisbane, he of the bags under his eyes, the rumpled and ill-fitting shirt, and the pallor of a corpse.

He lifted a paper cup in greeting, and his eyes had an amused glint to them. Behind him, Madge, their bosomy dispatcher, pecked quietly on her keyboard, her black headset disappearing into her great bob of dark brown hair. The harsh glare of the fluorescent lights shone in the white countertop like a deep scratch; the base of the counter was carpeted like the floor, in a swirling pattern of browns and blues. "Nice little dance step there," Brisbane said. "Man, aren't you a sorry sight. You fall in Big Dipper Lake or something?"

"I'm here to see Jeremiah," Gage said.

Brisbane, obviously in no rush, took a sip from his coffee. The office behind the front counter, a series of cubicles tall enough that the occupants were hidden, hummed with activity, clicks and beeps, a dozen murmuring voices on a dozen phone calls.

"We video the front door, you know. I'll have to get the tape. Upload it to YouTube."

"What's YouTube? The nickname for your toilet?"

"Bet it will get a million hits."

"You think? It can't be as popular as that time you wrestled naked with Trenton in hot mud. That move you pulled, grabbing his love handles, was really something."

Madge snickered, which for her was the equivalent of a lengthy soliloquy. For a dispatcher, she was remarkably quiet, hardly ever speaking other than through the headset. Brisbane glared at her, but she took no notice.

"Jeremiah," Gage said.

Brisbane downed the rest of his coffee, then leaned over the counter and tossed the cup into the garbage. Taking his time. He loosened his tie, which was already plenty loose. He propped himself up with his elbows, nodding, looking Gage up and down as if sizing him up for a fight. Gage wondered when Brisbane had last been in a fight, other than to fight into his clothes each morning, which was the only way to explain their consistently disheveled appearance. No clothes could get that wrinkled unless someone was trying to beat the crap out of them.

"Yeah, Jeanie Cooper called," Brisbane said.

"Imagine that."

"And we can't seem to get in touch with Arne at the moment. He was in the process of getting an attorney. If he'd gotten one, we wanted to make sure your visit was all right."

"You have one parent's approval," Gage said. "You shouldn't need another."

"Yeah, well, we like to cover our bases."

"Since when?"

"Since you got involved, Gage. Anyway, you can talk to the kid, but there's a hitch. I'm going to be your escort."

"Are you going to wear a tiara?"

Brisbane shook his head, rueful and sad as always, and motioned for Gage to follow. A short hall with locked doors, one of which was the interrogation room he and Zoe had been in the previous day, led to a thick metal door with a barred center window. The police officer on duty searched Gage, took his Beretta, then waved them past.

"Don't get your hopes up," Brisbane said. "The kid's been practically catatonic since we brought him in. Won't talk to anyone, not even his parents."

"You never know," Gage said. "I might surprise you. I'm a master conversationalist."

They stepped into a hall of bare concrete with a high barred window at the end and a security camera mounted inconspicuously above the window. The air was warm, almost balmy, and smelled of damp concrete. Gage hadn't been in the city lockup more than a handful of times over the years, and he was always surprised to find how much warmer it was inside. Soaked to the core as he was, the feeling wasn't unwelcome. There were five jail cells, all on the right, and all but the first and last were dark. A heavily tattooed man occupied the first cell, eyeing them like a caged tiger.

The last cell appeared empty—a rumpled cot in the corner, some comic books by the toilet. Gage was going to ask Brisbane if it was some kind of joke when he finally spotted Jeremiah sitting on the bed, head bowed. His plain gray T-shirt, camouflaging him against the concrete wall, may have had a fair amount to do with his being hard to spot, but his stillness, so statue-like it was inhuman, probably played a bigger part. Gage couldn't help but stare. It was mesmerizing, really.

"Hey, guy," Gage said.

Jeremiah didn't even glance in his direction. Not even a twitch of his eyebrow. There was something sadly profound about it, sadder than if he had broken down and sobbed.

"Hey, kid," Brisbane said, "wake up. Got a visitor here. Your mom okayed it. You want to join us for a minute?"

If Jeremiah was even breathing, Gage couldn't see it. Down the hall, the occupant of the first cell snickered. Other than a faint hum of an air duct somewhere beyond the ceiling tiles, there were no other sounds.

"Been like this since we brought him in," Brisbane explained. "Dad and Mom couldn't do nothing about it. You should have seen Arne. He was practically screaming in the kid's face. Nothing. It's like he's checked out. Maybe overwhelmed by guilt. I don't know. Some part of his brain is just gone."

"You know," Gage said, "Jeremiah *is* sitting right there. He can hear you."

"You think? I'm not so sure. Hey kid, you in there? Come on, talk to us?" Brisbane leaned between the bars. "Kid! Come on, man, you want to talk to Mr. Private Investigator here or what? He's probably the only friend you got!"

"All right," Gage said.

"What? Just trying to help you out."

"You can help me out by leaving us alone."

"Not going to happen."

"I plan to just be with him for a while. It could be a long wait."

"Fine, I got all day."

Gage shrugged and settled himself on the floor, easing himself down with the cane. He crossed his legs and tried to get comfortable, though the surprising coldness of the floor, his wet clothes, and his throbbing knee made any real comfort out of the question. Even this got no reaction from Jeremiah.

"You're serious?" Brisbane said.

"I could use the rest," Gage explained.

"This ain't no senior home, pal."

"Really? This smooth floor is perfect for shuffleboard."

Gage looked up to see if Brisbane was amused. He wasn't. It was hard to tell if Brisbane had ever been amused. The facial muscles used to show a smile were probably so derelict at this point that even if Brisbane *was* amused, he wouldn't be able to show it.

"I can wait as long as you," Brisbane said.

"Fine."

"The only reason this is happening at all is because even after being advised of his rights, the kid hasn't asked for a lawyer. And the parents haven't seemed all that concerned either. You know why that is? It's because everybody knows he's guilty. The kid knows he's guilty. Look at him. You think he'd act that way if he was innocent? No way."

Gage had to suppress the desire to whack Brisbane in the knees. "How about just five minutes alone?"

"No way."

"Fine. Have it your way."

So they waited. As expected, it was a long wait. Five minutes passed, but they felt more like ten. Ten minutes passed, and they felt more like fifty. Jeremiah didn't move, not even to scratch his nose. Brisbane made a couple of remarks, something about a heavy caseload this year, another about the drunk tourists really being out in force, but he stopped when Gage, emulating the kid, didn't respond. He may not have been able to sit as still as Jeremiah—there were too many little aches and pains throughout his body to tolerate it for long—but he did his best.

"All right, for Christ's sake," Brisbane said finally. "I'll give you your five minutes. I have to take a dump anyway."

"Enjoy the experience," Gage said.

"No funny stuff while I'm gone."

"Not even my Abbott and Costello routine?"

With a roll of his eyes, Brisbane left. Despite Brisbane's bravado, Gage got the sense that he may not have been one hundred percent certain that Jeremiah Cooper was guilty. Gage had never been a cop, but he certainly knew that gnawing feeling when the facts of a case just didn't add up to the conclusion, no matter how obvious that conclusion seemed to be.

"We don't have long before our pal comes back," Gage said. "You have something to tell me, you should do it now."

Any hope that Brisbane's presence had been the chief reason Jeremiah was pulling the silent treatment were dashed. Even a Tibetan monk, meditating with the weight of the world on his shoulders, would have been jealous of how supremely still Jeremiah was.

"You do any acting in high school?" Gage asked. "No? I bet you would have been terrific. Better yet, a mime. That's just real impressive, sitting as still as you are. Or how about those folks in the big cities? The living statues? Doubt they have a living-statue major at BBCC, though. Probably not a lot of call for it here. Maybe down at Berkeley, though. You think of transferring to another school? When we get you out of this place, I think you should consider it."

There was something, the barest hint of a reaction, the tiniest flutter of his eyelid, not really even noticeable on a conscious level, but Gage was sure he'd seen it.

"I know you didn't do this," Gage said.

Now there really was something. The kid frowned—not a frown by the usual standards, but a downward tuck of the corners of his mouth nonetheless.

"But I've got to prove it," Gage said. "I admit, there's a hell of a lot of evidence pointing to you as Connor's killer. This town is pretty much ready to string you up. I might be your only hope, the only one who really believes you're innocent. I need your help."

Jeremiah looked at him—or not quite at him, more of a sideways glance, staring at a spot somewhere between the two of them, but definitely turning in his direction. Now they were really getting somewhere.

"Who did it, Jeremiah?" Gage asked. "Do you know? If you know, tell me, and it will make my job a lot easier."

"You're wrong," Jeremiah said. His voice had the scratchy quality expected from someone who hadn't spoken in days. "You're wrong about me."

"Oh?" Gage said.

"I did this. I'm guilty."

"No way."

"I—I shot him."

Gage shook his head. "I take back what I said. You're a terrible actor."

"I'm not acting."

"Good to know. Who really did this?"

Jeremiah returned to his sacred mission of drilling holes in the floor with his eyes. But he wasn't quite as still anymore. Gage had broken through the kid's composure.

"Okay, I'll play along," Gage said. "Let's say you *did* do it. Why'd you shoot him?"

No answer.

"Pretty nasty business, shooting him in the back of the head like that," Gage said. "Probably didn't even see it coming. And yet, the way he was sitting, he had to know who it was. Somebody he was comfortable with, otherwise he wouldn't have turned his back, don't you think? Sure, that could have been you. You two were pretty close, I hear. Maybe you were hanging out in his room, he insulted you somehow, made a flippant comment about Spock's big ears or something, and you decided to show him who really knew *Star Trek*. You just knew this day would come, which is why you had your dad's revolver on you. You were waiting for it. Waiting for him to insult Spock one more time ..."

"Stop," Jeremiah said. His eyes were big and bright, his jaw trembling.

"Or was it Doctor Who? Help me out here. I'm not as up on all the science-fiction shows as you."

Jeremiah shook his head.

"But it wasn't that, was it?" Gage said. He briefly considered whether to push into more dangerous territory and decided he really had no other choice. "Okay, we're still going with you being the shooter here. What are other theories? How about this? You were in love with Connor, but he didn't love you back. You wanted a sexual relationship, and he wouldn't reciprocate, said he didn't see you that way."

This finally got the kind of reaction Gage had been hoping for: the kid leapt off his cot and sprang like a wild animal toward the bars.

"Fuck you!" he screamed. "You don't know anything! You don't know anything at all!"

Gage got to his feet, taking his time. Partly this was to give Jeremiah a chance to calm down, but mostly it was the pretzel knots of pain springing up in all kinds of places. There were days when Gage felt like a young man, despite his bad knee, but this wasn't one of them. When he was finally upright, he leaned in close to the bars and dropped his voice to a whisper.

"Help me out then," he said. "I can't help you unless I know more. Do you know who did it? Do you know why?"

The boy's lips parted a crack, and Gage knew it was right there, the answer. It was close enough to reach out and snatch it, but then Jeremiah shook his head. The fire in his eyes flared one last time, a final surge, then it was gone. His shoulders slumped, and once again he was this frail wisp of a kid who'd lost what little will he'd had before all this madness had started. When he spoke, it was in a dull, emotionless monotone.

"I did it," he said, nodding. "Go get the cops. I confess. I did it."

"Jeremiah—"

"I confess," he said.

"I don't believe you."

"I don't care. I'm confessing. I have to."

"What do you mean, you have to?"

"I confess."

"Jer—"

"I confess, I confess, I confess …"

The kid went on repeating it like a mantra, no matter what Gage said, no matter how much he pleaded with Jeremiah to really think about what he was doing. He went on until Brisbane returned, then he repeated it to Brisbane's face, with even stronger conviction. The glee on the cop's face sickened Gage. He wanted to punch him. He *would* have punched him, if he hadn't been too depressed to summon the effort.

Even then, as Gage felt the world closing its door on Jeremiah Cooper, he believed more than ever that the kid was innocent.

*Chapter 14*

On his way back to the house, Gage picked up a couple of turkey subs, thinking Zoe might have a late lunch with him. When he got there, he found a note saying she was at the bookstore doing some training with Alex, and, if it was okay with him, that she planned to spend the night at the Turret House to look after the cats. If it was okay with him? It was a nice gesture, but he knew she didn't really mean it. She wasn't asking for permission, and really, he didn't expect her to any longer. Not that he ever had.

Unlike most times, Gage was in no mood to be alone. He wanted to commiserate about his failures with someone. Since his first two choices were out, that left the pretty lady staying at the Inn at Sapphire Head.

The steady downpour had turned into a sporadic drizzle by the time he pulled into the inn's parking lot. The gray sky bowed low like a tarp stretched taut by the water cupped in its canvas. Ducking through the tunnel that separated the parking lot from the inn, under the highway, Gage was hit by a blast of cool, salty air with enough force that he would have lost his balance if not for his cane.

In the lobby, which was decorated in green marble and a low-nap purple carpet, a middle-age man dressed in khaki pants and an obnoxious Hawaiian shirt was asking when the next shuttle to the casino was expected to arrive. A woman, probably the man's wife, waited patiently at the white couches near the floor-to-ceiling windows, taking in the expansive view of the beach and the ocean. Gage punched the button for the elevator and spent the waiting time taking in the view himself.

He could go down there. Skip right past the pretty lady's room on the first floor and walk a few miles on the wet sand. It would be a good way to clear his mind. Maybe he'd find a few seashells, a sand dollar or two.

But why? What was he trying to avoid? He was just enlisting Karen's help on the case, that was all. When the elevator opened, he stepped inside and punched the button for the first floor. He was alone except for the many reflections of himself cascading through the mirrors, and each of those reflections looked tired and beaten, a middle-age man with thinning brown hair made slick by the rain, leather jacket and jeans rumpled as if he'd slept in them. He should hop the bus to the casino, join that old couple for an afternoon of fun in the blinking lights. That vacant stare of his was the kind of thing that he saw when he occasionally hit the poker tables. Most gamblers, he'd found, had already lost before they'd begun to play.

There he went again, trying to think of a way to avoid seeing Karen. She was young, attractive, and obviously interested. On top of that, she was whip-smart. What was the problem? Well, he knew what the problem was. There was Jeremiah in jail, Zoe dealing with her friend's death, and Alex struggling to keep it together while Eve underwent treatment for breast cancer. There was no room for anyone else, especially an FBI agent who, no matter how attractive, was obviously dealing with some issues of her own.

Dating her would just be like gambling with all the odds stacked against him. He was bound to lose before he even began.

Yet when she opened the door, it didn't help matters at all that she answered it wearing a gray Lycra tank top, hardly more than a sports bra, and black exercise shorts that showed off her lean and muscular legs. Or that her hair was pulled back in a tight ponytail, revealing her swanlike neck.

Her face was flushed and slick with sweat. She even smiled, as if she was happy to see him. Since most of the time he'd spent in her company, she'd acted as if they were on their way to a funeral, the smile caught him off guard. It really wasn't fair, that smile. She was so attractive as is, a man barely had a chance to keep his wits about him in her presence. When she deployed that smile, there was no hope.

"Oh," she said, winded, "you didn't call ahead."

"Yeah, I'm not so good with the calling thing," he said.

"Having a phone would help."

"Would it?"

"So I'm told." She mopped at her face with a white towel. A strand of hair stuck to the side of her face. "I just got back from the hotel gym. You mind waiting while I get cleaned up?"

"I can come back some other time," Gage said, nodding toward the elevator. "I was just in the neighborhood. Thought I'd say hello."

"In the neighborhood," she said.

"Right."

With a roll of her eyes, she grabbed his arm and pulled him into her room, closing the door before he could offer to wait upstairs. Not prepared for it, he stumbled on his bad knee, falling into her. There was the bump of bodies and somehow, when he managed to right himself, he had his hand cupped over her right breast. It was only there a second, but it was a long second, long enough to feel the smoothness of the Lycra, the warmth of her body, the firmness of her flesh. Like a boy who accidentally touched the stove, he yanked his hand away.

"Sorry," he said.

"Sure you are," she said. "Nice way to use the whole cane business to cop a feel. Bet you use that one a lot."

"It was an accident! It's never happened before. Oh wait. Maybe one other time. In this hotel, actually. But it was an accident, too, I swear!"

"If it happens twice in a row, it's not an accident," she said. "It's a pattern."

"Well, I'm not doing it consciously."

"I'm not sure that's better."

They were standing close enough that he could see how much her eyes were dilated, close enough that he could smell the sweat on her—and it wasn't an entirely unpleasant smell. It was time to change the subject, and fast. "Do you have a laptop? With Internet access?"

"Why?" she said. "You want to look at naked ladies on the Internet?"

"I want to research something."

"Something related to female anatomy?"

"Wow," Gage said. "You really are relentless, aren't you?"

"You just grabbed my breast, and you say I'm relentless? Come on, I'll get my iPad for you."

It was on the nightstand next to the bed, in a case that looked a like old parchment. As he held it in his hands, she leaned close, typing in a password and activating the screen. He felt the heat coming off her in waves. A bead of sweat trickled from her temple down to her cheek. She swiped her fingers across the screen, tapped an icon, and brought up an Internet browser. The way her hands moved, with such deftness and purpose, was like a miniature ballet.

"Judging by the look on your face," she said, "I take it you haven't used one of these before."

"I've played around with Alex's iPhone," Gage said. "But this is amazing."

"Rethinking your approach to technology?"

"Not in the slightest."

She laughed. This was a good laugh, the laugh of someone who'd forgotten to be self-conscious. He'd always been a sucker for a woman's laugh. As she laughed, he became mesmerized by her lips again. He noticed the slight residue of lipstick, a color of pink that nearly matched her lips, as if she wanted to wear lipstick but didn't want anyone to know. He noticed the chewed-up skin on the lower lip, where she obviously bit when she was nervous. He noticed the sheen of sweat under her nose.

She noticed him noticing, and, whether on purpose or not, leaned a bit closer. He felt her breath on his neck.

"What are you looking for?" she asked.

"What?"

"On the Internet."

"Oh. It's a forum. A fan forum. It's called SpacedOut or something. Jeremiah liked to hang out there."

She held his gaze a beat longer than was necessary, then clicked in the search box and brought up the on-screen keyboard. As she typed, her bare arm brushed against his jacket. He felt his heart pick up its pace, felt the flush on the back of his neck. With her intently focused on the screen, he was free to admire her, the flutter of her eyelashes, the curve of her cheekbone, the way the dangle of a single strand of hair caught the light from the open window. Click, tap, swipe, and there was the forum. It wasn't until she looked up that he realized that he'd been staring at her, and he swallowed.

"Thank you," he said.

"Knock yourself out. I'm just going to take a shower."

"Okay."

"Can I ask you something?"

"Um."

"Technology. Phones. The whole anachronism bit."

"Anachronism bit?"

She nodded, and just for a moment, crazy as it was, he was almost certain she was going to kiss him again—and this time he was disappointed when she didn't. "You seem pretty young to be such a ... I don't know. What's the right word? Old fogy? I don't quite get it. What is it that you have against the modern world?"

"Maybe the modern world has something against me. And I'm not *that* young."

"You're not even fifty yet. I checked."

"You checked?"

"It's almost like it's an act," she said. "Like you're purposely being obtuse just for the hell of it. Because you know it annoys people or something."

"Does it annoy you?"

He said it with a laugh, expecting a witty rejoinder in return, but she considered the question as if it warranted a more thoughtful response.

"Only a little," she said.

"Well, that's good."

"And not really in a bad way. It's kind of charming. You throw people off a little. They don't know what to make of you. Is that why you do it? To keep people off balance? Some master detective trick?"

"Ma'am," Gage said, "if I could explain the inner workings of my own mind, life would get a lot easier for me."

"That's just the thing," Karen said. "I think you know exactly what you're doing—even if you don't think you do."

"You're making my head hurt."

"But it's more than that, isn't it?" she said. "I'm overthinking it, probably. It's more about you. About you wanting to create a life that's, what, disconnected from everybody. Is that it? You want to cut people out, keep yourself safe, because caring about other people can cause pain."

"I feel like I should be lying down on a couch while you take notes."

"I'm just trying to figure you out, Garrison."

"That makes two of us. And what about you?"

"Huh?"

"Are you cutting people out, Karen?"

"No."

"What are you running from?"

"Running? I'm not running. I'm on vacation."

"Bullshit. This isn't a vacation. What happened that made you run for the hills?"

She stared defiantly, her eyes doing this little dance, a two-step shuffle back and forth. Somehow the distance between them had been cut to only a few inches. He could count the freckles on her nose. He could study the sweat on her eyelashes. She was searching his face, looking for something, and she settled on his lips. She shifted forward, as if she was going to kiss him, but then suddenly spun away and marched off to the bathroom.

"I have to take a shower," she said.

There was a certain smugness this time. She knew exactly what she was doing to him. He wouldn't have been surprised if she could even hear his heart, which was beating so hard it actually hurt. Watching the sway of her hips, the way those shorts clung to her body, all those wonderful curves, it was all he could do to keep himself from following her. It didn't help that as she closed the bathroom door, she glanced over her shoulder, her expression both seductive and mysterious, before she disappeared inside.

It wasn't until he heard the shower a few minutes later that he realized that he was still staring at the door.

He swallowed away a lump as big as a golf ball, then settled into the chair by the sliding glass door. He tried to concentrate on the iPad, but his mind wandered. It wandered right back to those tiny shorts. Her room, on the first floor, led directly to the beach, and even the slope of the sand reminded him of a woman's body. The ocean beyond the beach was dark and brooding, an undulating mass of grays and blues.

The next thing he knew, she was standing in front of him.

In a towel.

"Doesn't look like you've gotten far," she said.

"Huh?"

She pointed at the screen, which still showed the home page of the SpacedOut forum. When she moved her arm like that, the towel shifted, almost slipped, though she made no effort to grab it. Steam rose off her arms, her bare shoulders, her slicked-back hair. It was not a big towel. In fact, like most hotel towels, it was quite short. Minuscule, really—more of an oversized white hand towel. One little tuck was all that kept it in place, and when she shifted, her breasts shifted along with it, straining against the rough cotton.

"Been daydreaming?" she said.

"Mmm."

"What's wrong? Am I distracting you?"

Somehow he found the will to clear his throat. "You should—you should probably get dressed."

"Probably," she said nodding. The towel slipped a bit more. Now there was more breast showing than hidden, soft white flesh. "Probably should do that, yeah."

"Do you, uh …" he began.

"Yes?"

"Maybe—maybe I should …"

"You should what?"

Then the towel slipped and fell. She made no effort to stop it, nor even acknowledged that it had happened. She stood before him in all her glorious nakedness, skin glistening, the muscles taut in the right places, the flesh more forgiving in others. She was as fit as an Olympian, lean and powerful, a precision machine in the way all the body parts fit so perfectly together, but with still enough womanly curves that there was little boniness to her. She had a tattoo of a black rose on her hip, quite low. He tried to remain focused on her eyes, he really did, but no heterosexual male could fight off that kind of temptation for long. The strongest of them could only last a second. He lasted less than that.

"Karen."

"Mmm?"

"Your towel."

"Yes?"

"It, uh, fell off."

"Sure did."

"Um. I don't—I don't want to take advantage of you."

"Why not? What if that's what I need right now? Jesus, take advantage of me."

"But what happened to you that—"

"Forget about that. This is how you can help me. "

"Karen—"

She leaned into him, cupping both sides of his face and kissing him hard on the lips. Whatever protests he had, that kiss was like a delete button for his mind, wiping it all away. He tasted soap. Then her whole body folded against him, legs between his legs, her breasts on his jacket. Small as she was, she still seemed to envelop him, bare flesh crushing against him, a hot furnace of sexual desire.

In the beginning, other than sliding his hands onto her bare bottom without really thinking about it, he was not much more than a passive participant. She kissed him hungrily, on the lips first, then worked her way down, kissing his chin, his Adam's apple. Then she slid her hands under his polo shirt and across his chest, kissing her way down, his belly button, lower still, a few nips and bites along the way, reaching his belt buckle and working his belt free with the deftness of a street magician performing a card trick.

When she started working on his zipper, Gage decided it was time to start being an active participant. Or maybe *decide* was too strong a word. His own desire took hold, his qualms banished to some backwater part of his mind. It had been too long since he'd been with a woman, and his body, knowing this, was not letting him miss the opportunity. In an instant he was standing, clutching her bottom so hard she yelped, holding her against him as he carried her to the bed. His knee hurt like hell, but what did it matter?

The heat of her neck against his nose. The honey scent of her shampoo. He barely had time to take in these sensations before they fell onto the bedspread. She was laughing and smiling, happy in the moment, and seeing her in this state was the most powerful aphrodisiac she could have used on him. Somewhere along the way, with a fair amount of help from her, he shucked off his own clothes. Now, skin against skin, contact wherever contact was possible, there was no room for thoughts at all.

And for all their hurry in the beginning, there was no hurry in what happened next.

* * *

"NICE ROOM, by the way," he said.

She murmured in response, and with her head on his chest, he felt it more than he heard it. A single cotton sheet lay over their cooling bodies, her hand resting on his stomach, her leg draped over his legs. Gage didn't know what time it was, but judging by the position of the sun, a silvery wrinkle in a sky like aluminum foil, it had to be going on late afternoon. He should have cared, felt the rush of impatience to make something happen in the strange case of Connor Fleicher and Jeremiah Cooper, but for the moment he cared only about remaining where he was. Her hair, now dry, tickled his nose, and he breathed deeply, taking in the intoxicating smell of her.

"A little expensive, though," he said.

She lifted her head and peered out the window, as if noticing the view for the first time. Far away, too far for them to see into the hotel room, a woman and a child, both dressed in parkas, walked hand in hand by the surf.

"Yeah," she said.

"I'm not complaining, mind you."

"I wanted to treat myself," she explained. "I've been staying in Motel 6s mostly. And I thought, you know, if you were interested … I wanted a nice place."

Looking down at the side of her face, her head still lying against his chest, he could clearly see the rosy color in her cheeks. It was funny, blushing after everything they'd done to each other the past few hours. He'd known she was fit, but she'd certainly proved it. She'd proved it, proved it again, and proved it a few more times just to make sure there was no doubt. If it had been a scientific experiment to prove her fitness, there'd be no question of her thoroughness.

"It sounds like you've been planning on seducing me for a while," he said.

"Ever since I met you," she said.

"I'm that handsome?"

"Mmm. Try not to let it go to your head."

"Too late. I'm needy that way."

"You're a hell of a lover too."

"Wow," he said. "Now you're really in danger of overinflating my ego."

"I didn't think your ego *could* be overinflated."

"There you go. That's bringing me back down to size."

Her hand, resting on his stomach, strayed lower. "I bet I could bring you back *up* to size pretty fast."

"Ah."

"Cat got your tongue?"

"Or something."

She giggled. Her hand moved away, index finger tracing lazy circles on his chest hair. "Don't worry. I'll let you recharge."

"Thank you."

"But only for a little while."

They lay like that for a time. He heard voices through the walls, a man and a woman in the next room. He couldn't make out the words, but he could tell it was a pleasant conversation, an easy one. Maybe they were talking about where to go for dinner. Whether to walk on the beach now or later. The movie they'd seen last night. Easy chatter. The kind that he used to have with Janet years ago, and with Carmen when she was still in town. He hadn't thought he'd missed it, but now he saw how empty his life had been, how much of a hole Carmen had left in his life when she'd gone.

Now here was this woman, this lovely, beautiful woman, a strange combination of resolve and fragility, like a steel bearing inside an eggshell—or perhaps the other way around.

"Can I ask you something?" he said.

"Okay." Already he could hear the guardedness in her voice.

"You don't want to talk about why you're here. That's fine. I don't want to push you."

"I *told* you, I'm on vacation."

"Yeah. You said that. But you know I'm not buying it, so let's drop that charade, okay? I just want to know one thing right now. Are you still in the FBI?"

She didn't answer for a moment, then she rolled away, facing the wall. The rivets of her spine were like footprints left in the sand. He reached out and touched her back, gently pressing his fingers against her warm flesh. She pulled away from him, body half off the bed.

He sighed. "I don't know why you have to keep this from me. I want to help you."

"That's just it," she said. "Maybe I don't want your help."

"I just want to have some idea what I'm dealing with here."

Her voice, when she spoke, turned thick. "You're dealing with a woman who wants to make love to you. Why does it have to be more complicated than that?"

"It's *always* more complicated than that."

"Jesus. *Men.* You try to give them what they all say they want, sex without the complications, and all they can do is ruin it."

"Is that what men want?"

She didn't answer.

"Or," he said, "is it just what the men you've been with want?"

She rolled over, facing him again, and her eyes were watery and bright. "Are you *trying* to be cruel?"

"I'm trying to get you to talk to me."

"Maybe you should go."

"I could call Alex and he could log into the FBI database. He still does some part-time work for them, you know. I bet he could find out the answer to my question pretty quick."

"Jesus!"

"I'd rather have it come from you," he said.

"Get out!"

"Are you still in the FBI?"

"Leave!"

She shoved him hard in the chest. There was an animal-like rage about her now, her eyes dark, her face flushed with her anger. When he didn't move, she shoved him again, even harder. Her arms were so lean, her hands almost as small as a child's, but there was a focused power about her. He felt the bruises already forming.

Not reacting the second time seemed to slip something loose

inside her. She screamed and thrashed at him, pummeling his chest, arms, and face, not punches but wild swings that sometimes connected but mostly in a glancing way. Even so, the sum of all that fury was going to leave him bloodied pretty quickly if he continued absorbing it with his defenses down.

So he swept her up in his arms, squeezing her close, crushing her arms and breasts so tightly against his chest that she didn't have much room to operate. She went on struggling, bucking and kicking, a hysterical display that finally culminated with her biting him on the shoulder. Biting him! Absorbing *that* without resulting in a violent response of his own took every ounce of self-control he had, but absorb it he did—though not without a strangled yelp.

Whether it was the yelp or more generally his steely resolve, her fever of rage broke. The screaming turned into sobbing. She plowed her face into his shoulder, whole body convulsing, a seizure of tremors and shakes, hot tears planted against his skin. This took twice as long to burn out as the rage, but he held on just the same.

Eventually the fire burned out. The rocket fuel was spent. The smoldering remains lay cradled in his arm, a lovely woman who seemed much smaller and more fragile. Minutes ago he was wondering how any person who stood against her, whether as a lover or as a criminal, would have any chance. Now he wondered how she even had the strength to get through the day. Every person may have contained such a contradiction within them, but he couldn't think of a time when they had both been on display in such a short period.

Outside, the ocean in all its vast grayness continued its endless sweep against the sand. There was nothing out there but rotting logs and tangled kelp. The air whistled through the vent above them, and he could just feel it brushing his forehead. Karen was so still, he thought she might have fallen asleep, but then she sniffled.

"Sorry," she said.

"Don't be," he said.

"I made a mess of your shoulder."

"It's probably an improvement."

She replied with such a soundless laugh that he wouldn't have been able to tell if she didn't have her face pressed against him.

"Do you want to talk about it now?" he asked.

She shook her head.

"Okay," he said.

"Eventually. Eventually, I will. I just … not right now. In my own time."

"Okay."

"But I'm still in the FBI, okay? I'm just … I'm on leave. I answered your question. But wait on the rest. Can you do that? Can you wait?"

"I can wait," Gage said.

"Good. While we're waiting, I want to show you something."

"What's that?"

Her hand began to move again.

"Oh," he said.

THE AIR WAS still too charged with emotional electricity to spend time in her room with the iPad, so after getting showered, he took her to the inn's restaurant. It was going on five o'clock by this time, and they had the panoramic view all to themselves. The skylights and the floor-to-ceiling windows lining the west wall gave the place the feel of a cruise ship, especially since they were so high they could see only ocean, no beach. They could have been a hundred miles out at sea. The sun, quite low, strained to pierce the overcast skies like a silver sword lancing through wool. A gas stove burned low in the center of the room, pulsing out waves of heat.

They took a seat near the window, sitting side by side, her knee pressing against his thigh as they both leaned in close, over the iPad. He set his cane on the chairs on the other side, trying not to be self-conscious about it. At this point, what did he have to hide?

Since she was obviously more familiar with the iPad, she took the helm, navigating through SpacedOut's flashy front page, full of photos from all the current science-fiction movies, into the many layers of fan forums. The neon green text on a black background was tough for Gage to read, but Karen appeared to have no trouble, fast-tapping her way through the account-creation stage and plumbing the depths of the forums, dancing from one thread to another so fast Gage had a hard time keeping up.

It was also tough keeping his attention focused on the screen with her sitting so close. Even the smallest gesture, as she pushed a strand of hair over her ear, was mesmerizing. There was something about watching her work. The world disappeared for her. When they ordered, she barely looked up, simply mumbling that she'd have the same as him—a New York sirloin, medium rare.

"All right," she said, when the waitress had gone, "I think I got a handle on this place."

"I'm glad you do," he said.

"Sorry," she said, looking at him. Other than a bit of red around her eyes, there was little sign of her outburst earlier; a second shower and a bit of makeup had done the trick. "Didn't mean to leave you in the dust."

"I'm still with you. Barely."

She smiled faintly and squeezed his hand under the table. "You've already showed you can keep up with me in the most important way."

"I hate to admit, but I was running on fumes at the end."

"Hmm. Well, better eat that steak. You'll need that energy later." She must have seen the surprised look on his face, because she laughed. "Just kidding. I think I've done enough damage to you for one day."

"You think?"

She held his gaze for a playful second, then shifted her attention back to the iPad. "This is one popular site. Hundreds of different subforums, each centered around a different show, and inside each of those forums are hundreds of threads. The popular ones, like *Star Trek* and *Star Wars*, really dominate. The site does make you register to participate, but you don't have to use your own name. Most people post under anonymous handles."

Gage studied the screen. "Like MyBigWookiee2008?"

"Yes, they can get a bit nerdy."

"And I take it you searched for both Jeremiah and Connor?"

She nodded. "Nothing under their own names. Not really that surprising. But I've got a few more tricks up my sleeve. Take a look at this."

She tapped a few times on the screen, whizzed her way through a few pop-up menus, and suddenly they were looking at HMTL code.

"Scary," he said.

"Only if you can't read it," she said. "Lucky for you, I thought I was going to be a computer analyst at the FBI before I got hooked on field work. I'm a bit of tech nerd."

"Is there anything you *can't* do?"

"I can't play the piano."

"Well, that settles it, then," Gage said. "I can't be with any woman who can't play the piano."

"I'm not bad with the electric guitar, though." She pointed at the screen. "See, this site is actually fairly open. It lists their IP addresses if you know where to look. And if you have that—"

"—you can narrow down their location," Gage finished. And when she looked at him with surprise, he shrugged. "I may appear to be a Luddite, but I do try to have at least a passing understanding of things."

"That's more than passing," she said. She tapped and swiped and copied one of the addresses, then opened up another window, quickly loading another site that could identify the IP. She copied and pasted the IP address and a few seconds later had some information about its location. "See, this guy's from the Sacramento, California, area."

Gage saw where she was headed. "There's not nearly as many people in Barnacle Bluffs as there are in Sacramento."

"Right."

"So if we can find IP addresses based here, there's a good

chance it's going to be Connor or Jeremiah. Or at least we'll be able to narrow it down to a handful of people."

"My thoughts exactly," she said. "The problem is, without my handy-dandy friends at the FBI on speed dial, I'm left searching these IP addresses one by one. There's thousands of users. It can take a long time."

Gage thought about it, rubbing his thumb along his water glass, leaving a moisture trail on the cold glass. *"Red Dwarf,"* he said.

"Huh?"

"I saw a poster on Connor's wall. *Red Dwarf.* It looked like a British show."

"Yes, and what's your point?"

"Maybe it's not as well known. Which means—"

"—it's probably got a less active forum," she said, finishing his thought. "I get it. Fewer names to search."

"And you can also eliminate anyone who's posted since Thursday," he said. "With Connor dead and Jeremiah in jail ..."

"Right. Give me a second."

Her eyes glittered with her excitement. He felt the excitement himself. It felt good to be on the trail of a solid lead. More than that, it felt good to be working with Karen. He'd never had a partner. He'd never *wanted* a partner. Even when he'd been starting out back in New York working for his uncle, chasing down deadbeat dads and cheating wives, he'd chafed at working with anyone else. He'd always assumed that he wasn't the sort of person who could even have a partner, but now he was at least reconsidering the idea.

It took her more than a second. It took her the entire time before their meals arrived, steaks juicy, vegetables steaming. She whirled from one screen to the next, occasionally tapping a name in an open document before whirling onto the next. Even while they ate—it was the best steak Gage had eaten in a long time, tender and succulent, but he doubted she noticed—she kept returning her attention to the iPad. He made a couple of jokes about kids living in their parents' basements, pretty good jokes if he did

say so himself, but she ignored him. Finally, when he was decid-
ing whether he was really hungry enough to eat that cauliflower,
she looked at him and smiled triumphantly.

"Three names," she said.

"What?"

"Three names. Three people from the mid-Oregon coast who
fit that criteria."

"Three?"

She cut into her steak. "That's right. SpockLives2008. DWR_
forever. And Fireflyawesome. *Firefly* was a cult show in the late
nineties that was only on the air briefly. I don't know what *DWR*
stands for."

Gage remembered Connor's drawing right away, the one
with *DWR* surrounded by a bunch of animals. He described it
to Karen.

"Any idea what it means?" she asked.

"No idea, but there has to be a connection. So those three
people all posted before Thursday but not after?"

"Yep. And here's something else. I'm pretty sure that
SpockLives2008 and Fireflyawesome are Jeremiah and Connor.
Not sure which is which, but when I scrolled through their posts,
it's pretty clear they're teenagers. Every now and then one of them
will drop a reference to their parents or jerks at school."

"What about the other one?"

She swallowed a bite, closed her eyes and enjoyed it. "Mmm.
Nothing like a little exercise to make you appreciate a fine steak."
She opened her eyes and fluttered her eyelashes at him. "I don't
know, but I'm guessing he's not a kid. He made some digs about
women on their periods. He made a reference to Monica Lewinsky
that kind of dates him too. But here's the best part. They all made
a reference to private-messaging each other—about a week ago."

"Anything else to go on?" Gage asked.

"Not so far. A lot of nerdy posts about time continuums and
alien races. I went through them pretty quickly, so I can read
through them again a bit more closely. It's not like they posted
a ton, though. Especially DWR_forever. He was just in there a

couple dozen times, all of them in the past few months."

"In other words, since school started."

"Right."

"I just thought of something. The IP addresses … would BBCC have their own unique IP address?"

She put down her fork and marveled at him. "Are you sure you weren't a computer nerd in another life?"

"I've been told I was a ballerina in another life."

"I can see that. You're quite light on your toes."

"You should see me *en pointe*. It's a thing of beauty."

She was already tapping away on the iPad. It took her only a few seconds and she was smiling.

"What?" he said.

"All three of them have a couple different IP addresses, but all three of them also have at least one from BBCC. Probably means they were posting from other locations, too—home, a coffee shop—but the main ones are at BBCC."

"Bingo," he said.

"It gets better. Two of the IP addresses are almost identical. I'm guessing that's because they're in the dorm. The other one is different. It's DWR_forever."

"Could be another student," he said. "Maybe logging in at the library or the student union. He or she just doesn't live on campus."

"Or somebody who works there," she said.

"Or somebody who works there."

They let this thought settle. If the situation wasn't disturbing enough, the idea of a professor or staff member tied up in the murder definitely took it over the top. But why? That was the million-dollar question. Find out who DWR_forever was, and he had a sense that he'd be a lot closer to freeing Jeremiah Cooper from jail. The question was how. If Karen was on leave, he doubted she'd have access to her powerful friends, some of whom might be able to give him the actual names behind the handles. There was always Alex, who had his own contacts in the FBI, but Alex had his hands full dealing with Eve, and there was no way Gage was going to lean on him. There was the ever helpful Barnacle Bluffs Police Department, of course, but he very much doubted they'd agree to any kind of quid pro quo, no matter how nicely he asked.

Then Gage realized he was probably overthinking this. There might be a much easier way to find out who this person was.

"Can you post something?" he asked.

*Chapter 15*

After dinner, Gage decided to make a run to the Turret House to check on Zoe. Karen didn't ask if she could tag along. She simply did. The sky was dark. The air felt heavy and thick. A few pinpricks of water appeared on the van's windshield, but otherwise the rain had mercifully stopped—at least for a short while.

"Does it always rain this much?" Karen asked.

"It *is* Oregon," Gage said. "Technically, a lot of East Coast cities get more rain than us, but we just get it in lots of little drizzles instead of the occasional big storm. Spreads out the joy."

"How can anyone stand it? It'd drive me crazy after a while."

"It's exactly because it drives other people crazy that a lot of us like it. Keeps away the less committed."

"Maybe you should *all* be committed."

"Let me guess, you're from Nevada?"

"Arizona, actually. But mostly I was a military brat. Traveled all over the world. I saw all kinds of weather, but I guess I'm still a sun worshipper at heart."

She sounded as if she were on the verge of saying something more, but then she lapsed into silent contemplation, gazing out the passenger-side window as they buzzed over the highway. He didn't press. He saw what pressing got him, and he trusted that she'd come out with it in time. And if not? Well, he liked being with her, and he'd take whatever he could get.

That was an odd thing for him. He wasn't good at avoiding mental land mines. He was more the kind of guy who jumped on them with both feet. As they drove, he kept glancing at her, and each glance stirred up the same butterflies in his stomach. The headlights of the passing cars swept across her face, the shadows deepening and receding, accentuating cheekbones and jawline, eyes shadowed and then revealed. The fluttering in his stomach, the flush on his face, the quickening pulse—Gage had to force himself to stop looking at her or he was going to drive himself nuts.

She pulled out her smartphone, the screen giving her face a bluish glow.

"Any response yet?" Gage asked.

Karen tapped and swiped a few more times. "It *has* just been ten minutes, you know."

"Yeah, but you were thinking the same thing, weren't you?"

"I was just going to play Solitaire."

"Liar."

"Maybe we should have written something else. It was pretty vague."

"Nah, I think it'll work."

They'd settled on the screen name TheOneWhoKnows. They'd debated for a while what to write to DWR_forever in a private-forum message and finally settled on "I have information you don't want people to know." They thought about adding more, perhaps demanding to meet, but Gage figured it was better to leave the person wondering about their intentions. Gage had learned it was often better to play it tight for a while until you had a better read on your opponent, like in a poker game.

They turned west, dropping past stores crowding the highway, winding along a road lined with green Scotch broom, a few sad fir trees, and only a couple of small cottages. Every year, the Scotch broom, which would be blooming with explosive yellow flowers in the spring, encroached a little more, strangling what was left of the natural vegetation. The three-story Turret House Bed and Breakfast lay at the end of a long winding road with sweeping, expensive houses on either side, nestled on one side by a grassy dune. Brown shake siding, blending into the darkness, made the glowing windows that much brighter. The two wrap-around decks and the turret, which was technically a fourth story, gave the place the appearance of a castle.

There were two cars parked in the gravel parking lot in front of the Turret House: Zoe's white Toyota and a teal F-150 with black mud flaps. He didn't recognize the truck, and he felt a creeping anxiety. Alex had told him there wouldn't be any guests. When he parked along the street, Gage saw Zoe talking to a man at the front door. The man, dressed in a baseball cap and a green windbreaker, was tall and lean, a bit thicker in the waist than in the shoulders, like a slim pyramid. Gage recognized the windbreaker. It was just like the one Arne Cooper wore.

Hearing the Volkswagen's noisy motor, they both turned and looked at him. It wasn't until Gage got out of the van, stepping into the wind, that he recognized the man. It was one of the assistant coaches who'd been on the football field when he'd talked to Arne Cooper earlier that day. Zoe, dressed in a baggy black T-shirt and black jeans, didn't look unhappy; in fact, she looked almost pleased.

The wind was strong enough that Gage didn't dare leave his cane in the car, even though he was sorely tempted. He hated looking weak around the macho types.

"Hey there," the guy said, tipping his baseball bat. He flashed a wide grin, and despite a few crooked teeth, it was a handsome smile. "Just returning a book to Zoe."

Zoe held it up, a thick, well-worn paperback. "It's Stephen King's *The Stand*. I'd let Jeremiah borrow it. Mr. Weld was just bringing it back."

"It's autographed," Weld said, as if that explained everything. He extended his hand to Gage. "Paul Weld. I don't know if you remember me. I taught Zoe in biology three years ago. Figured because it had King's signature, Zoe really would want it back."

Gage shook the man's hand. He was expecting a macho grip for a macho man, but instead the handshake was like his smile, warm and welcoming. "I'm still a little confused as to why you ended up with the book."

"I've been a family friend of the Coopers for a long time. Jeanie found it, and she asked if I could return it. I emailed Zoe, and she said I could drop it off here. I hope that was okay?"

"It's fine," Zoe said, before Gage could reply. "I really appreciate you stopping by, Mr. Weld."

"It was no problem." He extended his hand to Karen. "Ma'am, I'm Paul Weld. Did I hear that you're an FBI agent, or is that just a crazy rumor?"

"It's not a crazy rumor," Karen said, shaking his hand. "But I'm not here representing the bureau. The name's Karen Pantelli."

"Vacationing?"

"Something like that."

"Well, I wish we could have given you better weather."

Nobody said anything for a moment. They stood there in the wind nodding at each other.

"I guess I better get going," Weld said.

"Sounds good," Gage said a bit too eagerly.

"Look," Weld said, "I know it's probably not my place here, but I wondered if maybe I could give you some advice."

"Uh-oh," Gage said, "this never goes well."

Weld's jovial smile faded a bit. "Excuse me?"

"People giving unsolicited advice," Gage said. "For some reason, the advice usually comes out as some sort of warning or threat."

"*Garrison*," Zoe warned.

"No, no, nothing like that," Weld said. "Look, I've known the Coopers for a long time. Both Arne and I grew up here. Both of us graduated from Oregon State. Me and Arne started teaching the same year. I even met Jeanie before I met Arne, in Bible school as a kid. I like the whole family. I know Arne doesn't have the warmest personality in the world—"

"Right off, I pegged him for a member of Toastmasters," Gage said.

Weld chuckled and adjusted his baseball cap. "Witty. I like that. No, listen, I just wanted to say maybe to cut him a bit of slack. This is very tough on both Arne and Jeanie."

"And Jeremiah," Gage added.

"Right. Of course. And Jeremiah. I'm just saying, Arne may not show it very well, but he really does love his son. I was with Arne the night before Jeremiah was arrested— we had dinner at my house, and we were watching video from the last game. He actually talked about him, how he really hoped Jeremiah would find his way now that he was on his own. If you could have seen his face … well, there'd be no doubt about how much he really cares about that kid. He just doesn't understand him. They're very different. You know that. And this whole thing, this is killing him. It doesn't help you riling him up all the time."

"Well, I'm truly sorry for riling him up," Gage said, "but you see, I'm working hard to prove his son's innocence, and it's not easy when nobody else seems to believe it except for me."

"I believe he's innocent," Weld said.

This surprised Gage. "You do?"

"Without a doubt. No way he could have done this. I don't have kids of my own, but if I did, I'd want a son just like Jeremiah. He's smart as they come. And brave in his own way. Did you know he once published an article in the school paper titled 'Ten Irrefutable Reasons Evolution Is a Fact'? That's pretty bold in this town. A lot of Bible thumpers around here. And with his own mother being such a fundamentalist Christian, well, it was even more brave …"

"I forgot about that," Zoe said. "It was neat to see Jeremiah come out of his shell a bit. I remember him talking to you about evolution a lot. He was really passionate about it."

Weld nodded, and when he spoke, his voice took on a new roughness. "Although he seemed to lose his way a bit his senior year, I still thought he would have found his way to a career in the sciences."

Gage found himself liking Weld despite himself. "So how long were you with Arne on Wednesday?"

"Oh, from practice after school until very late—midnight maybe. We'd often lose track of time like that, just analyzing plays and chatting. Why? Wait, you don't think *Arne's* a suspect, do you?"

"I treat *everybody* like a suspect. I try not to discriminate."

"Me included?"

"Sure."

"Hmm. I'll try not to be offended. In this case, Arne had a few too many beers, so I drove him home. Jeanie met us at the door. So unless he went out after that, I think you can safely cross him off your list. Considering he practically fell asleep in the car on the way home, I think him leaving again is highly doubtful. And my mother can attest to me coming home a few minutes later. She was having a hard time sleeping and was up making herself some tea."

"Your mother lives with you?" Gage asked.

"It's more accurate to say I live with her. I moved in after Dad died. Why? Is she a suspect too?"

"Could be."

Weld nodded. "She's ninety-two, mostly blind, and can't get around without a walker, but … she's deadly at pinochle. Was pinochle involved in this at all?"

"Too early to say."

"All right. Just assuming, for a moment, that my mother isn't guilty. Or Arne. Or me. Do you have any other possible leads? Honestly, it's the other reason I came over here. I was hoping to run into you. I've just got to believe that there's some hope for Jeremiah."

"You call him Jeremiah," Gage noted.

"Certainly. Why shouldn't I? That's what he prefers."

"And yet Arne calls him Jerry."

Weld sighed. "As I said, their relationship is complicated. But do you have any idea who might have done this?"

Gage nodded. "I'm not at liberty to discuss things yet, but

there's some possibilities."

"Ah."

"Anything else you know about Jeremiah and Connor could really help. Did Jeremiah mention any other friends? Maybe ones he just knew online?"

"I never knew Connor. And no, I'm afraid I don't know much about Jeremiah's online life. Though I can say that the last few years, he seemed to spend most of his time glued to that computer. Why, do you have reason to believe the person who did this met him—"

"I don't have reason to believe anything yet," Gage said, cutting him off. "I'm just exploring some possibilities."

"I see. Well, if there's anything you need—"

"I'll let you know."

"Right. I was just hoping there was something I might be able to do. I know it was a long shot. I just … I care about that family, Mr. Gage. I hate that this is happening to them. But you know that. You know the boy is innocent too. Now that I know that, it makes me feel better. Zoe, Karen, good night."

He tipped his baseball hat and, while they watched, departed in his truck. The taillights were still visible at the end of the street when Gage turned and raised his eyebrows at Zoe.

"Don't give me that look," Zoe said. "Mr. Weld's the nicest guy in the world. He was my favorite teacher. He used to run a little candy shop out of the back room. I didn't even care that all the money went to the football team." She looked from Karen to Gage and back again. "So are you two, like, an item now?"

Gage glanced at Karen, who, he was delighted to see, was blushing again. Her skin was a bit too dark for a bright stop-sign sort of red, but he still saw plenty of pink.

"Um," Karen said. "Well …"

"We are as far as I'm concerned," he said, rescuing her.

He wasn't sure how she'd take that, but the pleasure in her eyes was unmistakable. He'd been tempted to allow her to suffer in embarrassment a bit longer, just for the fun of it, but he didn't think Zoe would put up with it. She was already getting that nonplussed way about her, when his very presence seemed to irritate her. He would have asked to go inside, because standing in the cold air was making his knee ache, but he didn't want to press his luck.

"Quick question for you and we'll be out of your hair," he said. "You ever heard of the website SpacedOut?"

Her brow furrowed. "Is that one of those science-fictiony-type websites?"

"Exactly."

"I think maybe Jeremiah liked to go there."

"Did he ever talk about it?"

"Not really."

"Nothing about the people he met on there?"

Her eyes turned distant. The wind picked up, stirring the bits of grass on the dunes, launching fine particles of sand in the air. He couldn't see the ocean from where he stood, or hear it because of the wind, but he could smell it, the salty freshness of it, and he could sense it, too, the sprawling immensity just over the rooftop.

"You know," Zoe said, "I do remember him swearing off the Internet a couple months ago."

"Swearing it off?" Karen said.

"Yeah. He said everything just got ruined on the Internet anyway because when something's good, people just find out about it and ruin it. I mentioned Facebook, which was good when it came out, but then all the old people got on there and things just got crappy. No offense, by the way."

"None taken," Karen said. "I'm not old so I know it doesn't apply to me."

"I still can't even find the Facebook," Gage said. "I don't know what section to look for it in the bookstore."

"Anyway," Zoe went on, after a brief eye roll, "I thought that's what he was talking about, more of a general rant thing, but maybe he was talking about one of his sites. I didn't think about it until now. I didn't think it was a big deal."

"Why would you? It still may not be a big deal."

"But it may be?"

Gage shrugged. "So he didn't mention anybody he hung out with on there?"

"No. Why?" Her face turned grave. "You think whoever killed him was somebody from one of those forums?"

"I don't think anything yet," Gage said. "I'm just exploring possibilities. Think hard. You can't remember anyone, other than Connor, he may have mentioned that he met online?"

"No. Like I said before, Jeremiah wasn't much of a talker. And we weren't really that close. I mean, I had other friends, you know? I like Jeremiah, but it wasn't like … like I was going to hang out with him all the time. I kind of wish … well …"

Her voice grew hoarse. Karen reached over and squeezed Zoe's shoulder. Rather than shrug it off, which was what Gage expected, Zoe bowed her head. It was the kind of gesture that Karen did effortlessly but would have come off as forced and awkward if Gage had done it—if he had thought to do it at all, which, knowing himself, he doubted he would have. He admired Karen for it, was even a bit jealous. He didn't lack for empathy, despite the commonly held opinion of him. He simply had a hard time showing it.

"There's always a lot of what-ifs," Karen said. "But if you don't let them go, you'll never be able to move on."

There it was again, Karen brushing up against that dark place that haunted her. Both Gage and Zoe looked at her, waiting for it, and for a few long seconds Gage thought she might actually tell them what it was, but then she gave Zoe's shoulder a soft squeeze and let her hand fall limply to her side.

"Well," Zoe said, "if I think of anything more, I'll let you guys know."

"You have my number?" Karen asked. "You know, since this one here doesn't believe in modern technology."

"Ouch," Gage said.

"Modern technology?" Zoe said. "Try *any* technology."

"Double ouch," Gage said.

"But no, I don't have it. You want to text me and then I'll have it?"

Karen pulled out her phone and Zoe told her the number. While Karen typed on the little keys, Gage stepped closer to Zoe.

"Everything okay at the Turret House?" Gage asked

Zoe shrugged. "No guests, so not much to do. Kind of worried about the bookstore tomorrow, but since it's only open from noon to five on Sundays, hopefully it won't be too bad."

Gage almost offered to come down and help her, but he suspected that Zoe would only take this to mean he didn't believe she could handle the bookstore on her own. "You heard from Alex?"

"Yeah, they called a while ago just to say they were going out for dinner."

"Good for them," Gage said.

"Oh boy," Karen said suddenly.

"What?" Zoe said. "You need my number again?"

But Gage knew, just from Karen's face aglow from the phone's light, that her comment was about more than a wrong phone number. She looked like somebody had just told her she'd won the lottery.

"They message back?" he asked.

She smiled up at him. "They did."

"What did they say?"

"They said, 'Who are you?'"

"Hmm. Even somebody who had nothing to do with Connor's murder might write that."

"That's not the best part, though," Karen said. "The best part is where the person wrote it."

Now it was Gage's turn to smile. "Let me guess," he said. "The IP address, it's from the college?"

"Not only that," Karen said, "but the person just sent it. Which means—"

"—that they're probably still there," Gage said.

## Chapter 16

There weren't a lot of tourists who visited Barnacle Bluffs in November, but there were obviously more than a few, judging by how clogged Highway 101 was as Gage rushed to the college. What were all these people doing here? There were tons of them.

Or maybe not tons. Maybe it just seemed that way, since it was one of the rare times Gage was actually in a hurry since he'd moved to the town.

"You know," Karen said, "that guy's bumper won't move any faster because you're so close to it."

Gage peered through the whirring windshield wipers at the mud-stained Taurus ahead of them. The rain had started again shortly after they left Zoe. "What are you talking about? I've got at least fifty feet."

"Fifty inches maybe," Karen said. "I can read his bumper sticker, and it's in tiny font. It says *God Bless the NRA*. Maybe you should take it as a sign that rear-ending him might not be a good idea."

"You're such a worrier," Gage said.

"You have a plan?"

"Get to the college and find this person."

"Not much of a plan."

"How many people can there be at the college on Saturday night, especially when the school's been shut down?"

"Good point," she said.

"I also have a backup plan."

"What's that?"

"Tell you about it when we get there."

She smirked. "Tease."

It seemed logical that the college would be mostly abandoned when there was no school for a week, but there were actually still lots of cars in the parking lots—not full by any means, but when it was all added up, several dozen vehicles. As Gage cruised around the campus, he saw that plenty of dorm and office windows were lit.

"Should we go door to door?" she asked.

"Nope," he said. "Now's the time for the backup plan."

It took him a minute, but he found the right area to park the van, in the lot near the front. He killed the engine, listened to it tick in the stillness for a while, watched the campus. Nobody was coming or going. The rain, which had lessened to a mist, streaked the cones of yellow light beneath the streetlamps.

"Okay," Gage said, "I want you to send another message. Write, 'I left an envelope for you taped to the bottom of the mailbox at the IGA. It explains what I want. Come get it before I change my mind.'"

Karen pulled out her phone and started typing. "You think he'll actually go for it?"

"Would you?"

"Depends on how worried I was."

"Exactly. And the IGA is just down the road. Even if it's a kid here without a car, they could still walk to it."

"So what, we just sit and wait?"

"I can think of something else to do, but not sure now's the time."

"Dirty bastard," she said.

"What? I was thinking you'd teach me how to play *Angry*

*Birds.*"

"Is that what the kids are calling it these days?"

"I don't want to *know* what the kids are calling it these days. Hold on, here's somebody."

A girl in a red trench coat, a wisp of a thing, left the student union and walked briskly across campus to the dorm. She disappeared inside. After that, nothing happened. They waited, the heat seeping out of the car.

"What if somebody leaves and it's not our person?" Karen asked.

"If somebody leaves, we follow them to the IGA. If they don't go to the IGA, we go to the IGA anyway and wait there."

"Not much of a plan, really."

"Well, even great detectives can have off days."

"Somebody told you that you were a great detective?"

"I was thinking of you. I'm pretty sure this plan was your idea."

"Ah. You sure you weren't really in the FBI? You've already got what some of us call post-responsibility realignment down pat. And anyway, I'm not a detective. I'm a special agent. Emphasis on the *special.*"

"I'll say," Gage said. Then, since they were waiting and he knew he had to get around to it eventually, he decided to tell her about what had happened at the police station. "I need to tell you something about Jeremiah. He confessed this morning."

"What? And you're only *now* getting around to telling me?"

"He didn't mean it. He's protecting someone."

"Who?"

"I'm hoping it's DWR_forever."

"But *why* is he protecting someone?"

"I have no idea."

"Hmm. Who, exactly, called you a great detective again?"

"Well," Gage said, "I don't know about the detective part, but I distinctly remember you calling me great a couple hours ago."

"Touché."

This word had barely left her lips when they saw a new figure emerge, from the administration building, a tall muscular man in a leather jacket, tan slacks, and a red scarf. Provost Dan MacDonald. He walked quickly and with purpose, head down and hands shoved into his jacket pockets.

"Oh my," Gage said.

"You were hoping it might be him all along, weren't you?" Karen asked.

"He's heading to that Porsche over there."

"You going to follow him?"

"Does it rain in Oregon?"

"I'll take that as a yes."

MacDonald was in the black Porsche and peeling out of the parking lot before Gage even had the key in the ignition. When he was sure the car was well past them, Gage started the van and followed. To avoid being detected, he needed to stay a safe distance back, but he was afraid of getting so far behind that MacDonald would be in and out of the IGA parking lot before Gage even got there. When he crested the hill, he saw the Porsche's red taillights veering left onto the highway.

"He's going the right direction," Karen said.

"Indeed he is," Gage said.

The road was an inky blur. Though it wasn't raining, the moisture in the air was thick enough that Gage had to occasionally turn on the wipers to clear the glass. By this time, traffic had lessened considerably, which meant it was easy to keep the Porsche in sight, though it also meant there wasn't a lot of cover on the highway.

As it approached the IGA, the Porsche appeared to slow, and Gage tensed, thinking this was it, they really had their guy, but then the Porsche sped on without stopping.

"Damn," Gage said.

"Maybe he just got cold feet," Karen said.

"Or maybe he isn't our guy."

"You want to stop anyway?"

Gage considered it. They could stop at the IGA, go back to the college, or just follow MacDonald. He thought about all those photos on the walls of MacDonald's office. He'd assumed at the time that MacDonald had been accompanied by young women, just like the girl working at his front desk, but his companions could have just as easily been men. He decided to keep following, and as he did, he explained his reasons to Karen.

"It seems like a distinct possibility," she said. "But why would he kill Connor?"

"Maybe Connor threatened to expose him?"

"Okay, but it doesn't seem worth killing over. You can give up your career and start over somewhere else."

"That depends on what's being exposed."

She lapsed into silence, her face contemplative in the sweeping lights of the passing cars, and he sensed that she was right there again, on the verge of talking about whatever sharp-edged memory was haunting her past. Instead, she offered only more silence. He had to agree with her, though. No matter how homophobic MacDonald thought his colleagues were, it was hard to believe that such a self-possessed man would result to murder to keep his sex life private. Gage doubted it was all that much of a secret anyway, knowing how college campuses were. If he asked some professors, Gage guessed that more than a few would have an inkling at their provost's sexual leanings.

But what if his sexual leanings were a bit more … perverse? What if he was mixed up with Connor and Jeremiah in a way that, if it came to light, would do more than end his career? The motives for murder were endless and varied. It was hard to tell what would pull a man into the dark places where the urge to kill would take hold.

They drove well past the Barnacle Bluffs city limits and along the winding coast until they reached the fringes of Newport, where big houses were separated by the natural slope of the land and strategically planted pine trees. There the Porsche slowed and turned right onto a long drive with a single house at the end, a modern, three-story Frank Lloyd Wright wannabe with an ocean view. The top floor was already lit, and Gage, driving past, thought he saw the shadow of a person passing one of the windows.

Two driveways down, one of the houses had a For Sale sign planted by the road, and the house was dark, so Gage pulled into the driveway. He killed the engine, cracked the window, and waited to see if anyone would emerge from the house. Cool ocean air flitted into the car.

"What do you plan to do?" Karen asked.

Gage had a queasy feeling about this, a familiar churning in his gut. He checked his Beretta, ensured that the clip was in, the safety on, then put it back in the holster beneath his jacket. He looked at her.

"Wow," she said.

"Just a precaution," he said. "You have the Glock on you?"

"Yes." She patted her side, as if to make sure.

She swallowed. He already knew she was packing; he'd seen her put on the holster back in the hotel room. He'd asked because he'd wanted to see her reaction—and it wasn't good. She looked like someone in the first throes of food poisoning. Carrying a piece was one thing. Being comfortable carrying a piece was another. A person who was armed and was nervous about it was worse than a person who wasn't armed at all. Accidents were more liable to happen when the trigger finger was already twitchy.

"You can stay here, you know," he said.

"I don't need to stay here."

"I don't think anything will happen. I just don't know how he's mixed up in this, and that makes me uncomfortable."

"What's the plan?"

Her voice had grown terse. She thought he didn't believe in her. That he didn't trust her. By probing her state of mind now, he was only making matters worse.

"We watch him," he said.

"That's it?"

"That's it for now. Come on."

They got out of the van. Wind buffeted them from all sides, strong enough that Gage had to clamp his hand over his fedora. The ocean, blocked by the house, was a steady whisper in their ears. He hated to bring his cane, but the ground was too uneven to do otherwise. Rather than take the road, where they might be spotted, they scaled the small hill, through pines made thin by the constant wind, and crossed in front of the house next door, where they could plainly see a family of four eating at a kitchen table. With the darkness as their ally, Gage and Karen passed another house before reaching MacDonald's, emerging from the sand onto the gravel drive.

A wooden enclosure, waist high, had been built for the garbage cans, and that's where they crouched. The tangy scent of spoiled apples rose from the cans. Sand had made its way into Gage's socks; he felt the grittiness of it between his toes. Behind them, up the drive, cars buzzed past on the highway. It was now dark enough that the ocean was nothing but a black canvas behind the house, made all the blacker because of how bright the second-floor windows glowed in the night. He saw cherrywood cabinets in the kitchen, forest-green walls, and a golden chandelier that must have been hanging over a table.

It was a long time before a person appeared, long enough that Gage's fingers, gripping the base of his cane, had grown numb. Finally, there was MacDonald, dressed in a tight black turtleneck, his hair slicked straight back as if he'd just taken a shower.

At the sink, MacDonald filled a glass and stared into the night, his face clouded with worry. For a moment, Gage was struck with the uneasy feeling that MacDonald could see them, but then MacDonald turned, glass in hand, and walked into the room with the low-hanging chandelier. He took a drink and put his glass down on a table they couldn't see, then crossed his arms and stared out the bigger window. He said something. There was a moment's pause, then he shook his head and said something else.

A bare-chested young man walked into view, blond buzz cut, chiseled chin, possessing the kind of muscular body that could have graced the covers of any number of romance novels. If he was twenty, he was a young-looking twenty. He put his arm around a clearly distressed MacDonald and pulled him in for a hug, kissing him tenderly on the cheek. MacDonald, as rigid as cardboard, didn't return the favor, but he didn't push him away either. He wasn't a short man, a little over six feet from what Gage remembered from seeing him at the college, but the young man was at least a head taller.

"Oh my," Karen said.

"If I worked out, I'd look like that too."

"Sure you would. You'd be that tall too. Well, you were right about him. Now what?"

They watched the two men. MacDonald was talking, the young man listening and nodding. The young man tried to grope his way down MacDonald's pants, the lust on his face unmistakable, and MacDonald slapped his hand away and stepped closer to the window. Worried about that message Gage had sent him, maybe? Worried as only a murderer who's afraid of getting caught can worry?

"I'm going to knock on his door," Gage said.

"And then what?"

"And then I'm going to confront him with what we know."

"Direct," she said.

"Sometimes it's best to be direct. We could sit around the bushes all night and not learn anything more than that he has a male lover. If I put him on the spot, we might get somewhere fast."

"What do you want me to do?"

"Stay here," Gage said.

"Come again?"

"I want you to have my back."

"Hard to do if I'm out here and you're in there."

"If I go inside, I'll be back at the door within five minutes. If not, it means you should call the cops."

She checked her cell phone, her frown visible from the light of her screen. "I've got signal. But after I make the call, I'm not just standing around. I'm coming in there."

"I'm counting on it. But I'm not expecting a fight. I'm just making sure we have a way to call for help if I get one."

She nodded, though he could clearly see that she wasn't happy. Then, surprising both her and himself, he brushed his thumb across her cheek in a gesture of tenderness. He started to rise, but then she grabbed him by his leather jacket and pulled him in for a kiss—and there was nothing tender about it, a hot crush of lips that set his spine on fire. Stay another minute and he knew the two of them would be ripping at each other's clothes, so he pulled away and ambled toward the house. His knee, bent for so long, buckled under his weight, and he was glad for his cane.

Pampas grass in black pots flanked the door, the ribbed ceramic shiny under the porch light. There was a security camera mounted in the corner. He rang the doorbell and waited, watching the opaque glass window in the center of the door. The shadow of a head appeared. He heard the low mumble of voices. There was a pause, then the door opened and there was MacDonald.

"What are you dong here?" he said.

There was worry in his voice, but it wasn't the kind of worry Gage had been expecting. He'd been expecting the worry of a man who was afraid his secret—that he was a murderer—was about to go public. Why else would Gage be at his door? But MacDonald sounded more perturbed than afraid, perplexed and a bit nervous, but not afraid for his freedom. Or maybe Gage was just reading him wrong.

The scent of baked bread slipped out the door. Frank Sinatra, faint but unmistakable, was playing from somewhere within the house.

"I need to talk to you," Gage said.

"About what?"

"Can I come in?"

"I don't think so. This isn't a good time."

"Let's make it a good time," Gage said.

"Excuse me?"

"If you don't give me five minutes of your time, I'm going to the police right now."

MacDonald responded with comically big blinks, cartoon-character blinks, so phony that they couldn't be anything but real. "I'm sorry, did you say you're going to the police?"

"That's right," Gage said.

"With what?"

"With what I know."

MacDonald shook his head. "This is nonsense. I don't know *what* you're talking about. Is this about Connor Fleicher?"

"You know very well what it's about."

"No. I don't."

"Oh yeah? How about the guy who was just kissing you a moment ago? You think *he* might know what it's about?"

Whatever color was left in MacDonald's face—and there wasn't much—drained away. When he spoke, it was in a strained whisper.

"My private life is none of your business," he said.

"It is if it involves murder."

"That's crazy! I had nothing to do with the boy's death."

"Can you prove it?"

"I was home. I don't have any proof."

"Then I'm going to the police."

Gage turned to go. He hadn't even gotten off the porch before MacDonald called after him.

"Wait!" he said. "Please. Don't drag me into this. It won't—it won't help anything, and it will just drag my personal life into the public's eye. Please. Please, come in. Let's talk about this. I'll answer any questions you have. Just don't do that. Go to the police. Not without hearing me out."

Without making it obvious, his back still to MacDonald, Gage looked in Karen's direction. He couldn't see her. She was well hidden behind the garbage enclosure. With deliberate slowness, he turned and looked at MacDonald. There was genuine fear on the man's face, the kind of fear Gage had expected to see when he first opened the door. "Afraid for your career, huh?" he said.

"My career is fine," MacDonald said. "It's not me I'm worried about. Come in, please. Hear me out."

He stepped aside and gestured for Gage to enter. Because Gage knew exactly how big and muscular MacDonald's companion was, he went inside without letting his guard down—and yet because the attack was so sudden and overwhelming, Gage was still somewhat surprised.

The bare-chested guy was so thick and blocky, it was like being mowed down by a pop machine. The two of them went crashing to the tiled floor, knocking over a glass vase of dried flowers. The crackle of glass only preceded MacDonald's cry of surprise by a split second, and both sounds were equally grating. Gage, thudding onto his right shoulder, took a right hook on the cheek before he managed to connect with his cane, jabbing the young man squarely in the solar plexus. It was a good thing Gage was moving with his cane *before* he took the punch, because the young man's fist blacked out his vision momentarily.

"No, Thomas!" MacDonald cried.

But Thomas, the big gleaming sweaty muscle of a man, was not stopping. Recovering from the blow, he was winding up for another punch, both he and Gage on their sides on the cold floor. Before he could let it rip, Gage kneed the young man in the balls. That did the trick, because Thomas, as big as he was, still turned into a mewling ball of pain, cupping his genitals and rolling away from Gage.

"Hold it!" Karen shouted, bursting into the room.

She swung her Glock from Thomas to MacDonald and back again. Gage, his eyes blurred and black-spotted, saw her as a rippled shadow, but he marveled at the authority in her voice. *The command.* If she wasn't a natural at this, she'd certainly trained well enough to come across as one.

He tried to speak and managed only to cough out a choked *"Stop."* Raising his hand, he struggled onto his knee—his bad knee, the pain splintered up his leg—and then got his other foot under him. By then, Karen was at his side helping him to his feet. Somewhere along the way he got his cane. The world was spinning so badly he felt like a bowling ball crashing into the pins.

"Oh God," MacDonald whined, "I'm so sorry. Thomas, why did you? *Why?*"

Thomas, he of the naked chest and the big muscles, was still curled into a fetal position, and no words were forthcoming. He did manage to glare at Gage with enough hatred to melt steel.

"What happened?" Karen said.

Gage rubbed his stinging cheek. "We were just making our introductions."

"This—this asshole—" Thomas managed finally, and Gage was delighted to find that Thomas had the kind of high-pitched falsetto that would perpetually make him sound like a haughty teenager. "This asshole, he comes into our house, making accusations—"

"That's enough," MacDonald said.

"I won't let him ruin us!" Thomas protested.

*"That's enough!"*

Thomas, having apparently recovered enough feeling in his nether regions that he was capable of doing something other than writhing on the floor, staggered to his feet. His hatred for Gage palpable, he made quite a show of arching his back and jutting out his chest, but his face was so pinched and pale that Gage had to stifle a laugh. Laughing now would not be a good idea. That usually didn't stop him, but he decided to make an exception in this case.

Karen had lowered her Glock and pointed it away. MacDonald bowed his head and rubbed his temples vigorously with both hands, pushing so hard that the skin there turned white.

"Maybe we should start over," Gage said.

"This is a nightmare," MacDonald said.

"Oh, it's not that bad. I'll have a bit of a headache tonight and Thomas might not be able to pee straight for a few days, but neither of us should have to cough up any co-pays."

"Jokes," MacDonald said. "Jokes, at a time like this."

"I find it helps lower the blood pressure."

MacDonald stopped massaging his temples and squinted at Gage with the kind of attention that an entomologist might give to a rare breed of beetle. In the other room, a grandfather clock marked the time with eight gongs. MacDonald went on staring, his eyes red and weary. Nobody said anything. Gage stifled the urge to crack another joke. He needed MacDonald to come to terms with whatever he needed to come to terms with without Gage getting in the way. Thomas stepped over to MacDonald and attempted to put an arm around him, which MacDonald slapped away. Karen busied herself by shutting the door.

"Maybe we should all sit down," Gage said.

"Maybe *you* should leave," Thomas said.

"Thomas, please," MacDonald said.

"A bourbon would be nice," Gage said. "You got any bourbon?"

MacDonald sighed. "What is it you want? I didn't have anything to do with Connor Fleicher's death."

"I'll be the judge of that, thank you very much. Do you have an account on the SpacedOut website?"

"What?"

"The message forum."

"I don't even know what that is. I've never heard of it."

He sounded pretty convincing. Then again, so did Ted Bundy and plenty of other killers. It didn't mean anything. Gage looked at Thomas. "How about you, Mr. Bench Press? You hang out on SpacedOut?"

"Fuck you," Thomas said.

"That's a no, then?" Gage said.

"I've never even heard of it."

Gage looked at MacDonald. "So if I checked your computer, I wouldn't find that you've visited that forum?"

"No, you wouldn't."

"So let's go check then."

"No. Not without the police. And even then, only with a warrant."

"Got something to hide?"

"I've got plenty to hide," MacDonald said. "None of it is illegal, though. Just private. And I'm not surrendering my rights simply for your convenience."

"Convenience," Gage said. "That's a funny way of talking about a teenage boy who was murdered."

"I already told you, *I* had nothing to do with that!"

There was something about the way MacDonald phrased his denial that was all wrong. "But you know something, don't you?" Gage asked.

"No!"

"What is it you're hiding?"

"I'm not hiding anything!"

Gage raised his eyebrows at Thomas, then looked at MacDonald again. "Not hiding anything?"

"That's different," MacDonald said. "Not everyone would understand. You see, it's not about me. Thomas is … Thomas works with younger children. He's a kindergarten teacher in Newport. If it got out he was a … a …"

"A faggot," Thomas said, spitting out the word. "A homo. A queer."

"Thomas," MacDonald said.

"Might as well make it clear," Thomas said.

MacDonald shook his head in exasperation. Gage got the feeling he spent a lot of time being exasperated with Thomas, which was when Gage knew this was no dog-and-pony-show kind of relationship. This was the real deal. Nobody got that exasperated with somebody they didn't care about.

"Anyway," MacDonald said, "we're really keeping our relationship under wraps because of him, not me. I just didn't want any unwanted attention."

"That's the part I don't understand," Gage said. "Attention for what? There's still something you're not telling me."

MacDonald shook his head, but there wasn't a lot of conviction in the gesture.

"They wouldn't have a reason to talk to you," Gage said, "unless you knew something worth talking about."

Still, MacDonald said nothing, his eyes distant and glazed. Thomas, reading something on MacDonald's face, touched MacDonald gingerly on the elbow.

"Daniel?" he whispered. "What is it?"

"Nothing. It's nothing."

"Did something happen?"

"No."

"Then what's wrong?"

MacDonald went back to rubbing his temples. They all waited. Gage hoped that for once his patience would be rewarded. MacDonald crossed the room and stood in front of one of the side windows, staring out as if he could actually see something through the frosted glass. It was quiet enough that Gage thought he could hear the hush of the ocean even through the walls. He glanced at Karen, who raised her eyebrows but said nothing.

"I think you need to leave *now*," MacDonald said quietly.

"Daniel—" Thomas began.

"You too," MacDonald said.

"What?"

"Everyone," MacDonald said, turning to face them. The anguish on his face was so palpable that it caught Gage off guard. "Everyone needs to leave now."

"It really would be easier if you—" Gage began.

"I don't think so," MacDonald said.

"The police," Gage said.

"Go to the police, then. Do what you have to do."

"It doesn't have to be this way," Gage said. "If you tell me whatever it is you know, we don't necessarily have to bring in the police."

MacDonald shook his head. "You don't understand."

"No, I don't. That's why I need your help."

"And I told you, I *can't* help you. I really don't know anything."

"But you know *something*."

"It's not relevant. It has nothing to do with the boy's death."

He said it with as much conviction as he could muster, but his expression did not match it. There was doubt. Gage wanted to go on arguing, but MacDonald opened the door and swept his hands forcefully for them to go. Gage glanced at Thomas for support, but the younger man folded his arms and glared at Gage. Apparently his doubt about his partner took a backseat to his re-sentiment toward Gage and Karen. There was nothing to do but go, which Gage did reluctantly, turning on the porch to give one last effort to pry MacDonald away from whatever was haunting him. The breeze stirred the pampas grass.

"This isn't over," Gage said.

"I'm sure you're correct," MacDonald said wearily, "but I won't be a willing participant in my own destruction."

"But *what* is going to destroy you?"

"I can't say anything more."

He started to close the door. Karen put her hand on it.

"Please," MacDonald protested. "I'll call the police if you don't leave."

"Well, that will certainly speed things up," Gage said.

"One question," Karen said. "Whatever you're not telling us, even if had nothing to do with the murder, was Connor or Jeremiah involved in any way?"

There was a bit of hesitation, a hitch as he closed the door, and in that moment Gage saw just how troubled MacDonald really was. He was adrift in an ocean of torment, and it was all he could do to keep his head above water.

"I wish I could help," he said, and then he was gone.

An image of Connor's bloody pulp of a head flashed through Gage's mind, and he felt a furious assault of rage course through him. He steeled himself against it. He stepped off the porch and walked a couple of paces away from the door, then turned and looked at the house, considering his options. One option was to throw his cane at the window.

"What do you want to do?" Karen asked.

"Call the police," Gage said.

"Right now?"

"Yep."

"But we don't have any proof."

"No, but I was assaulted. I can press charges, or at least make a lot of noise about doing so. We can make his life miserable. Maybe he'll crack."

"It'll also make Quinn pretty pissed off at you."

"He's always pissed off at me. Go ahead, make the call."

With a shrug, Karen pulled out her phone and started to dial, then her expression turned quizzical. She tapped a few times on the screen, read for a moment, then looked at Gage.

"What?" he said.

"We just got another email from DWR_forever," she said.

Gage looked at the house. Would MacDonald really be so bold to send the message while they were still standing outside? "What does it say?"

"It says, 'I don't know who you are, but whatever crazy game you're playing, I think you have the wrong person.' But it's not what it says. It was when it was sent, according the date stamp on the message."

"What do you mean?"

"It was sent eight minutes ago," Karen said.

"Eight minutes," Gage said, and then he realized what she meant. Eight minutes ago, they were still standing in MacDonald's entryway. If either MacDonald or Thomas had sent a message, Gage certainly would have seen them do it.

## Chapter 17

They rode in silence on windswept Highway 101, Gage contemplating the question Karen had asked when they'd gotten back in the van. If not MacDonald, then who was DWR_forever? Gage certainly couldn't rule out MacDonald's being involved in some way, despite the time stamp on the forum message, but if he was, he wasn't alone. More than that, the IP address was the same as before, from the school, which meant that DWR_forever was affiliated with the college in some way—student, faculty, staff. As Karen had pointed out earlier, this didn't mean he was literally at the college when he sent it, since he could have done so remotely, but there was a good chance he was.

The night air was thick, but it wasn't raining. The puddle streaks in the uneven road shimmered in the wind.

"Back to where we started?" Karen asked, as if reading his mind.

"Couldn't hurt. Let's grab some coffee on the way."

"There's coffee places open in Barnacle Bluffs this late?"

"Nope. Have to do with the stuff from the machines at the mini-mart up the road. With enough cream, it's almost drinkable."

"What if I like my coffee black?"

"As I said, you need cream."

She said she'd pass, but he bought her one anyway. She took one sip, claimed it was terrible, and immediately drank another. They returned to the same BBCC parking spot they'd been in earlier that night, but now, with the time closing in on ten o'clock, most of the lights in all but the dormitory were dark. They sat there for half an hour, drinking bad coffee, making idle chitchat, and watched two students cross the campus from the student union to the dorm. The student union had been the only building that appeared open, and they watched those lights go out too. Soon a couple of staff members appeared, chatted in the parking lot across the way for a moment, then got in their cars and left.

"Follow either of them?" Karen asked.

Gage sighed. "Nah."

"Kind of grasping at straws, aren't we?"

"I don't even know if there are straws."

"You want to go?"

Before he answered, Gage spotted another person pass under a lamp near the administration building, the beam of a flashlight bouncing along the sidewalk. With the thick night air, he could only see that it was stocky man in a gleaming parka. He got his hopes up until the man, heading generally in their direction, passed under another lamp and Gage saw the gray-and-blue uniform. Campus security. The man looked left and right, as if scanning for trouble, and eventually his gaze settled on the van.

"Uh-oh," Gage said.

"But we weren't even necking," Karen said.

The man approached cautiously, a hand on the baton attached to his belt, the flashlight shining directly at them. When the man got a little closer, and Gage saw the blocky gray hair and saggy, flushed face in glimpses around the flashlight's halo, he recognized him. It was the head of security, the guy who'd stopped them when they wanted to enter the dorm to retrieve Connor's drawing pad. What was the name? Jantz. Good old officer Jantz, doing a sweep of the campus grounds.

Jantz, stepping over to the driver's side, shone the light in

Gage's face. Squinting, Gage rolled down the window, the heavy night air slipping into the van.

"Mind pointing that thing somewhere else?" Gage asked.

Jantz didn't lower the flashlight. "What are you doing here, sir?"

"I'll make you a deal. You lower the flashlight, I'll answer the question."

Mercifully, the flashlight lowered.

"Much better," Gage said.

"The campus is closed to the public, sir," Jantz said.

"Is it? Then my yoga class is canceled?"

"All classes are canceled."

"That was a joke."

Jantz didn't laugh. If anything, he looked even more serious, eyes narrowing, the lines in his face as sharp as carved wood. Gage wondered if Jantz was one of those poor souls born totally bereft of a sense of a humor. If so, Gage wondered how Jantz even found the will to live.

"You need to leave, sir," Jantz said.

"Sure. Question, though. You notice anything unusual the night Connor Fleicher was murdered?"

"I wasn't working that night," Jantz said. "I already told the police that. I was at Tsunami's watching the game. I … I wish I had been here. I could have—could have stopped it, maybe." He stopped abruptly, as if realizing he'd said more than he'd meant to say. "I really need you to leave now."

"Guilt can be terrible thing," Gage said. An image of Janet, drowned in the tub, one naked arm draped over the side, rose up in his mind. "Believe me, it can eat at you like a cancer, hollowing you out from the inside."

"I don't feel guilty," Jantz said, but the tone of his voice said the opposite.

"I'm just telling you, it can help to confide in others. Tell them what you're feeling. I wouldn't have thought so, but it's true. Take it for what it's worth."

Jantz said nothing for a long time, but there was something

fragile about him, something thin that could break. It was hard to see his face clearly in the weak light from the streetlamp, but Gage thought he noticed a tear forming at the corners of the man's eyes.

"Sir—" he began.

"I know, I know," Gage said. "We need to go. Fine, going."

With a nod, Gage rolled up the window. He started the van with Jantz watching silently, his right hand still hovering over his baton. As Jantz back-stepped away from them, he moved closer to the cone of yellow light under one of the street lamps, affording Gage a better look at his anguished face. Gage had seen a similar face many times in the years following Janet's death—in the mirror every morning.

"Job probably pays crap," Karen said, "and then he's got to live with something like this happening on his watch."

Gage, sensing that she might not be talking entirely about Jantz, looked at her. She met his eyes and looked away. Rumbling their way out of the parking lot, he debated about whether to broach the subject. Weaving their way back to the highway, through firs steeped in darkness, he debated some more.

"Karen—" he began.

"Save it," she said, her breath fogging on the passenger-side window.

"If you want to talk—"

"I don't."

They turned onto the highway, heading north. They had the road to themselves. The ocean was nothing but a dark expanse to their left. It could have been a desert or an alien landscape. Gage looked at Karen and found her staring out the window, not at the darkness where the ocean was but at the darkness on the east side, where they were passing the forested hills that led to the college and, beyond, three thousand miles of continent that somewhere contained whatever was troubling Karen.

"I think we should call it a night," Gage said.

Karen didn't answer. As they passed under a streetlamp, her weak reflection in the passenger-side window leered back at him like a skull.

"You want me to take you back to the inn?" he asked.

He detected a slight shrug of her shoulders.

"I'm going to break this thing open tomorrow," he said. "We're right there. MacDonald knows something, and I'm going to find a way to shake it out of him."

"Sounds good," she said.

It was spoken with all the excitement of someone headed to the DMV. He was losing her again. He needed to toss her some kind of lifeline, but he didn't know how. He mulled over what had set her off. Gage had mentioned guilt to Jantz. She had made a comment about his having to live with something like this happening on his watch. He decided to take a chance.

"Did someone die?" he asked.

She turned to him sharply. "What?"

"Who was it? Another agent?"

She sighed. "Garrison—"

"I've been racking my brain for what kind of mistake could bring a tough cookie like Karen Pantelli to her knees, and I figure it's got to be pretty big. Were you protecting someone?"

"It wasn't like that," she snapped.

"Then *what* was it like?"

"I told you, I don't want to talk about this."

"I think you do."

"What?"

"I think you do," he repeated. "I think you want to talk about it. You just don't know how to get there. So I'm taking you there. I'm forcing the issue. You've got to get whatever this thing is off your chest before it crushes you. So let's talk. How did it start? Give me some details."

"No," she said.

"What kind of mistake was it? Were you drinking or something? Sleep through your alarm?"

"Oh, fuck off."

"Must be getting close," Gage said.

"You're not getting close at all. You don't know anything!"

"Then help me understand!"

Even in the dark, he could see that her eyes were big and glaring. It was right there, about to surface, all that pain and rage and guilt. She was so close to letting it all out, teeter-tottering on the edge, and he waited in anticipation for the big reveal. But in the end, she merely shook her head and turned back to the dark window.

"Just take me back to the inn," she said.

"Fine," he said.

"It's not you," she said. "I just … can't go there. Not now."

"Not with me, anyway. I'm just some guy you slept with."

Even this wasn't enough to rile her up. She said nothing. He wondered if she'd open up if he tapped her on the head with his cane. At this point, he was willing to try anything. They drove to the inn's parking lot without either of them saying a word. He crossed through the tunnel under the highway and pulled into the roundabout by the front door. When they stopped at the curb under the red awning, he expected her to hop out in a hurry, but she just sat there.

"You think I should stay at the Turret House instead?" she asked.

"What?"

"With Zoe," she said. "I was just thinking, she's all there by herself."

"By design," Gage said. "Alex didn't book any guests. She's just watching the house itself."

"Yeah, but I know you'd feel better if she wasn't alone. And if you offered to stay there, she'd get all offended. But me? I could just tell her that the inn was a bit pricey and I wasn't expecting to stay here this long, so if I could save a few dollars, I could stretch out my visit a bit longer."

"A bit longer," Gage said.

She studied his face. "If you want me," she said.

"You know I want you. I think we've established that without a doubt."

That got her to smile. "So it's okay then?"

"You'll have to ask her, since she's the one Alex left in charge, but if you show up with bag in hand, I doubt she'll refuse you."

"Then I better get my bag."

"You better. But you don't want to drive your own car?"

"I'll come back for it later."

While she disappeared, he waited at the curb, the van's engine idling. It was more of a smoker's cough than an idle, all rattle and wheeze, and he could see the mustachioed night clerk beyond the double glass doors eyeing him with annoyance. Karen wasn't gone long, five minutes at most, before she was back at the same desk paying her bill. It occurred to him that he could have offered to have her stay at his place. He wondered if it had occurred to her too. Probably, and yet she hadn't asked. He pondered what that meant. He pondered why he hadn't thought of it until now, and why even now, he wasn't sure it was a good idea.

When she hopped back in the car, she must have seen that something was troubling him, because she raised an eyebrow.

"What?" she said.

"Nothing. All set?"

"Sure thing, boss."

"We haven't received any response from DWR_forever, have we?"

She pulled out her phone, swiped and clicked, and a moment later shook her head no. Gage put the van and gear and headed back to the lonely highway.

"You know," Karen said, "he might not have anything to do with Connor's death at all."

"He might not," Gage said, nodding.

"But you think he does?"

Gage tapped the steering wheel. "I think we need more information, that's all. And I think he—or *she*—might be able to give us some. Can you search his posts and tell me anything more?"

"I already looked at all of them. It was just the same sci-fi stuff as everybody else. He didn't really post that much. Only a handful of times, maybe a dozen. It was the same as the other two, SpockLives2008 and Fireflyawesome."

"Who showed up first?"

"Good question. Let me check." A moment later, she had the answer. "DWR_forever was the last to post, a couple weeks after the other two. He also has only eight posts. The other two have more, maybe twenty each. Hmm. Get this, he *only* posted in discussion threads that other two were in, and only after them … I'm reading … Yeah, not a lot there. But you know, he kind of parrots the other two. It's not like he has any original thoughts."

"So maybe he's not as interested in the subject matter and he's just there for them?"

"Could be," she said.

"Brainstorm the name with me. What could it stand for?"

This time, she took longer to respond. They were halfway to the Turret House, rattling along the empty highway, the van's high beams cutting a swath through the darkness. Behind them, a distant pair of lights was approaching, but otherwise they had the road to themselves. At this point, the highway climbed to a bit of a crest, a guardrail on the left protecting them from the bluff's drop-off to the beach, a deep drainage ditch to the right that climbed into the forested woods. Barnacle Bluffs was a long and narrow city, the eventual merging of tiny coastal hamlets from long ago, and this was one of the gap areas. In moments, they'd be back down into the shops and houses again.

"Well," she said, "given the forum, there's a good chance it's science-fiction related."

Gage nodded. "A good chance. How about … Darth Will Rule Forever?"

"Not bad. Hmm. Demons Wish Rage Forever?"

"Doctor Who Remembers Forever?"

Karen smiled. "That's really good. You're sure you're not a closet science-fiction fan?"

"I always thought it would be neat to have a TARDIS," Gage said. "Then I could jump around in time and cause all sorts of havoc."

"There you go again," she said. "As a bit of fangirl myself, that kind of talk does get me a little hot and bothered. Be careful or I might ask to see your light saber."

"Dirty girl," he said. He glanced in the rearview mirror. Those headlights, once distant, had closed the gap between them in a hurry.

"Like that surprises you about me," Karen said. "I'm thinking about Connor's drawing, though, the one with *DWR* and all those animals. Not sure how that's science-fiction related."

"It did seem almost religious," Gage said, "with all those animals mixed with people. A Noah's ark feel."

"Ducks Want Rights?" she offered.

"Somehow, I don't think so. How about Dreams Will Realize?"

"Too hokey for these boys, I think. But there's something … it's like we're so close to it. You know what I mean?"

Gage did. It was the same feeling when he was trying to remember someone's name and he was close but not quite right. Jonathan instead of Jacob. Suzie instead of Sally. But why would he feel that way? That would imply he'd already heard what the initials stood for, but that couldn't be the case, could it? That drawing had seemed so out of place from the others in Connor's sketch pad, but there had to be a reason it was there.

The headlights behind them suddenly loomed large in the van's rear window, high and spaced wide apart. A Hummer? It was dark blue if not black and so close it could have been attached to the van by a trailer hitch.

"Guy's certainly a little close, isn't he?" Karen said.

"Probably drunk. Hold on. When we get off the hill, I'll pull off the road and let him pass."

Only Gage never had a chance to pull off the road. He'd barely finished the sentence when the Hummer gunned it, the big engine roaring like a locomotive's. There were no approaching cars in the oncoming lane, so Gage eased off the accelerator, intent on just letting the jerk pass—but then the Hummer did something unexpected. It veered not to the left but to the *right*, into the gap between the highway and the drainage ditch.

"What the—" Karen said.

It was right at that moment, just before the Hummer slammed into the van's right side, that Gage realized that this wasn't some drunken asshole they were dealing with here. He may have had the realization only a split second before the truth of the situation would have been obvious to anyone, but that split second was just enough lead time to get him to jerk the wheel to the right, toward the Hummer, instead of to the left, which was what instinct was telling him to do.

The two vehicles collided with a bang, the metal impact as loud and as powerful as a grenade going off between them. Gage felt the reverberations right into his bones. The Hummer may have had twice the size and heft of the Volkswagen, but he'd actually turned the wheel harder, veering with more force, and that action had prevented the van from being cue-balled across the road and into the barrier.

Or no barrier.

He saw, as he swerved back and forth trying to regain control, that they'd just passed the area where there was no barrier. On the downhill slope of the hill, there was a gap in the metal structure that had been missing for the better part of a year, a gap big enough that if the van had careened in that direction instead of holding its own, it would have allowed Gage and Karen to sail off the edge of the cliff to the beach below. Instead of metal, the only things blocking them from the drop were three flimsy free-standing orange road signs.

The Hummer's driver, who must have realized he was missing his chance, came at them again with a renewed fury.

Gage lifted his foot completely off the accelerator, but the Hummer smashed into them a second time before the van started to slow. The van's passenger-side window splintered but didn't break. Even strapped in with seat belts, he and Karen bounced around like balls in a lottery machine.

This time all the weight and bulk of the Hummer kept coming at them, sweeping them across the highway and toward the gap. No more than three seconds had passed since the first impact, but it felt much longer. The heartbeat in his ears and the adrenaline coursing through his veins lit the world on fire. He smelled smoke and gasoline, but he didn't know if it was all in his mind. He caught a glimpse of a man's silhouette in the window, but it was nothing but a black shape, obscured even further by the moisture on the glass.

"Gage!" Karen cried.

There may have been other options available to him, but only one flashed into Gage's mind. He turned the wheel hard to the left, toward the gap, and slammed on the brakes, thinking if he could gain even a few inches of breathing space between the van and the Hummer, that room might be all he needed to screech to a stop and let the Hummer pass.

At first, that's exactly what happened. The van, losing all momentum, began to drop back from the Hummer even as the gap loomed dangerously close. If he'd had his hand out the window, Gage could have touched the orange road signs that sat in place of the metal barrier.

The problem was the Hummer's massive size. Gage had enough time to feel the thrill of the matador who has managed to get the bull to pass under his red cape before the Hummer, still veering toward them, hit their right front fender with its back corner.

The crackle of metal was like two giant pop cans smashing together. He saw that the Hummer wasn't black, or even dark blue, but forest green flecked with bits of gold. Tiny details. This time Karen's window, already spiderwebbed with cracks, shattered completely, spraying them both with glass. Even worse, the corner-to-corner impact—combined with the screeching brakes of the van—caused the van to spin.

The roar of the wind in the broken window. The red glare of the Hummer's taillights. The pressure of the seat belt straining against his chest.

Gage had only an instant to take in these sensations before the world tilted on its axis with such ferociousness that Gage had no time to do anything but white-knuckle the steering wheel. The van flipped. He thought he heard Karen scream, but it may have been the shriek of the metal on the road.

Then there were a series of bangs and smashes, the world

flashing through blackness, his body pulled in every direction at once.

Gage may have blacked out. If not, time appeared to skip a beat, because one moment he was still hanging onto the steering wheel, floating weightless, and the next he was on his side, hanging in his seat belt as if it were a twisted hammock.

They were spinning. He was on a merry-go-round of crumpling metal. Something was burning. He caught a glimpse of Karen's face, eyes shut, a bloody gash on her cheek, before there was another impact, one so jarring that it felt as if he'd been punched in the back.

Scraping metal, roaring engine, a rumble like an earthquake—then, mercifully, all the tortures of the moment came to a whimpering conclusion.

He was on his side in darkness, the seat belt cutting into his ribs. Complete darkness. He tasted blood in his mouth. For a few seconds, all he heard was the ringing in his ears, and when this subsided, the patter of rain on the asphalt. The whisper of wind. His own ragged breathing.

"Karen?" he said.

His voice sounded odd to him, as if he were trying to talk with a mouthful of marbles. There was no answer.

"Karen, are you all right?"

Still nothing. Panic began to swell inside him. Was she dead? He blinked, focusing, trying to get a sense of things. Shapes took form. He could just make out the edge of the dashboard. Who punched him in the jaw? Somebody had, by the feel of it. His eyes adjusting to the darkness, he finally saw the line of the road through the cracked windshield. He rolled his head to the right, a sharp pain shooting up his neck, and for an instant it looked as though Karen wasn't there.

The seat was gone.

But then—as the first sirens rose above the wind—he saw that the seat wasn't gone. It was turned, the back of the seat facing him. Somehow it had dislodged during the crash, and Karen, if she was still in it, was face down, pressed against what was left of the passenger-side window.

The sirens grew louder. Gage fumbled for the buckle of his seat belt, found it, and was careful to swing his legs around and prop himself against the dashboard before unbuckling himself. Now both knees hurt like hell, though he didn't think anything was broken. *Everything* was bruised, but not broken.

Planting first one foot, then another, on the side of the van, he managed to get his legs under him. The sirens were now almost as loud in his ears as his beating heart. He heard the screech of tires. He settled his weight onto his legs, and it felt like standing on toothpicks. He grasped at the ripped seat cushion, fingers slipping, found purchase, and with immense effort began to tilt the seat on its side.

By the weight of the thing, she was still in it. Voices shouted outside. He heard more tires screeching. Blue and red lights strobed through the interior. Bright lights illuminated the map of cracks on the windshield and allowed him to see inside the van. What was left of it. The seat felt like it weighed more than the van, but he got it around, and there she was, blood all over her face, eyes closed. She was dead. He was sure she was dead, and he felt disbelief and rage and sadness that she'd been taken from him, taken from the world.

Of course it would be this way. Of course Gage would lose her. He lost everyone eventually. It was the way it was. It was like the sun rising in the east and the moon never showing its dark side and seven billion people taking a breath.

But, defying the universe, her eyes fluttered open.

"Karen—" he began.

"I killed her," she said. "I killed a little girl."

Then her eyes closed.

## Chapter 18

The ambulance was halfway to the hospital, sirens screeching through the night, when Karen spoke again. "It happened—happened at a drug house," she said. "A drug house outside Boise, Idaho."

"Shh," Gage said.

"No," she said. "No, I've got to say this. I've got to say it now."

Her voice rattled, throaty and deep, and she coughed. On the gurney, she tried to roll on her side to face him, but the paramedic in the back with Gage restrained her. Like Gage, he urged her to be still, but his voice was tuning in from a distant planet. It was just the two of them in the jostling little cave inside the van, Gage and Karen, him crouched on a bunker seat, her on the gurney. Miraculously, Gage had survived the ordeal with only minor bumps and cuts, at least as far he could tell, but the paramedics wanted him to be checked out at the emergency room anyway. He wouldn't have argued with them. It wasn't like Gage would have let them take Karen without him.

It was too soon to say how beat-up Karen was. If it was bad, it was all internal—which of course would make it all the worse.

"I've got to say it," she said.

"All right."

"I should have told you. Should have told you before. I'm sorry I didn't. I don't know why."

"You don't have to be sorry."

"Oh yes I do. I have—have a lot to be sorry about. I'm just ashamed. That's all. A coward. Don't want to face it. But I'm going to face it. It was like this. We'd ... we'd gotten a tip from a meth addict, me and Ben, about a drug house. We were in Boise on another thing, following a lead on a possible homegrown terror cell, a bunch of skinheads, but it didn't—didn't—didn't —"

"Karen," Gage said.

"It's all right. Just got to get my breath. It didn't pan out. But while we were there, we got this tip and end up at this ranch house with weeds as tall as the roof. It's one of those streets with shit cars parked up and down the street. Hot August day. Blistering hot. We knock on the door, just to see if we can shake out what's going on without a warrant, and this Hispanic woman with no teeth opens the door. She's wearing a big Tweety Bird T-shirt but nothing else. Her eyes are like saucers. And right there, right there behind her, we see two skinny white guys on a ratty couch, needles and bags of meth laid out on the coffee table like a Thanksgiving dinner. Shirtless. One in boxers, the other in briefs. Funny how I remember that. And this little girl. This little girl, this little skinny thing all bruised and wasted, sitting between them, dressed in a black tank top and black panties. I found out later she was actually nine years old, but she looked more like seven."

"We're almost there," Gage said.

"And we pull out our badges and tell them who we are and this chick, she drops to her knees and starts to cry. Both guys jump and run, both for the hall behind them, the one in the tighty-whities snatching up the little girl. We got our guns out and shout for them to stop, but they're so jacked up they're probably not even hearing us. I don't even think. I just go after the guy with the girl. Ben's shouting at me to stop, but I'm not letting this guy button down a hostage situation."

The ambulance swerved around a corner, bumped over a pothole, and Karen groaned. Gage reached for her hand, but the paramedic shook his head at at him.

"The guy without the kid bolts into a side room and the other keeps going, to the master bedroom at the back of the house. I follow him. Ben must have gone in after the first guy, because then it was just me and the guy with the girl in the master. Piss-stained mattress, clothes and fast-food packaging all over the floor. Smelled like they were using the closet as a toilet, which it turned out they were. The guy with the girl, he's got short bleached-blond hair set in cornrows and tattoos up and down both arms. Thin as the curtain rod—which was the only thing on the window, no blinds or curtains."

The ambulance made the hard right turn onto Big Dipper Road, the last leg of the journey before the hospital. Leaning forward, peering through the front windshield, Gage glimpsed the lake through the Douglas firs, a black tarp flecked with occasional spots of yellow from the house lights surrounding the water.

"A minute away," he said.

"Let me—let me finish," she said. "Got to get this out. So this guy, I yell at him to stop, but he doesn't listen. He's still got the girl under his arm. She's got blond cornrows just like him. The way she lays limp in his arms and doesn't blink, it's like she's a doll. I figure her to be in shock. The guy's fishing under some rumpled jeans next to his bed and he comes out with a revolver. A little piece, a Colt Mustang. I'm screaming at him to drop the weapon, but he's got it in his hand and he's swinging ... swinging it around."

"Jesus," Gage said.

"Got that right. So here I am, alone in the back room without my partner. In a meth house we weren't even supposed to be in. A jacked-up druggie with a human hostage bringing his weapon to bear on me. I don't have a clear shot. He's really got the girl in front of him, and the gun is coming around, it's coming around and it's going to be pointing at me in a second. I'm screaming at him so much my throat will be hoarse for three days. I'm screaming and screaming, telling him to drop it, and that gun is coming around. It's coming around, Garrison. It's—it's coming around."

"All right," Gage said, giving her hand a squeeze. The ambulance tore into the parking lot. He saw the *Emergency Room* sign glowing green in the darkness just ahead. "Save your breath. We're almost—"

"No. Got to say it now or I won't later. So this guy, he's just about got his gun pointed at me. I have no shot. I'm telling him to drop it. I'm thinking he won't fire. He's just scared. I'm taking the chance of a lifetime, but I'm thinking he won't fire. But bam! He fires. He fires again. Three times, just clicking them off. Plaster flying off the walls behind me with the first two shots. The third one rips a hole in the sleeve of my leather jacket. No choice, I pull the trigger. I hit the guy squarely in the chest. I miss the girl. I don't know how, but I miss her."

The paramedic scurried around Karen's gurney, preparing it for the move.

"So this guy, this meth head, he crashes against the wall. His piece goes flying. So does the little girl, crashing to the mattress. Blood sprayed all over the wall, like some kind of abstract art. He's got his hand behind him and I'm thinking he's got another piece in his back pocket, so I rush him. Kick his arm out. That must have been all the life he had left, though, because when I kicked him, he sort of spasmed once and that was it. Gave me the long dead stare. And my heart is pounding hard in my ears and I'm thinking it's a miracle. It's a miracle, right? I made the one-in-a-million shot and saved the hostage. That's when I turned to look at her."

The ambulance screeched to a stop in the roundabout under the emergency-room overhang.

"She's crouching on all fours. She's looking up at me and her eyes are all dead inside. Nothing there. Probably shock, I think. I finally notice the bruises on her arms and legs. Little bruises, not big ones. Like the kind you'd get when somebody grabs you too tight. I also notice that the black tank top and the panties are lace. Lace! Like what you'd buy at lingerie shop, not right for a little girl. That's when I see the ... the sex toys on the bed."

The back doors to the ambulance flew open. Both paramedics wheeled the gurney out, and an attending doctor in a white coat and two nurses in blue uniforms were there to greet them. One nurse reached for Gage and he shrugged her off, hobbling after the gurney as a bevy of medical professionals barreled Karen into the hospital. They ambled through the cool night air for only a second before they were under the bright fluorescent lights and into the warmth of the hospital.

"Garrison?" Karen called after him.

"Right behind you."

"I got to—got to finish." They tried to shush her, but she wouldn't listen. "So this girl, I found out later her name was Bo Peep. Named by … by a meth head, what can you expect? Bo Peep reached for something in front of her, still staring at me … staring at me with dead eyes. I see that it's the gun. The Colt. She's reaching for it. I still don't really register what she's doing. I tell her she's safe. I tell her it's over. Her hand, her wasted little hand, grips the handle. Now I finally get it and I shake my head at her. I say, 'Don't.' That's all I say. One word, the whole time. She doesn't even blink. She's got the piece now and she's bringing—bringing it up."

Double doors loomed ahead. They were almost to the operating room.

"She's almost got it pointed at me. I'm shaking my head, but she's not even there. The gun goes off and I'm sure it's hers. I even flinch. But it's not hers. It's mine. I shot her. I shot this little girl, right in the chest. I shot her and she flopped back like a rag doll, like she never had any life to begin with. I let some meth head get off three shots before taking him down and this little girl … this little girl, I shot her … before she could even … pull the trigger once. Little Bo Peep. I shot her dead. Shot her right in the heart, it turns out. And that's … that's not the worst part."

The gurney crashed through the doors, speeding away from Gage. Two nurses held him, restraining him from following her. He heard Karen's final words before the doors swung shut.

"Her gun," she said, "was empty."

*Chapter 19*

The first cops, hounding him with questions, showed up only seconds after Karen was wheeled into the emergency room. What was the other vehicle involved in the crash? Did he see the license plate? The driver? If Gage didn't have a headache already—and he did, a steady throbbing at the back of his skull—this would have guaranteed it. They followed him into a smaller exam room, where Gage received five stitches to patch up the gash on his left arm. The rest of his wounds were superficial; some antibacterial cream and bandages took care of them.

He was only vaguely aware of what he told the cops, but he must have said something that satisfied them, because the next time he looked past the flank of blue uniforms and white coats, they were gone.

Another doctor, an old guy with vaguely Japanese features and thinning black hair, stopped into his room when the last nurse was disposing of all the gauze and wrappers.

"She's going to be all right," he said. "A mild concussion. Two broken ribs. She'll have a minor scar from that cut on her cheek, but it won't be too bad. No internal bleeding, which was the worry."

"Can I see her?"

"Probably another hour before she's in a room. And she's unconscious right now. Let the charge nurse know. They'll come get you when she can have visitors." He patted Gage's shoulder gingerly. "Your friend got very lucky. Maybe not as lucky as you, but considering the circumstances ..."

The doctor didn't have to finish the thought. Considering that someone had tried to run them off one of the famous cliffs of Barnacle Bluffs in a vehicle that had no business being driven outside a military engagement, they were lucky to be alive at all. Lucky. He wondered if Karen would use that word. If she'd stayed away from him, none of this would have happened. Story of Gage's life.

A few minutes later, Gage was alone with his guilt in the emergency room's crowded waiting area, surrounded by the coughing and the wheezing and the moaning. A nasty flu going around, the nurse told him. The orange vinyl seats looked like something out of a bad seventies movie. The magazines on the end tables were only slightly newer. He picked up an issue of *Time* about a school shooting back East and flipped through it without seeing the words. He was still flipping through it when someone sat down next to him. He smelled the cigarettes on the man's breath before he even spoke.

"She gonna be okay?"

It was Chief Quinn. Droplets of water pebbled his trench coat, and his slicked-back gray hair shimmered under the fluorescent lights. Often Gage found Quinn's kindly, Mr. Rogers let's-all-get-along face irritating, but this time he actually found it mildly reassuring.

"A little banged up," Gage said, "but she should pull through all right."

"That's a relief. Want you to know, we found the Hummer abandoned at the cable company a quarter-mile from your accident. It was reported stolen a little while ago. Some tourists staying in a beach house and they didn't know how long it had been missing. They were all in the back in the hot tub and said somebody must have stolen the keys right out of the house. We're combing the Hummer for evidence."

"Okay."

"Now," Quinn said, his tone getting a bit more stern, "you want to tell me exactly *why* somebody was trying to kill you?"

"You know me well enough by now to answer that question yourself, Chief. It's the effect my winning personality has on people."

"Let's just pretend that's not it. Come on, Gage, you've got some idea who did this. Make my life easier and tell me who it is. Who have you pissed off recently?"

Gage rubbed his chin. "There's just so many ..."

"This is related to Jeremiah Cooper, isn't it? You know the boy confessed. I hope you're not still out there poking at the rattlesnakes. You got some other theory, don't you? Some crackpot theory and you won't let it go. What is it?"

The trouble was, Gage really had no theory. It may have been an aftereffect of his brain getting knocked around in the accident—the world still felt slightly off-kilter—but everything was all jumbled up, faces and names floating in and out of his consciousness. Jeremiah. Connor. Arne. Berry. Provost MacDonald. His first thought was that it was Dan MacDonald, that he got nervous that Gage was getting too close, and he decided to get rid of the threat before it exposed him.

But it didn't add up. They'd already established that DWR_ forever couldn't be MacDonald, not unless he had some amazing program that could post messages for him when he wasn't there to do the sending, which was technically possible but seemed far-fetched. But was there something else going on? Maybe MacDonald was involved in something else entirely, something not involving Jeremiah Cooper or Connor Fleicher, and that something was enough to kill over.

For once, Gage decided to play along with Quinn. He wasn't going anywhere until he was sure Karen was all right, not just physically but with what she'd told him in the ambulance, and something about MacDonald screamed guilty. He might not be guilty of *this*, but he was guilty of something. Maybe if the cops showed up to rattle his cage a little, he'd break.

When Gage was finished explaining to Quinn his encounter earlier that night with MacDonald, including his professional wrestling audition with MacDonald's friend, Thomas, the chief merely shook his head.

"But what made you go there in the first place?" he asked.

"Following a lead. We thought he might have been communicating with Jeremiah and Cooper on the Internet. Through a message board on a science-fiction website."

"About what?"

"Not sure yet."

"They were using their real names?"

"No, they had handles."

"Uh-huh. And why did you think it was MacDonald? Or any of them, for that matter? Was it something they wrote?"

"The IP addresses. They were from the college. And we know this was one of Jeremiah's favorite websites, from what his friends told me." Gage left out that this friend was Zoe. He also wasn't quite ready to tell Quinn about MacDonald's sexual orientation. If none of this panned out, Gage didn't want to be the one to shine a bright light on the man's bedroom, not in a town like Barnacle Bluffs. "Look, can't you just send a car over there? Even if we eliminate him as a suspect, it would be a load off my mind."

Quinn shook his head. "Let me get this straight. You want me to send a car over to the house of the provost of Barnacle Bluffs Community College based on, what, a little voice in the back of your head?"

"You're going to have to trust me on this one."

"Right," Quinn said. "Because that's always worked out so well for me."

"Chief. Percy, listen—"

"Oh, it's Percy now, is it?"

"Listen, someone just tried to *kill* us," Gage said, and he heard the agitation rising in his voice. "They almost succeeded. Don't you think that buys me just a little bit of leeway? Maybe just this once? All I'm asking is that you send an officer down there to knock on the door. Tell them I was involved in a bad accident and foul play was involved. You're just checking out the people I talked to that day. Find out his alibi. Shake him up a bit. You know as well as I do that sometimes when you shake people up, stuff shakes out."

That got at least a wry smile out of Quinn. "Is that a passage from *Detecting for Dummies* by Garrison Gage?"

"I think it might have been Yogi Berra who said it first."

Quinn narrowed those grandfatherly eyes, studying Gage for a long time before finally tipping his chin in a slight nod.

"Okay, I'll have someone check them out," he said. "But you have to make me a promise. Nothing comes of it, I want to know *everything*. No more secrets. I want to know everybody you've talked to lately and everything you've talked about. Any cocka-mamie theories you've got rattling around in your brain about Connor Fleicher, I want the nitty-gritty details on those too. You got it? That's the deal."

Gage nodded. "I'll tell you everything I can."

"Hmm. Sounds like you're threading a needle again. Gage, no bullshit on this. Either you're straight with me here or forget it. If you got some next move you're about to make and you're not telling me, I'm gonna be pissed as hell."

"Chief, if this doesn't pan out, then I don't even know what my next move is. I'm in the dark."

"Well, that makes two of us at least. All right, fine. We'll check out MacDonald. You planning on going anywhere?"

"I'll be here for a while. I want to finish this article on Princess Diana. Besides, the van might need a few repairs before it's driv-able again."

"Gage, pal, that van won't *ever* be drivable again. I saw it."

"We'll see. People said something similar about me once, too, and here I am."

Quinn stood. He adjusted his trench coat and tightened the belt, regarding Gage with the kind of ruefulness he might have re-served for a dog who'd dropped a load on his carpet. "You know, I *am* sorry about this. No matter how I feel about all your meddling, you don't deserve this."

"If I was judged by all my past sins," Gage said, "I probably deserve a lot worse."

"Don't we all." He turned to go, taking a few steps away from the orange vinyl seats before turning back to Gage. "Got another theory for you. You remember what I told you about wearing out your welcome in this town?"

"Sure."

"Well, it's possible you've already done it."

With that, Quinn walked toward the glass sliding doors, his cell phone already out of his pocket.

IT WAS ANOTHER forty-five minutes before Karen was allowed to have visitors and another fifteen minutes after that before she opened her eyes and peered at Gage in the dimly lit hospital room. A bandage as big as an oven mitt covered the left side of her face, a face so swollen and bruised he might not have recognized her if he'd only seen her in passing. Her hair, usually wispy, was slicked straight back. The bedspread couldn't have been that heavy, but her body under the covers was hardly even there, just a few bumps and wrinkles in the tan fabric. She may have always been small in stature, but the force of her personality compensated for this; it was hard to think of her as physically tiny after he'd known her a while.

But the eyes, those liquid green eyes, there was nothing different about them. He would have known them anywhere. Even as droopy as she was, there was a fierce vitality to them that few people possessed.

"Hello, beautiful," he said.

"Don't—don't make me smile," she mumbled. "It hurts."

"How about laughing?"

"Even worse."

There was no clock in the room, but the one over the nurse's station outside had showed that it was half past midnight when he walked inside. It may have technically been Sunday, but it was still truly Saturday night, and it was hard to believe all that had happened since Quinn first showed up at his house Thursday morning with news that Connor Fleicher had been murdered. If the following week was anything like the last one, Gage didn't know how he'd survive it. He'd barely survived this one. And Karen, she'd come even closer to having her name printed on a death certificate.

"I think I'm going to have a scar," she said.

"They say it'll be pretty small. Besides, it'll make you look pretty badass, I think. Nobody will mess with you now. When you get back to the FBI, all the other agents will be jealous. You'll probably start a trend. Pretty soon we'll have another public-health scare on our hands, people giving themselves self-inflicted knife wounds on the cheek so they can look like badass Special Agent Karen Pantelli."

This time she *did* smile, a little, at least until it morphed into a wince. "Ouch," she said.

"Sorry."

"It's all right. I don't think you could *not* make me laugh if you tried."

"Hmm. I think there might be an insult in there, but I'm too dim-witted to find it."

"It's okay," she said. "I like you for your body, anyway. But you probably shouldn't call me a special agent anymore. I'm not going back to the FBI."

"You never know," he said. "Give it time."

"No. I'm done with that part of my life."

She held his gaze for a beat, then looked away, at the window on the other side of the room—the curtains open, the night deeply dark, a streetlamp casting a soft net of light on the tops of the fir trees that bordered the parking lot. Rain streaked the light. More rain. Always more rain. Gage, seated in the chair next to her, reached across the bedspread and touched her hand. She pulled it away. He reached for it again, clasping it firmly, and this time she let him. Her fingers were warm, burning up.

"About what I told you," she said.

"It was a terrible thing you did," Gage said.

She turned to him sharply, surprise and confusion clouding her face.

"What?" Gage said. "You expected me to say something different? You expected me to say it wasn't your fault? It could have happened to anyone? Or maybe some cheap platitudes, like when the going gets tough, the tough get going? When life gives you lemons, you make lemonade?"

"I don't—I don't understand what—"

"You did a terrible thing. You shot a little girl. It's crappy, and you have to live with it. Sorry, them's the breaks."

Her eyes flashed wide. "Are you *deliberately* trying to be an asshole?"

"Yes."

"Why?"

"Because that's what you need, Karen. You want me to tell you I'll be there for you? Of course I'll be there for you. You want me to tell you I understand? I can't do that. I don't know what it's like to shoot a little girl."

"I wish you'd stop saying that."

"No, that's just the thing. You have to be okay with saying it. You need to say it more often. You think to yourself, If I just don't talk about it, it'll go away. I can pretend it didn't happen. But that's not the way it works. You don't talk about it, it festers. It eats you up. You have to find some way to grapple with it, and the only way to do that is to go at it head-on. I may not know anything about shooting a little girl, but I do know a thing or two about what guilt can do to a person. My wife died because of me."

"But you didn't—you didn't shoot her," Karen said. "You're not the one who killed her. You're not the one who—"

"Stop."

"But—"

"No, I mean it. Those are all equivocations. Justifications. Rationalizations. Call them whatever you want, but it doesn't change that she died because she was married to me. There might have been a drugged-up Iranian strongman who actually drowned her in the tub, but he wouldn't have been there at all if I hadn't pissed off a Jersey Mafia man named Anthony Bruzzi. No way around that one. Them's the breaks. I have to live with it."

She shook her head and looked away, at the ceiling this time. "It's not the same."

"No, it isn't. That's just the point. Every time guilt rears its ugly head, it shows a different face. All I'm saying is that you have to confront this one instead of running from it. I spent five years running from mine. I buried it in bourbon and crossword puzzles. I lived a half-life, walking through life like a ghost. Anything but facing the cold hard truth that Janet would be alive today if it weren't for me. Then something changed."

"What?"

"I started working," Gage said.

"You started—"

"A dead teenage girl washed up on the beach. I could have let the police handle it, but I didn't. I got back to doing what I'm good at. And you know what it did to all that guilt?"

"What?"

"Absolutely nothing."

"Oh. Then why—?"

"Because when I was focused on something else, I wasn't focused on *that*. And when I wasn't focused on the guilt, my life slowly started to fill up with other things. Zoe. My pal Alex. A place for love in my life. The guilt is still there. It will always be there. There's no making it go away, so you shouldn't even try. You just have to get on with things. And when you get on with things, those things start to matter again."

He could see that she was close to tears, but she blinked them away. He squeezed her hand. She placed her other hand on top of his and tried to smile.

"It's hard, isn't it?" she said.

"Never really gets easier," he said. "It just gets more familiar. Like that scar you're going to have. At first it will really jump out at you. You'll see it every time you look in the mirror. But eventually, you'll get used to it, and then it will just be part of you. A badass part of you."

The door opened behind them. Gage turned, expecting a nurse or a doctor, and was surprised when Quinn walked through the door. That wasn't the biggest surprise. The biggest surprise was that Quinn wasn't alone. The droopy-faced Brisbane and a young uniformed cop accompanied him. The young cop, who had the body of a linebacker and the face of a twelve-year-old, looked like he wanted to throw up. His hand hovered over his sidearm.

"Chief?" Gage said. "What did you find—"

"Stand up," Quinn said.

"What?"

Brisbane, looking all too pleased with himself, grabbed Gage by his leather jacket and started to yank him to his feet.

"Hey!" Gage protested. "What the hell is going on here?"

"You're under arrest," Quinn said. "That's what's happening here."

"Are you nuts?"

"Get up now or this is going to get a lot more unpleasant for you."

Brisbane's glee at this turn of events—if Brisbane could be said to show anything remotely close to glee—prompted him to be a little too rough, from Gage's point of view. There was a bit of a scuffle. The young cop, his baby face reddening like a shiny ripe tomato, pulled his gun. Quinn stepped in, hands raised, repeating the word *whoa* like it was some sort of mantra. Gage, still baffled by what was happening, shrugged off Brisbane and climbed to his feet on his own power. His right knee buckled a little, but fortunately it didn't give out completely.

"What's going on?" Karen said.

"Can he put that thing away?" Gage said, nodding toward the cop. "I'd like to know why I'm being arrested before someone shoots me, if that's all right."

Quinn, in the kind of low, soothing voice he might have used to talk to a wounded dog, told the cop to put the gun away. When he did, and Brisbane stepped away, Quinn turned back to Gage.

"You have the right to remain silent," Quinn said.

"Oh Jesus," Gage said.

"Anything you say or do—"

"This can't be happening."

But it was. Not to be deterred, Quinn finished with the Miranda rights, then pulled a pair of handcuffs out of his trench coat. The metal glinted like fine jewelry in the soft glow of the lamps.

"You've got to be joking," Gage said.

"Got to do it, pal. Murder is serious business. Turn around."

"What? Murder who?"

"Turn around!"

"All right, all right! Just give me some kind of clue what's going on here, okay?"

When Gage turned, he was facing Karen. He imagined that his own face must have looked as confused and shocked as hers. It had been a long time since he'd felt the clinch of handcuffs on his wrist—it had happened twice in his New York days—and it was just as unpleasant as he remembered. Right away, he could feel the metal biting into his flesh. Quinn fished around inside Gage's jacket and pulled out the Beretta, handing it to Brisbane. Gage heard the gun drop into an evidence bag.

"Fine," Gage said. "Fine, I'm handcuffed and unarmed. Now do you mind telling me who I supposedly killed?"

"Two people," Quinn said. "Dan MacDonald and Thomas Kelton."

"What? They're dead?"

"Come on, let's go," Quinn said. "You're going down to the station."

"Not until I get some answers!" Gage said.

"Buddy," Brisbane warned, "you're in no position to make demands."

"I got this," Quinn admonished his detective. Then, to Gage, he continued in a low, flat voice: "When we went to MacDonald's house, we found them murdered in the living room—stabbed to death. We also found that MacDonald had a security camera mounted on the side of his house and pointed at his drive. The tape clearly shows that you were the last person to show up at his house. The only person that day, in fact."

"That doesn't mean I killed them! I already told you I was there! Doesn't that seem a little odd to you?"

"We also found a knife on the road by your van. It has blood on it. I'm guessing forensics will match that blood to the victims."

Now it was immediately clear to Gage what was happening. He was being framed. He was so out of it after the van crashed that he must not have heard the Hummer returning and dropping the knife.

"The security footage," he said. "Did it show anyone earlier? Maybe not the same day, but earlier in the week?"

"There was only one day's tape there. The rest were gone."

"Gone? You mean someone stole them?"

"Or maybe MacDonald only keeps one day's worth, who knows. Come on, let's go. Meloy, make sure you get his cane." He raised a stern finger toward Karen. "We're not done with you either. Still sorting out whether you were part of this or not."

Quinn took Gage by the arm and guided him toward the door. Gage, over his shoulder, told Karen not to worry, this would be sorted out soon, and he was out of the room before she mustered a response. The clerk behind the counter, a black man with graying hair, gaped at them, as did the nurse and the old man she was helping into a wheelchair. To Gage, it felt like more people than that. It felt as if the whole town was gaping at him, thinking, Good riddance, we didn't want you here anyway. In that moment, it didn't just feel like the driver of the Hummer was out to get him. It felt as if the whole city of Barnacle Bluffs had turned against him.

"This is crazy," Gage said. "Think about this. Why would I kill them and then tell you to go back and talk to them?"

"I haven't thought that far ahead," Quinn said.

"The killer never expected me to send you back there," Gage said. "And why take the earlier tapes but leave the one that incriminates me?"

"We also had a complaint on you," Quinn said.

"What? From who?"

"Security at the college called in. They said you two were prowling around the campus earlier tonight. When they told you that you had to leave, they said that you displayed aggressive behavior."

"Like hell!"

"Yeah, it was totally out of character for you."

"This is insanity."

"It is what it is," Quinn said.

They left the hospital and walked into the dark parking lot, Quinn guiding him by the elbow, Brisbane and the young cop behind them. The air felt even heavier than earlier, hitting his face like a damp paintbrush. He could sense a storm coming, a big one. Quinn directed him to an unmarked police car, no lights on top but still a rabbit cage in the back. A regular police cruiser was parked next to it. Quinn took off the handcuffs, then refastened them so that Gage could wear them with his hands in his lap rather than behind him. He opened the back door, and Brisbane, obviously enjoying himself immensely, was a bit rough as he positioned Gage into the backseat.

"You ride back with Officer Reginald," Quinn said to Brisbane.

"Sir?" Brisbane said.

"Do as I say. I'll be behind you shortly."

Brisbane shrugged and slammed the door, then went with the young cop. Gage, still handcuffed, locked in the back of a police cruiser that didn't even have door handles, didn't think escape was an option even if he was so inclined—which he wasn't. This was all going to get sorted out, the evidence was too flimsy to keep him, but knowing how slowly the wheels of justice turned, that might be weeks or even months. By then, whoever had killed Connor Fleicher—as well as MacDonald and his friend—would be long gone. Quinn climbed in the police cruiser, glancing over his shoulder at Gage. His face, through the thick metal mesh, was inscrutable. Still, Gage took hope from the fact that Quinn had specifically asked to ride with Gage alone.

"No funny stuff," he said.

"Listen to me," Gage said. "You know I didn't do this. You know this is a mistake."

"What I *know*," Quinn said, "and what the law compels me to *do* are not always the same thing."

"Come on. You've got to admit, this looks like a frame job."

"Yep. I won't argue with you there."

"But you're still going to throw me in jail?"

"Got to," he said.

He started the car. While they sat there, the engine idling, Gage raced through some way to persuade Quinn to let him go. He felt as if all the puzzle pieces were on the table in front of him; he just didn't know what the puzzle was supposed to *be*, so he didn't even know where to begin.

Quinn gestured for Brisbane and the other cop to leave. They did, and yet still Quinn waited in the parking lot with the engine idling.

"What are you doing?" Gage said.

"Waiting," Quinn said.

"Waiting for what?"

"Waiting for them to leave."

"Why?

After the cruiser finally left, Quinn put his car in gear and slowly eased out of the spot. He took his time about it. The odd behavior made Gage uneasy. For a moment, he was struck with the wild possibility that somehow Quinn himself was behind the murders. Certainly being the chief of police gave him all sorts of power and leverage that ordinary people didn't have. When they reached the road, instead of turning right, which would have led straight to the police station, Quinn turned left, which was the long way around the lake, back to Highway 17, the road that led back to the Willamette Valley.

"You're going the wrong way," Gage said.

"I'm going the long way. We'll double back along the highway and come into town that way."

"Why?"

"Maybe I just like the scenic route."

Gage felt a prickle of fear along his spine. He envisioned the chief pulling into an empty lot behind the lake and putting a bullet in Gage's head. This nutty theory lasted only for a few seconds before Gage, realizing the absurdity of it all, discarded the idea. What could the motive possibly be? The idea of a cop being involved, though, stirred something in the recesses of his mind. There was something he was missing. It was staring him in the face.

"I know you didn't do it," Quinn said.

"What?"

"Might seem funny, me taking you in, but the law's the law. I just wanted to have you alone for a few minutes. You know some things you're not telling me. Maybe you don't want them officially out in the open, but I figured I'd give you the ride to the station to let me in on what you know. You might not be my favorite person in the world, Gage, but I have no desire to throw you in prison. At least not yet."

"Believe me," Gage said, "if I had any critical information that could convince you I'm not in on this, I'd tell you."

"Well, let's start with *any* information. I figure you have about five minutes, and that's if I drive slow."

"And if I say I want to talk to my lawyer first?"

"Then I drive a lot faster," Quinn said.

"That's what I figured. "

"Why were you prowling around the college earlier tonight?"

"I wasn't *prowling*," Gage said.

"Why were you there at all?"

"I was thinking about taking a philosophy class."

"Gage, this is serious."

"So is philosophy. Especially Immanuel Kant. Very serious guy."

"I'm rethinking my generosity of spirit here."

"How do I know *you're* not involved? A minute ago, I thought you were going to drive me out to the woods and shoot me in the head. That's just as crazy an idea."

"We're going to be at the station in two minutes."

Gage sighed. "Someone at the college was involved with Connor and Jeremiah in some way. They corresponded on a science-fiction message board online. They used a handle, so I don't know who they are, but they sent the message from the college. We got a message earlier tonight, and since there's not a lot of people on campus right now, that really narrows it down. So it would have to be someone ... have to be ..."

There it was, what he'd been missing. Maybe it was giving voice to the crazy idea that Quinn was involved, but his mind finally made the link.

"Campus security," he said.

## Chapter 20

They were nearly to Highway 17 when Gage made his realization. Through the gaps in the firs, Gage saw the lights on the far side of Big Dipper Lake shining like low-lying stars.

"Campus security?" Quinn said. "What are you talking about?"

"Jantz," Gage said. "You said campus security called in a complaint on me. Was it this guy Jantz?"

"Patrick Jantz, yeah," Quinn said. "He grew up in town, been here forever. He's the head of—"

"I know who he is. What time did he call it in?"

"What difference would that make?"

"Was it before or after the Hummer tried to push me off the road?"

"I suppose it must have been after. Not long after, though."

"But definitely after?"

"Yeah. I didn't hear about his call until I was already on my way to see MacDonald."

"Don't you see?" Gage said. "Once he'd realized that his original plan of running me off the cliff didn't work, he wanted to make me look even more suspicious as a murder suspect. Otherwise, why would he wait so long?"

"Maybe he just got busy. Maybe he was in the can. I don't know."

"Let's go to his place," Gage said. "Ask him some questions. He seemed like the sort of guy who might break under pressure, especially after the kind of night he had."

"Right now?"

"No, I thought we'd stop at the Dairy Queen for a sundae first. Of course right now!"

"Are you nuts? You're under arrest! I can't take you anywhere but the station. And anyway, your idea is pretty flimsy. If I didn't know better—scratch that, I *do* know better—I'd say you're just grasping at straws, hoping to delay the inevitable."

"It's not flimsy at all," Gage said. "It makes perfect sense. Who else would know that the security camera in the dormitory wasn't working? Or maybe even make sure that it wasn't? Who would have easy access to Connor's room? Who would know just how to get in and out to kill Connor without being seen? And that drawing pad that Berry Fleicher wanted—why was he so resistant to getting it for me? It's not because he *knew* something was in it that incriminated him. It's because he *didn't*. It was an unknown. A wild card."

Quinn was silent. He took the exit off Highway 17, merging onto Highway 101. They passed the Safeway and, a block behind the grocery store but looming like the top of a huge barrel, the Golden Eagle Casino. The strip of lights along the roof glowed like a parade of fireflies in the darkness. Inside, even at this late hour, people were gambling away their life savings. Gage knew from his early years playing poker, as he put himself through college back in Montana, what it felt like to bet big on a small stack, when your back was against the wall and one more loss would mean washing out of the game. He felt the same now.

As if in answer to this thought, rain began to pelt the windshield. It started as a few drops as big as quarters smacking against the glass, but this only lasted a few seconds before it turned into a deluge. Quinn turned on the windshield wipers, but this barely made a difference. It was like driving through a waterfall. Quinn slowed the car to a crawl. At least it gave Gage a little more time. Maybe his luck wasn't all bad.

"Five minutes," Gage said.

"What's that?"

"Five minutes! That's all I ask."

From the back, Gage saw Quinn shake his head.

"You said you knew I was innocent," Gage said, raising his voice to be heard over the roar. "Can't you at least give me this one last chance to prove it?"

"You're definitely not innocent," Quinn said. "There's nothing *innocent* about you. But guilty of killing MacDonald and Kelton? No, I don't think so."

"Then let's go see Jantz."

"Gage—"

"Five minutes."

The rain was so intense, a tsunami coming down on the roof, that Quinn was forced to pull the car over to the side of the highway, parking by the curb in front of a closed coffee shop. No cars passed. A red neon *Donuts* sign was barely readable through the sheet of water, as if the letters had been warped and bent. They waited out the storm, Quinn tapping the steering wheel. Finally, after an ocean had been dumped on Barnacle Bluffs and little rivers ran alongside the highway, overflowing the gutters and carrying debris under the streetlamps, the rain eased up to *only* a downpour.

"Motive," Quinn said. "I need some kind of motive here. Why would he do it?"

"I can't give it to you yet. I don't know."

"Then we're going to the station."

"Chief! I'm telling you everything I know."

"I don't think so. I think you're still holding something back. You really think this was about some kind of science-fiction message board? What was really going on? Jeremiah and Connor were wrapped up in something, and it got Connor killed. And now Jeremiah won't talk, so he's afraid of something. Exposing somebody."

"Maybe he's protecting his family," Gage said. "Maybe he's afraid somebody will hurt them if he comes out with the truth."

"But what truth?"

"I wish I knew." And then, seeing the light dim in Quinn's eyes, he added, "It's got to be obvious to you that they were both gay, right?"

"It crossed my mind," Quinn said.

"At first, I thought that was all Jeremiah was trying to keep secret. That he and Connor were having an affair. But to go to jail just to keep that secret, when it's pretty obvious to anyone who knows them what their sexual preference was? I don't think so. It's more than that. Jeremiah found Connor dead. He was so distraught, he picked up the gun, probably in a daze. He decided to kill himself."

"I'm with you so far," Quinn said. "Not that I buy it, but it's one theory."

"Why did someone kill Connor? To keep him quiet. There was something going on at the college, something that involved MacDonald and Jantz. Connor found out about it. Maybe Jeremiah doesn't even know. All he knows is that his friend is dead and he wants to die. Maybe he doesn't have anything to tell us at all. Only I don't buy that either."

"Why is that?" Quinn asked.

"Because he confessed to a murder he didn't commit. Someone really does have leverage over him. And since he's not protecting Connor, then I have to believe he's protecting someone else—maybe his parents, like I said. Come on, Chief. Let's go see Patrick Jantz. Rattle his cage a little."

The rain slowed. The rivers pouring into the gutters turned into streams. Quinn, with a deep sigh, tapped the steering wheel three times, as if to a beat, then nodded. The road ahead was drivable, even if nobody would be going out for a pleasure cruise in it.

"All right, five minutes," he said. He reached for his radio. "I'll have dispatch give me his address."

"One more thing," Gage said. "You need to take off my handcuffs."

"What?"

"And sit up front with you."

"No. Out of the question."

"Chief," Gage said, "this isn't going to work if Jantz thinks I'm in custody. It's only going to work if he thinks we're showing up together to ask him questions."

"No."

"You know I'm right," Gage said.

"Just no."

"Then take me to the station. It won't work otherwise."

Quinn leveled the kind of menacing stare at Gage that wasn't at all neighborly. This was the real Quinn, the hardened cop underneath, the guy nobody wanted to face in a dark alley. It was in those rare moments when Quinn showed his real self that Gage knew the grandfather act was just a way to get people to lower their defenses so Quinn could get a better read on them. Gage was more than happy to allow Quinn to get a read on him. For once, he really had told Quinn everything he knew, so there was nothing to hide.

Grinning, he raised the handcuffs.


THEY DIDN'T HAVE far to drive. It turned out that Jantz lived three blocks away, in a shabby little duplex within spitting distance of the casino. A red Ford Ranger, twenty years old with a rusty bumper, was parked in the spot on the left. The spot on the right was empty. Closed curtains hid both duplexes from view, but the main front window of the place on the left was rimmed with light, made hazy by the steady downpour.

"He rent or own?"

"Own."

"He lives in the one on the left? With the Ford Ranger?"

"Yep."

"Who's renting the other one?"

"I have no idea. Does it matter?"

Gage didn't answer. He found it hard to believe that some-body who had something big to hide would live in a duplex with only a thin wall separating him from a nosy neighbor. The rain pelted the overgrown rhododendron bushes, flattened the tall grass, and drained into the cracks along the sidewalks out front. On the side, in the narrow gap between the chain-link fence and the tall laurel bushes separating the duplex from the white cottage next door, were a couple of mountain bikes without wheels and the kind of exercise machine, with metal wires and weights in strange places, that was probably bought while watching a late-night infomercial.

"Remember," Quinn said, "I do the talking."

"You do the talking," Gage said.

"Don't make me regret I took those cuffs off."

"What fun would that be?"

"Gage—"

"I'll be a perfect Boy Scout. Promise."

They got out of the car and quick-stepped up the cracked driveway to the little overhang over the stoop on the left, Gage lurching because he didn't have his cane. They were only out in the rain a few seconds, but even so, Gage's hair was flattened and soaked, the water so cold it bit at his ears. It crackled like popcorn against both of their jackets. On their way, he saw the curtains part just a little, not enough to see someone inside but enough to know that someone *was* inside, looking at them, sizing them up. It was exactly what Gage was hoping would happen—and why it was so important that he not be wearing cuffs.

Quinn rapped on the door. There was a bit of a wait, some shuffling and knocking from within the house, and just when Quinn was about to knock again, the door opened. There was Jantz, dressed in blue jeans and a sleeveless muscle shirt that didn't do much for him because he didn't have the muscles to go with it, just two pasty white arms that hung from his side like wet noodles. His gray hair, just as before, was as blocky as cut granite. His face had an unnatural pink flush, and when he spoke, Gage got a good whiff of whatever booze the man was drinking.

There was so much nervous energy wound up in the man that Gage feared that if it came unspooled, it would knock the duplex down. For just a moment, Gage saw Jantz's eyes dart to the left, to the complex next door, and Gage suddenly understood why there was no car parked in the other spot.

"What do you want?" Jantz said.

"Mr. Jantz," Quinn said, "I'm sorry to bother you, but we just have—"

"You know exactly what we want," Gage said. "We want you to open up your place next door and show us what you're hiding inside."

"Gage—" Quinn began, sternly.

"What?" Jantz said, eyes doing the rattlesnake dance, his hands balling into fists. "I don't—"

"You're in big trouble, Patty," Gage went on, talking over both of them. "You know it and I know it."

"I didn't—"

"Let's make this easy instead of hard. You want to open the door or do we have to—"

Jantz slammed the door. It was so abrupt that it took both Gage and Quinn a few seconds to react to it.

"What happened to being a perfect little Boy Scout?" Quinn asked.

"That *was* me being a Boy Scout."

"I'd bet a thousand dollars you were never in the Boy Scouts."

"You'd win that bet," Gage said. "But did you see his face? He was panicked beyond belief. He's definitely got something over there. Let's find out what it is."

"Not without a warrant," Quinn said.

"Chief—"

"Gage, you may be able to play fast and loose with the rules, but I—"

Gage, knowing they would blow their opportunity if he argued any longer with Quinn, banged on the door. "Open up!" he shouted. "Open up, Jantz! Make this easy rather than hard!" He pounded on the door again. "Open up or we're kicking this door down!"

He raised his fist, but this time a cursing Quinn grabbed his arm and yanked him away from the door. They fell off the stoop into the rain. Gage took a few backward, stumbling steps, feet sliding on the slick pavement, and would have gone down if Quinn still wasn't gripping his arm. The icy deluge soaked through his clothes as if they were made of tissue paper. He ripped his arm from Quinn's grasp, and the two came back at each other like boxers in a ring. In a tiny back compartment of Gage's mind, he knew this was a bad idea, but his frustration had overwhelmed him.

That's when he caught the flicker of yellow behind the curtains.

It was behind the curtains on the *right*, not the left, and it wasn't a steady yellow but a pulsing yellow—from a fire! All at once Gage realized what was happening, that evidence was being destroyed, and if he didn't act *right this second*, then whatever hope they had of convicting Jantz was literally going to go up in smoke.

He was at the door on the right before these thoughts had barely taken coherent form in his mind, running despite the knife-jab of pain in his knee, Quinn hollering at him, kicking at the door with everything he had.

The first blow splintered the frame, but the door didn't give. He was raising his foot to kick again when he heard a scream from inside, a terrible scream of a man in agony, and Gage put even more force into his next kick.

The door blew open in a crackle of wood.

A wave of heat and smoke rolled over him. He heard Quinn shouting, but Gage was already inside, stepping into what first appeared to be an empty living room—blank walls, no furniture— until he saw the wall of flames to his right, and beyond them, totally engulfed in fire, some kind of cheap computer desk with bookcases on either side filled with DVDs. All melting to nothing before his watery eyes. Gage smelled gasoline.

From the back of the duplex, he thought he heard another

sound almost lost in the cacophony of the fire—a click and a thud, like a door closing.

He thought it might have been Jantz fleeing from the back until he saw a figure on the floor in front of the desk, writhing and spasming, a black slash in the fire. Gage took a step toward him, but the heat pushed him away. The smoke found his eyes and his lungs, burning and choking, seizing him in a death grip. If Gage didn't get out of there, he was going to end up like the man on the floor.

He heard sirens approaching.

The barrier of heat had only strengthened, pummeling him, shoving him back toward the door. There was no help for Jantz. There was no help for the duplex either. Gage's survival instinct was compelling him to turn for the door, but, remembering the sound from the back of the duplex, he breathed into his arm and dodged past the flames. Through an empty kitchen with green Formica countertops. Down a narrow, bare hall, turning on lights as he went. Past an empty bedroom, the heat chasing, to a master bedroom with a couple of stained mattresses on the floor, cheap blinds over the windows, and nothing else.

Except for a handful of DVDs.

They were unmarked DVDs in transparent cases, the kind someone would buy and record themselves. The sirens grew louder. The fire trucks were on the street. The rain tapped on the roof and the windows. There was a sliding glass door, and when Gage tried it, he found it unlocked. *Unlocked.* Had that been the sound he'd heard, someone leaving through the back door? He heard Quinn shouting at him from the front of the house.

The DVDs. Why were they there? There was no TV in the back room, no way to play them.

They'd been left there intentionally.

Why?

Someone wanted them to be found. And the sirens? They'd arrived so quickly. Quinn may have called them in, but it was also possible someone had called 911 *even before setting the place ablaze.*

If Gage hadn't come inside, or if he'd backed out instead of running down the hall to the bedroom, the cops would eventually have found the stack of DVDs. That meant whoever had left them wanted the cops to have them, not Gage, which meant Gage needed to take them.

Or maybe he was imagining all of this. Maybe he hadn't heard a sound at all. Maybe these were just Jantz's favorite DVDs.

This all went through Gage's mind in the span of a few seconds. He snatched up the DVDs and, with the fire raging behind him, fled through the back sliding door and shut it behind him. He heard—even as he doubled over gasping for breath in the rain, coughing—the shouts of men, the blast of water from hoses. Big brakes screeching to a stop. More sirens. He'd stumbled onto a small patio, exposed to the rain except for the house's slight overhang, the whole area enclosed with a chain-link fence and, behind the fence, a wall of unkempt arborvitae. Nobody was there. There were no signs that anyone had been there recently.

He looked at the DVDs clutched in his hand. He had to make a decision fast. The right thing to do, the thing Quinn would undoubtedly *want* him to do, would be to circle back to the front of the duplex and hand over the DVDs to Quinn.

But Gage had to know what was on them first.

As risky as it was, he had a hunch that it might be his last opportunity to find out who was really behind all of this.

Gage shoved the DVDs into the inside pocket of his leather jacket. With the room behind him graying with smoke, he fled for the chain-link fence, picking a spot where a gap in the bushes on the other side would let him pass. Rain hounding him, he struggled over the top of the fence, dropping with a thud on the other side on his bad knee. He bit down so hard to stifle his own shout of pain that he drew blood. He heard men shouting on the other side, rounding the duplex, and he rolled through the bushes into another backyard—this one with a rusty swing set and a sandbox filled with puddles.

Now he just needed to go somewhere to play the DVDs, somewhere Quinn wouldn't think Gage would go.

And he needed a way to get there. Without his van, without his cane, that was no easy problem to fix.

By the time he'd reached the gate, though, he knew both where to go and how to get there.

## Chapter 21

AT NEARLY THREE in the morning, the hospital floor was quiet except for a single orderly pushing a rattling cart over the tiles, making it easy enough for Gage to slip into Karen's room unnoticed. Her room was dark. He thought he might discover her asleep, still recovering from her injuries, so he was surprised to find her sitting up in bed, the bandage covering half her face lit up from the pale light of her iPhone. When she glanced up, her eyes widened. He was pleasantly surprised at how much more lively she seemed, how much more alert and present.

"You're—you're free," she said.

He closed the door behind him, and when he spoke, he kept it to a whisper. "Technically, yes. I'm glad to see your iPhone survived the crash. Now I can truly sleep easy tonight."

"What happened? How, how did you get here? Where's Quinn?"

"I took one of the free shuttles from the casino. Quinn? He's probably prowling the streets looking for me—if he's not helping put out the fire."

"Fire? What?"

He explained. He made it fast, raising a hand holding the DVDs when she started in with the questions, and nodded to-

239

ward the TV in the corner. "I need to play these," he said. "I figured the last place Quinn would think I would go would be back to your hospital room. Do you know if it works? No, of course you wouldn't. You're watching YouTube videos of funny cats."

"Dancing babies, actually," Karen said. "What's on them?"

"We're about to find out."

Gage crossed over to the window, limping like a madman, his cane currently sitting in Quinn's backseat. He could go without his cane for short periods and make a good show of it, but more than that and all he needed was a humpback to look like Igor. He glanced at the parking lot. No police cars so far. The hospital might not be the first place Quinn would search for him, but he'd send someone over eventually, if only to ask Karen if she'd heard from him. He turned on the television, took out the first DVD, and slipped it into the player beneath the television. The screen, blue at first, flickered to static, then went black.

They didn't have to wait long to be appropriately shocked. Within seconds, the black screen dissolved to a close-up of Dan MacDonald's face, his eyes open, his stare as vacant as a dead man's. In fact, Gage thought he *was* dead until he finally blinked, his expression was so flat and emotionless. That wasn't what was shocking, though. The camera, shaky and slow to focus, quickly zoomed back, and there was Jeremiah Cooper on his knees in front of MacDonald. They were both naked.

"Oh my," Karen said.

"I don't know if I'm old enough to watch this," Gage said.

"Is that—?"

"Jeremiah, yes. And Dan MacDonald."

"It's like a bad porn movie."

"That's exactly what it is," Gage said. "Jesus."

The two were in a windowless basement with concrete floors and exposed yellow light bulbs among the maze of pipes on the ceiling—MacDonald on a folding chair, Jeremiah kneeling on the kind of padded, fold-up mats used in gym classes everywhere. Jeremiah's head bobbed up and down on MacDonald's lap with plenty of vigor, but when the camera caught his eyes, he wore the same flat, zombie-like expression as MacDonald. These were not two people who were in love with each other. These were not people who were even in love with what they were doing, or even trying that hard to fake it.

"Now we know what MacDonald was hiding," Gage said.

"And Jeremiah. But why leave these behind?"

"Let's look at the other DVDs."

"I don't know if my stomach can handle it."

"You can watch dancing babies later to clear your mind," Gage said.

"I'm not homophobic. It's just, Jeremiah …"

"I know."

Gage didn't think he was homophobic either, but he wasn't so sure. He was only slowly coming to terms with his own unease about the whole thing. He liked to think that because he was at least *aware* of his unease meant he was making progress. He'd always believed in gay rights and gay marriage and the whole "It Gets Better" campaign, but that was all on an intellectual level. There was still something about two men engaged in sex acts, displayed vividly on a screen in front of him, that elicited some deep revulsion. He didn't like himself for it, but it was there. Maybe it was the Montana boy in him. He just knew he didn't like that part of himself, even if it was known only to him, and he was going to keep working on getting rid of it.

The other DVDs were more of the same, MacDonald and Jeremiah in various sex acts, always in the same room, though sometimes in the chair and sometimes on the floor. They never looked like they were enjoying it. There was one difference on the third DVD, and it was a big one. Toward the end, Jantz stepped in front of the camera and slapped Jeremiah's bare bottom, and, when the kid jumped, laughed heartily. Jantz, though only in view for a few seconds, was dressed in his uniform and was clearly recognizable.

"Bingo," Gage said.

"What?" Karen said.

"Don't you see?" Gage said. "This evidence is supposed to

lead us to where these sex videos were filmed. Probably beneath one of the buildings on campus. And when the cops search the place, they're going to find all kinds of evidence implicating Jantz. These DVDs were chosen so it looked like Jantz did this on his own."

"But who?"

"No idea. But whoever it is, I'm guessing he was already planning to do this when Quinn and I showed up unexpectedly at Jantz's place. Otherwise, where was his car? He must have parked it on a side street, which was why he was able to escape out the back just like me. It was his plan all along. He wanted it to look like a suicide, that Jantz was so distraught by it all that he killed himself. He was going to kill Jantz, slip out the back, and call the fire department from a cell phone so they'd get there before the entire place burned. He just wanted the other DVDs and the computer to be destroyed."

"He still managed to carry out his plan," Karen said.

"Except for me getting the DVDs. So right now there's no link to this basement sex dungeon."

"But why kill Connor?" Karen asked.

"Maybe he found out about what was happening. Maybe he threatened to expose them all. Killing him might have been the only way to stop him. And he made it look like Jantz, distraught by it all, committed suicide."

"And without Dan MacDonald around—"

"There wouldn't be anybody left to tell a different story."

"Except for Jeremiah."

"Yes," Gage said. "He's in prison, though. But for some reason, he doesn't want to expose whoever's really behind this."

"*Who* is behind this? That's the question."

"It is indeed."

Gage stepped to the window, peering through the crack in the curtains. Still no cops, just a rainy, windswept parking lot. The long day was finally catching up to him. The aches and pains, the pinching in the joints, the soreness of the muscles, it was all taking hold. He'd splashed some water on his face at the casino before the shuttle had arrived, cleaned himself up a little, but he still felt as if a mountain of dried sweat coated his body. Despite the late hour, he wasn't sleepy at all, but he did feel a deep fatigue settling into his bones.

But he had to keep pushing. He felt as if he were in a sinking ship, trying to find something before it disappeared into the ocean.

"DWR_forever," he said.

"It's got to mean something," Karen said.

He rubbed at his temples. "I've been focusing too much on that directly. What am I missing here? Let's focus on Jeremiah again. He walks in on Connor, finds him dead, then goes crazy with grief and threatens to shoot himself … wait a minute. Wait a minute here."

"What?"

"When I found him the first time on the beach with the gun, that was weeks before school started."

"So?"

"So," Gage said, "it's not very likely he'd met Jantz, right?"

"Probably not."

Gage started to pace. His knee buckled, nearly put him on the floor, but he didn't care. He'd gotten the dragon by the tail. He could feel it. "On the beach that night, Jeremiah told me he was a coward. I thought he was talking about not being able to kill himself. And later, when he *did* try to kill himself, that made even more sense. But what if he'd wanted to shoot someone else? What if he couldn't go through with it, and that's why he thought he was a coward?"

"Who?" She sat up straighter in bed. "You don't think it was Arne Cooper taping those videos, do you? God, this gets even more twisted by the minute."

Gage considered it. "The problem is, Arne has a rock-solid alibi the night Connor was killed. He was drunk off his ass. And as hard as he is on Jeremiah, I just don't think he'd do that to his son. No, Jeremiah had someone else in his life. Someone who lured him into that sex dungeon, somebody he trusted. It also had to be somebody who'd known both Jantz and Jeremiah a while."

"Everybody in this damn town knows everybody," Karen said. "The regulars, I mean. You're either a tourist or you grew up here."

"It does seem that way sometimes. It doesn't help that most people think of me as the guy who brings a lot of bad publicity to the town." He scratched his chin. He had enough stubble there now to qualify for an entry-level beard. "Jeremiah had a pretty small circle of people he knew. Most of his world was the high school ... wait. Wait, that's it. I can't believe I didn't see it right away!"

"Shh! The nurses are going to hear you. What?"

"High school. The same high school."

"Huh?"

"Arne's alibi. He was drunk. Who dropped him off that night? It was the good old family friend, Paul Weld. The assistant coach. The biology teacher. Remember, he dropped off Jeremiah's book with Zoe? Of course! He was fishing for information. He wanted to see how much we knew. And both Jantz and Weld grew up in this town. They both told me. I bet if we start asking around, we'll find out they were friends in high school."

"So they had this little sex dungeon before Jeremiah got sucked into it?"

"Maybe. Somehow they got MacDonald roped into it too. Probably with some kind of blackmail."

Karen rubbed her forehead. "What a sordid web this is. My head already hurts like hell, and trying to make sense of all this is just making it worse."

"Yeah, but I think we're definitely onto something here. Jeremiah was a pretty confused kid, just ripe for being seduced by a teacher he respected. Both he and MacDonald might initially have been willing participants in those sex videos, but I'm guessing Jantz and Weld used the videos as blackmail to keep them involved. Maybe Connor secretly taped them all with his iPhone, which is why it went missing. Jantz took it. Connor was in love with Jeremiah and maybe he was trying to force Jeremiah to cut loose from all the sex games."

"But he didn't know the hold Weld had on him."

"Right. And he also underestimated what a sadistic monster Paul Weld is. This is a guy who killed not only MacDonald and Thomas but also his sex buddy, Jantz. All to keep his little secrets from getting exposed."

"DWR_forever," Karen said. "What would a biology teacher who moonlights as a football coach use as his handle?"

All at once, Gage knew. "Darwin! Darwin Was Right! He told me himself! Remember the article he said Jeremiah wrote in high school, the one about evolution? And Connor's drawing, the one with *DWR* and all the animals—that fits too."

"Darwin was right ... forever." Karen nodded. "It seems like a pretty good bet. Survival of the fittest. Maybe that's the way he sees himself. But now what are you going to do about it? He's not just going to admit to murder if you accuse him."

"No. And it's pretty likely that there's no evidence at that sex dungeon linking him to any of this. Or anywhere, for that matter. And the only witness is currently sitting in jail, having confessed to murder. Even if Jeremiah agreed to point the finger at Weld, who would believe him?"

"We would," Karen said.

"And we'd be the only ones. No, I've got to find another way, and I've got to find it quickly ... All right, I think I have an idea. Can you post on that website, SpacedOut?"

Karen brought up her phone and, with a few clicks, was ready to go. "Of course. But what kind of message are you going to send him? Meet me at the O.K. Corral at high noon? He doesn't need to meet you at all right now. He can just sit back and wait for the net to close around you. He's not really afraid of being caught at this point."

"Yes, he could. But I don't think being caught is what he fears most. Not if we judge him by all that he's done lately. There's something he fears a lot more."

"What's that?"

"Being exposed. This is a respected small-town biology

teacher, a beloved assistant coach. Rumors can be a lot more deadly than the police. And if a rumor has enough truth to it that it can plausibly be true? It's even worse."

"Okay. So what do you want to message him?"

"Oh, I didn't say I wanted to message him. I asked if you could post on the site."

"Post on the site?"

"Yep." Gage crossed over to her, sitting on the bed. "Out in public for all to read. It's going to be about a small-town biology teacher who was very, very bad."

"You know," Karen said, "there is a chance you're wrong about this. If you are, you could ruin an innocent man's—"

"Oh, I'm not going to use his name. Not yet. That'll be Part 2, the coming attraction. If this works right, we won't need to go that far."

"What are you hoping he'll do?"

"I'm hoping he shows up for a shoot-out at the O.K. Corral."

"You're not serious?"

"I'm completely serious. Part 1 is going to be the general details, including a teaser about Part 2—which will include not only his name but pictures of his lair."

"But where is his lair?"

"Somewhere at BBCC. There are probably only a couple of buildings that might have a basement like that. The dorm. The library. The student union. I might have to sneak into a few."

"How do you know he's left anything behind?"

"He probably hasn't. It won't matter. When he sees we haven't posted pictures yet, it will gnaw at him. His first instinct will be to go there just to make sure he hasn't left anything that will incriminate him."

"But—"

"Trust me. I don't have enough evidence to put him behind bars. I need to take matters into my own hands. Don't post the message quite yet, though. I'm going to need to get over there and find that sex dungeon first. I just want you to have the post ready when I tell you to put it up."

"How do we know he'll see it?"

With a smile, Gage pointed at her phone. "Because you're going to message him and tell him it's there."

*Chapter 22*

**G**age knew he had the right place. The basement beneath the library had the feel of a dungeon—dusty floors, exposed pipes, one odd-shaped room after another dimly lit by fluorescent panel lights, half of which didn't work. He was only in there a moment when he realized why the word *dungeon* was the first thing that came to mind, and why the place seemed oddly familiar. Except for minor differences—there were no chains affixed to the walls, after all—it matched the drawing he'd seen in Connor's sketch pad, the one of the detailed dungeon.

Connor had left them another clue in plain sight.

Gage shuffled from room to room, the disposable 35-mm he'd bought at the mini-mart in hand, his leather jacket still dripping water on the floor. He'd taken a couple of pictures, just for the heck of it, but there wasn't anything of note except for hundreds of blue plastic totes full of boxes of student records dating back half a century. Gage was in the central room, where he'd been for some time, when he heard the telltale creak of the door at the top of the stairs. Shortly after that, he heard footsteps.

When he turned, there was Paul Weld, dressed in his green windbreaker and matching baseball cap. The slick jacket glistened. Seeing Gage, he paused halfway down the flight of stairs, the two of them sizing each other up, the basement as silent as a crypt. It was raining when Gage had entered the basement, but it could have been a snowstorm outside for all he knew. There was no way to tell.

"There's nothing here," Weld said.

Gage surveyed his surroundings, as if taking them in for the first time. "I can see that," he said.

"I'm guessing you're disappointed."

"A little. It looked so different in the movie. Must be the magic of Hollywood, huh?"

Weld responded with a limp smile, then continued down the steps, keeping his gaze locked on Gage the entire time. The smile might have been limp, but the eyes were as focused as a tiger's. Gage raised the camera, thinking he'd snap a photo, but Weld was out with a Ruger revolver before Gage had even centered Weld in the photo.

"Put it on the floor," Weld said.

"Wow," Gage said, "I'm a little camera shy myself, but this is taking it a bit far."

"Put the camera on the floor. *Now.*"

Now the voice was as deadly as the eyes. His other hand raised where Weld could see it, Gage lowered the camera to the floor.

"Kick it over here," Weld said.

"What?"

"You heard me."

Gage gave it a gentle kick. He hadn't given the kick much force, but the plastic box still skidded across the concrete floor like a hockey puck. Weld stopped it with his foot. Without looking away from Gage and keeping the revolver pointed at Gage the entire time, he eased himself to the floor and picked up the camera.

"A little old-school, isn't it?" Weld said. "What, you were going to get these developed at Walmart, scan them, then load them on the Internet?"

"What's the Internet?"

"Very funny. All right, now your gun. Take it out, very easy, and slide it on the floor too."

"I don't have a gun."

*"Do it."*

Gage, taking his time about it, reached behind him and under the jacket, bringing out the Glock he'd borrowed from Karen. Weld tightened his grip and zeroed his aim on the center of Gage's chest. Keeping the gun at arm's length, held by the barrel and not the grip, Gage lowered it to the concrete a foot away from him, then kicked it across the floor. Weld picked it up, eyed it for a moment, then shrugged and slipped it into the side pocket of his windbreaker.

"Too easy," Weld said. He looked at the camera again. "You got any pictures of your lady friend on here? I mean, from before. She's not so photogenic now, is she? Terrible accident, that was. A lot of crazy drivers in this town."

"Crazy indeed," Gage said. "Especially when they're driving stolen Hummers. How about you, Paul? You drive any Hummers lately?"

Weld shook his head. "I don't know exactly what you were trying to accomplish here. Did you really think you would find something here to implicate me? Did you really think you'd just waltz in here and find everything you needed to clear your name and put me behind bars?"

"A man can hope," Gage said.

"You're a fool."

"I've been called worse."

Weld smiled, and this time it wasn't a limp smile at all, but a deeply sinister one that revealed a man who was fully capable of trying to run someone off the road with a Hummer, as well as much worse. "How about a murderer? A twisted homosexual? A blackmailer and a recorder of disturbing sex videos?"

"What?"

"Let me guess," Weld said. "You have a tape recorder of some kind in your pocket? Or a video camera positioned somewhere on one of these boxes? Maybe you thought if I showed up, you'd get me to confess, is that it? You'd get me to confess on camera to all of those terrible things I supposedly did, then you'd just call the police and let the law run its course. Was that the plan?"

Gage said nothing.

"Don't worry," Weld said, "after you're dead, I'll find anything you've got on you—or anything you've placed in the room. Oh, does that surprise you? Yes, you're going to die, Gage. Not only that, but I'll be the hero that saved the town from a sadistic monster. All of those things you were hoping to find down here? They're in my car. And when you're dead, I'll bring them down here, so when the police arrive, there will be plenty of proof that *you* were the one teaming up with the poor unfortunate Patrick Jantz, who of course isn't around anymore to say anything differently. In fact, *no one* is around who will say differently."

"Jeremiah is," Gage said.

"No one would believe him even if he did. And besides, he's a murderer himself. He confessed, didn't you hear?"

"I don't believe it. What do you have over him?"

"Believe anything you want," Weld said. "The boy's a murderer. When his pretty little friend threatened to expose his, um, after-hours habits, well, Jeremiah couldn't have that, could he? It would absolutely destroy Arne and Jeanie. Now, I want you to give me the password so I can erase that terrible lie you posted on the Internet. I don't think it will cause too many problems—if someone has seen it, I'll just say you were trying to blackmail me—but better that it goes away."

"I'm not telling you anything," Gage said.

Weld shook his head. "You know, before I followed you from the hospital, I stopped by the Turret House looking for you. Zoe was there. She was sleeping. She didn't even know I was in the house with her. Very pretty girl."

Gage clenched his fists but didn't say anything. Now, more than ever, he needed to remain in control.

"Ah," Weld said, "I see I got to you. I can't promise you that lady friend of yours will, um, survive her injuries, but Zoe, well, she doesn't have to die."

"Bastard," Gage said. "How dare you threaten her."

"I'm not threatening anyone. I'm just saying that the ones you love may die before their time. Oh, and that frumpy old bookseller friend of yours? He might get very depressed at losing you and drive off one of the bluffs. Awful things happen, Gage."

"Why are you doing all this? What made you this twisted?"

"The password."

"I don't know it."

"Liar."

"Why would I know it? It's Karen's account."

"Give it to me or I'll cut your daughter into little pieces."

"You shouldn't make threats like that," Gage said. "The police are in the other room right now. They're hearing every word."

Weld laughed. "Desperate. You surprise me again, Gage. I'd heard such great things about you. Of course I was waiting outside when you got here. I waited a good long while to make sure you were alone. Though I don't know why I bothered, really. You're alone, Gage. You're a suspected murderer on the run. And more than that, no one in this town likes you. They don't like you and they don't want you here. They're all going to be willing to believe the worst. So you really blundered into this one, Gage." He snickered. "The great Garrison Gage, who turned out to be a sexual deviant and a murderer. It kind of erases all those laudatory things that have been written about you in the press, doesn't it?"

"But why MacDonald and Thomas? Why kill them?"

"Hmm? I don't know what you're talking about."

"You needed to tidy up those loose ends, too?"

"Could have been a break-in, I suppose."

"You must be ashamed," Gage said.

"What?"

"Even now, you won't admit to what you've done?" Gage said. "You're going to kill me and you won't admit it? You must be ashamed of it all. You may be a sick perverted bastard, but you must *realize* you're a sick perverted bastard. How's that for evolution. Do you think Darwin would see it the same way?"

Weld's face changed. That limp smile, that placid expression, it began to melt away, leaving something more brittle underneath. "You'd best stop talking now. I was going to shoot you in the heart, but I think I'll shoot you in the stomach instead. Let you bleed out on the floor for a while before I put you out of your misery."

"What did you have on MacDonald? You take pictures of him with his lovers and threaten to go public with them unless he played your twisted game?"

"Stop."

"Or how about Jeremiah? You've known him since he was little, haven't you? I bet this didn't start with the college. I bet you're a child molester too."

"No! It was never like that. I—I loved them. I loved them all."

"But you killed them."

"No, I—"

"Do you always kill the people you love?"

"I didn't—"

"It was you Jeremiah was talking about when I first found him on the beach, wasn't it? He called himself a coward, and I thought it was because he couldn't commit suicide, but it was really because he couldn't kill *you*. How does it feel to have him spend the rest of his life behind prison for a murder *you* committed? Is that what love is?"

"I didn't do that! I—"

"What a pathetic liar you are," Gage said. "Do you actually believe—"

The revolver fired. Gage took the shot like a punch to the stomach—or more like a baseball bat, from how the blow felt. He got a glimpse of Weld's surprised face before he stumbled backward, then crumpled into a heap and landed hard on his back. If there was any air left in his lungs, the fall would have knocked it out of him, but the bullet had already done the trick.

Gasping for breath, he clutched at his chest and groped around the hole in the leather.

No blood.

Thank God there was no blood. Gage couldn't breathe, his

ears were ringing, but there was no blood.

"I don't—I don't—" Weld began, but then he was cut short by the shouts of men and the stampede of feet.

There were the sounds of struggle, the clatter of Weld's gun hitting the floor, then the clink of handcuffs. By the time Gage, who could finally breathe again, summoned the strength to sit up, Chief Quinn was kneeling at his side. Behind him, Brisbane and Trenton flanked Weld, who had his hands cuffed behind him. Two twitchy-faced cops, young enough that they were probably wearing diapers under their uniforms, still had their guns out, though at least they had the decency to point them away from everyone.

"You all right?" Quinn asked.

"I was just shot," Gage said. "What do you think?"

"Technically, the *bulletproof vest* was shot. You seem to be okay."

"Details, details. You know, you and your friends took your time there."

"Needed to make sure we had enough proof, you know that."

"Or maybe you just wanted to see me shot."

"There could be some of that. Let me help you up."

It wasn't easy to stand up straight, not with the pain burning in the center of his chest like the tip of a branding iron, but Gage managed. He refused to look weak in front of Weld, who was staring at Gage with the kind of astonishment that could only come from someone whose view of the world had been turned upside down. Handcuffed with his arms behind him, surrounded by cops, he looked so much smaller and more pathetic than he had even moments ago.

"But I—I watched the library," he sputtered. "I saw—saw you come in. Nobody followed."

"I called them before we posted the message at SpacedOut," Gage said.

"You—you called the police? When you're a suspected murderer?"

"It was a risky move," Gage said. "But you were wrong, Weld.

Barnacle Bluffs is my home now. You may have grown up here, but it's not home to you, not the way it is to me. I decided to see if the other people who see it as their home too would give me one more chance. Even if they didn't like me all that much. For once, I didn't need to go it alone."

"All right, enough with the Hallmark moments," Quinn said, then stepped in and read Weld his Miranda rights.

Whatever fury was left in Weld drained out of him; his face hardened into a blank white plaster mold. When Brisbane and Trenton led him to the stairs, Gage couldn't help but wonder how long a sick deviant like Weld would last in a maximum-security prison. When his new friends found out what Weld had been doing with Jeremiah when Jeremiah was still a minor, they might not be too forgiving about it. Even the most hardened criminals had their standards.

"Two weeks, tops," Gage said.

"What?" Quinn said.

"Nothing. Thanks for coming through for me, by the way. I know I don't say that word enough."

"Thanks? Yeah, I didn't know it was in your vocabulary. You don't make it easy to help you, you know that."

"It's my nature."

"Yeah, well, you're lucky it's not *my* nature. I keep looking for a reason to help someone even if they don't want it."

"Everyone has their flaws," Gage said.

"One thing, though. What happens if Weld is right about Jeremiah's gun? What if the ballistics report shows that the bullet that killed Connor came from it?"

"It won't happen," Gage said.

"Weld might be telling the truth," Quinn said. "We've still got him for the other murders, but maybe Jeremiah was the one who set this whole thing in motion by killing his friend. If that's the case—"

"It won't happen."

"How can you be so sure?"

But Gage didn't have an answer to that. He just knew, deep

down, that Jeremiah Cooper was not guilty of murder. That was the truth. Sometimes he just knew the truth because it felt right, and this was one of those times. Eventually, when all the smoke had cleared, the evidence would come around to this point of view because it had no choice. The evidence would reflect the truth.

"Just wait," Gage said. "You'll see."

TWO DAYS LATER, they did. The ballistics report showed that the bullet used to kill Connor Fleicher did indeed come from Jeremiah's gun.

## Chapter 23

It was the kind of Thanksgiving dinner that only Eve Cortez could host, a feast of both the eyes and the stomach.

As might be expected from a Greek woman who was thoroughly Americanized, the spread before them was a unique mixture of Mediterranean and American cuisine. There was a turkey, of course, a splendid one, brown and glazed and mouthwatering just to look at, but there was also strawberry baklava, crisp on the outside, tart on the inside, like only she could make it. There was mashed potatoes and gravy, but there was also red-pepper hummus, balsamic chicken, and a tangy tzatziki dip to use with pita bread. They hadn't even eaten a bite yet and already Gage felt full.

Even better, the dining room was awash with the warm glow of the setting sun shining through the windows in the Turret House's dining room. Gage wasn't taken to sentiment all that much, but he couldn't imagine being anywhere else.

"I'm glad it finally stopped raining," Zoe said. She'd surprised them all by showing up in a burnt-orange sweater patterned with brown oak leaves instead of her usual all-black attire. When Gage had asked her about it, she'd said she was being ironic, whatever that meant, but Gage caught her admiring herself in the hall mirror.

"I'll agree to that," Karen said. When everyone glanced at

her, she self-consciously touched the scar on her right cheek. It was a nervous habit he hoped she would soon break, though he was glad to see she'd finally given up wearing that bandage all the time. In fact, the surgeon had said that far from being a terrible scar, when it finally healed, it would be fairly faint—a beauty mark, he'd called it. And Gage didn't think it made Karen any less attractive. "It's nice to see the sun for once," she added.

"For the time being," Alex said.

"In Oregon—" Zoe began.

"Oh, I know," Alex said. "We'll take it. What do you think, Berry? It's nice to have a little break from all the storms, isn't it?"

Gage looked at Berry Fleicher, who was seated between Zoe and Gage. She stared down at her empty plate as if she were trying to divine some meaning there, and she didn't react to Zoe's question. She wasn't wearing black either, her pink cashmere and tan slacks all but the opposite in their tasteful perkiness, but she might as well have been wearing black for how the color seemed to hang over her like a cloud.

"Berry?" Zoe said.

She jumped a little as if she'd been pricked, then looked around the room like a doe that had just hopped onto a busy road. When this passed, any energy in her face disappeared right along with it.

"Hmm?" she said.

"The rain," Zoe said. "It's nice that it's not raining."

"Oh, right." She nodded.

There were concerned glances exchanged between Zoe, Gage, Karen, and Alex, an unspoken worry for the woman who'd lost her son, but what could they do? Inviting her to Thanksgiving had been Alex's idea, and Gage, when he'd passed the invitation along to her, had never expected her to accept. Didn't she have other family she wanted to spend a holiday with, especially after everything she'd been through? But no, like Gage, she didn't.

It had been two weeks since her son was murdered, and while the multiple murders that followed had shaken the inhabitants of Barnacle Bluffs, life in the town was slowly getting back to normal. After a week's closure, the community college re-opened. Both the local and statewide news turned their attention to other tragedies. Jeremiah had been transferred to the county lockup, awaiting his trial, and though Gage had asked to see him, Jeremiah was refusing all visitors—even his own parents. Gage still couldn't believe the boy had actually killed Connor, but it was hard to argue with the evidence.

It still gnawed at him, though. And knowing himself, it always would.

"Where's my wife, anyway?" Alex called into the other room. "Eve, are you going to join us here?"

"Coming!" came her reply. "Just getting some more lemon tea, dear!"

A moment later, she came bustling in wearing one of her patented radiant smiles, the yellow teapot she was carrying trailing steam from its spout. She hardly looked the like a woman who'd had a double mastectomy only two weeks earlier, her green eyes bright, her black hair, pulled back in a ponytail, long and lustrous and bright. The blue satin blouse and pleated tan pants looked as if they'd just been bought at Nordstrom's. Except for the occasional wince when she lifted something heavy, which Alex rarely let her do, perhaps the only sign she'd had the surgery at all was that underneath her cotton apron, her chest was truly flat where once she'd had a fairly ample amount of cleavage. That she'd opted not to have reconstructive breast surgery, and that she made no attempt to hide this fact, either with padding or even baggy clothing, Gage found both brave and not surprising of Eve at all. She was always about getting on with things.

As were they all. These people, they were survivors. They got on with things. That's why he couldn't imagine being anywhere else on Thanksgiving. Everyone in the room had, at some point in the past few years, survived something terrible—and yet here they were, giving thanks.

"Well now," Eve said, depositing the tea on the table, "I suppose we better eat before it gets cold."

"Thank you for inviting me," Berry said, and her voice was so sad and lonely that even she must have realized how out of place it was in such a warm setting, because she quickly added, "I know I'm probably not fun to be around right now."

Eve reached across the table and patted her hand. Her skin, with that Mediterranean complexion of hers, was several shades darker than Berry's. "Nonsense, dear," Eve said. "I love having you here."

"Do you have children?" Berry asked.

"Alex and I have two daughters," Eve said, as if afraid to admit it, and then hurried through the rest. "Both grown, both with kids, and both spending the holiday with their husband's side of the family this year, alas. Shall we say grace?"

Before Berry could respond, Eve bowed her head and started in on the Lord's Prayer. It was good she did, because Gage could see the moisture forming in Berry's eyes. Maybe it was because of this that they all dug into the food with such fervor. Berry was a bit slower, nibbling here and there, but a little white zinfandel seemed to relax her, even if it didn't make her more talkative. Her shoulders, as straight as a coat hanger, began to relax, as did the muscles in her face. Her eyes took on the distant cast of someone peering far into the distance. Still, she smiled and nodded now and then, so Gage stopped worrying about her until she suddenly blurted out to everyone.

"You could have invited them, you know," she said.

They all looked at her.

"Who?" Alex said, a butter knife coated with tzatziki in one hand, some pita bread in the other.

"The Coopers," she said. "You could have invited them. I—I wouldn't have minded them being here."

"Oh, we never even—" Eve began.

"I just didn't want you to think it would have bothered me," Berry continued, talking right over Eve. "I don't blame them. It's not their fault."

And they all just looked at her, because what could anyone say to this? Even Berry didn't have a follow-up. She merely stared at them, blinking, for a few seconds, before picking up her fork and prodding the edges of her mashed potatoes. They followed her lead. There was a long moment of silence in which nobody spoke, then Karen, mercifully, asked how much busier Barnacle Bluffs got in the summer. There were lots of opinions about tourists, of course, so the conversation soon turned lively. The voices grew loud and overlapping, not in disagreement but in passion, and Gage couldn't help but think they'd released some dammed-up reservoir of energy that had been tamped down by their hesitation around Berry.

Zoe thought the town would be better off without tourists at all, to which Alex agreed, surprising everyone, including Eve, since both of his businesses survived on tourism.

"Don't all jump on my case," Alex said. "I've just never liked tourists all that much. I know it's an odd thing for me to say."

"While I agree with you," Gage said, "I have to say that bookshop of yours would be a pretty expensive hobby without making any sales."

"Oh, I'd still have you picking up those Harlequin romances you like so much. Stacks of them! I could survive on that alone."

This got quite a laugh out of everyone, and in the middle of the laughter Berry suddenly bolted to her feet. It had the effect of tossing a bucket of water on a fire, smothering all the mirth in a second. She stood there swaying. They waited expectantly. Gage noticed that while she had barely touched her food, her wine glass was empty.

"Excuse me," she said, and fled from the room.

"Berry—" Karen began, rising.

"No, let me," Gage said.

By the time he reached the kitchen, she was already gone. He started for the back door, thinking maybe she'd gone out to look at the beach, then heard a muffled sob from the living room. She stood in front of the window, her back to him, her shoulders hunched. She was so small and thin, an insubstantial figure, the bumps of her spine jutting through her sweater. He approached cautiously, stopping a few steps behind her. The ocean, visible above the boxwood hedge at the edge of the grass, was a vibrant turquoise, the sun a golden orb hanging low in the western sky. It was a good view, but certainly not the best in the house.

"Connor liked those," she said, surprising him. He hadn't even known if she realized he was in the room.

"What?" he said.

"Those romance books. He never admitted it to me. I just—I'd find them under his bed. Stacks of them. I think he picked them up from the used bookstore down the road."

"Oh," Gage said.

"I know he was gay."

"He was?"

"I'm sure you knew. I knew from an early age. I know about ... I know about him and Jeremiah. That's why I always found his love of romance books so funny. It didn't really make sense. But I guess—I don't know, maybe none of us are that simple."

"You got that right."

"I didn't even think of it until Alex made that joke. It just made me so ... sad. You know? Sad that he's gone."

A million clichés popped into Gage's mind, but he was wise enough not to speak any of them. Instead, he thought about the view, about its power to make people forget about their own pain, if only for a moment.

"Let me show you something," Gage said.

"What?"

"Come on, follow me."

He held out his hand. With some hesitation, she took it, her fingers so small and limp that it felt like holding a string. Without his cane, stepping carefully, he led her back to the narrow hallway that joined the kitchen and the living room. There, next to the coatrack now weighed down by a rainbow array of their coats, was an unadorned door that most people took for a closet. He opened it, and there was the metal winding staircase leading up into the darkness.

"Where—?" she began.

"Just wait."

Still holding her hand, he turned on the light and led her to the door at the top, using his other hand to grip so that he didn't have to put too much weight on his bad knee. The air felt cooler in the stairwell, slightly dank, but once they'd opened the door and stepped into the little octagonal room, it was just as warm as in the main house.

"Oh, my," she said.

That was the reaction most people had to the little room at the top of the stairs, and for good reason. He didn't bother turning on the light; with the sun so low in the sky, the three westward windows were filled with the soft orange and yellow hues of the sun. The dark-stained hardwood floor, the oak bookshelves, the books themselves, the well-worn leather chairs, the beaded lamps—they were all laid out before them just as the Thanksgiving meal was earlier, like an invitation. And the view? Unless you stepped nose-to-glass to the window, there was nothing visible but the endless sweep of that turquoise ocean.

"This is the reason it's called the Turret House," Gage explained.

"It's beautiful. So cozy. You don't think Alex minds us being up here?"

"Are you kidding? He would have suggested it."

"He lets guests up here?"

"Only special ones."

He smiled. She smiled back. For a moment, they were just two people enjoying a very special place, and they could forget about all the tragedy that had swirled around them the past few weeks. The reprieve didn't last long, as Gage knew it wouldn't, the serenity glimpsed in her face a fleeting thing, the dark clouds returning.

"I hope I didn't spoil things downstairs," she said.

"Don't worry about it."

"I just, I don't want people to think I'm just full of hate all the time. I don't hate the Coopers. They suffered too. Whatever happened between our sons … they were only victims."

Gage wasn't sure he believed that—it hewed too close to a

blameless view of society that he abhorred—but he didn't think it was time to argue the point either, especially since he still couldn't convince himself that Jeremiah had pulled the trigger.

"She sent me a Bible, you know," Berry said.

"What?"

"Jeanie Cooper. She sent me a Bible."

"Oh. That seems a bit—"

"I thought it was nice of her, actually. I'm not all that religious, though I do think of myself as somewhat spiritual. Are you religious, Garrison?"

"No."

"Spiritual?"

"Afraid not. Not unless you count the reverence I hold for a fine glass of bourbon in the still hours of the evening."

"Hmm. Anyway, she wrote a little note inside. 'There's hope in here for all of us.' It was nice. I didn't think it was preachy. I think she was reaching out to me. We're kindred spirits, you know. We've both lost our sons. We've both suffered. I think she wants me to forgive her son. I think that's what she wants. I thought maybe, you know, if I could do that, if I could … but I'm not sure I can. I thought if she was here … but I'm not so sure. I just don't know if I can do it. So maybe it's good she isn't here. Is that awful of me? She's reaching out to me, trying to connect, but I'm not sure I can do it. What do you think? Does that make me a terrible person? I don't want to be a terrible person. I want to be bigger than that … but it's so hard …"

She'd been looking out the window, her face shaded by the wooden hues of the room, and as she turned, the sunlight gleamed like a diamond in her eyes. He wished he could tell her that this hurt she felt would go away, but he knew from experience that it wouldn't. He could tell her that there would come a point when she would be glad that the hurt didn't go away, strange as that sounded, but it wouldn't mean anything to her now.

"You're not a terrible person," he said. "You just love your son."

Then, all at once, he knew what he had been missing.

## Chapter 24

The Coopers were still eating their Thanksgiving dinner. When Arne opened the door, Gage spotted Jeanie at the table in the other room, a bountiful buffet spread out on the tablecloth before her that rivaled the one he'd just left at the Turret House. The smell of turkey and baked bread and mashed potatoes drifted out to greet him. Jeanie was the only one at the table, though three places had been set. One of the plates was empty, the water glass full, the silverware untouched.

"What are you doing here?" Arne snapped at him.

Following Gage's stare, Arne stepped to the side to block his view. For once, Arne wasn't dressed in a green windbreaker and blue jeans, but judging by the wrinkled chinos and the tightness of his pinstriped blue shirt, this wasn't something that happened often. Gage looked up into the man's face and saw that Arne, though just as big and broad as always, had aged in the past few weeks. The crow's feet at the corners of his eyes had extended, and his hair, what little he had in his buzz cut, sported a bit more gray around the temples.

"Can I come in?" Gage asked.

"Are you kidding?"

"Just for a few minutes. It won't take long."

"Are you here to take my gun away again?"

"Do you want me to?"

"Listen, pal—"

"Arne, let me in. I have to say something I think you need to hear."

"Oh yeah? My son is in jail for murder. So is my best friend, Paul. Turns out he's some kind of twisted monster who was carrying on having sex with my son for years right under my nose. And you think there's something else I need to hear? Man, I can't wait."

"Five minutes," Gage said.

"You need to leave."

"It's what really happened, Arne. It's the missing piece."

"I don't—"

"It's what really happened to Connor Fleicher. And your son, why he confessed. Don't you want to know?"

He watched something flare up in Arne's eyes, the kind of rage that could have led to violence, but before anything could happen, Jeanie spoke softly behind him.

"Let him in, dear," she said.

At first, Gage wasn't sure Arne had heard her, since his face didn't change, but then, with a huffy shrug, he stepped aside. For all the anger seething from Arne, there was nothing of the sort from Jeanie, only a sad emptiness. Like her husband, she was not a small person, but sitting there in her white cardigan and blue silk dress, he got the sense that there was nothing there but clothes. The person inside them had been hollowed out and removed. Gage, careful where he put his cane on the vinyl entryway, stepped into the house.

The door closed. Nobody said anything. Gage made his way to the table, standing behind the empty spot. Jeanie watched him, her eyes as flat and unblinking as the eyes of the porcelain angel figurines that decorated the room. Gage nodded at the empty plate.

"I don't think he's going to make it," he said.

"Habit," she said.

"Mind if I sit here?"

Arne snorted. "Oh, come on—"

"Don't worry," Gage said. "I've already eaten. I just want to tell you a little story about what happened to your son and his friend, and my knee's killing me. It won't take too long. In fact, since one of you already knows this story, it shouldn't take long at all. Isn't that right, Jeanie?"

She blinked a few times but didn't answer. A mask of confusion fell over Arne's face. Gage took advantage of their hesitation to pull out the chair and settle into it.

"It's something you said when I came before that made me finally put it together," he said. "That and the Bible you sent Berry Fleicher. You remember what you said to me, Jeanie? I asked you why you liked angels. Do you remember what you told me?"

There were tears threatening to spill from her eyes now. "That they reminded me to walk God's path."

"And what else?"

She stared at him.

"You told me that if more people would just read the Bible and stay true to it, the world would be a better place. You said we can all be redeemed. And when I asked you about Jeremiah, if he could be redeemed, too, you said there's hope for all of us. You said you had to believe that or there would be no reason to go on living. I thought you were talking about Jeremiah, but I realize now that you weren't talking about him at all. You were talking about *you*."

This, finally, roused Arne from his comatose state.

"What?" he said. "What are you talking about?"

"Somehow you found out about them," Gage said, focusing on Jeanie. "About your son and Connor. Did you overhear something?"

Jeanie hesitated, and when she spoke, it was in a monotone. "It was a letter," she said.

"Connor wrote Jeremiah a letter?"

She nodded.

"What did it say?"

"It was very ... *dirty*. It was all ... all about how much he loved him. All the—the ways he wanted to touch him. He said he wanted him all to himself, that they were—oh God—"

"Go on," Gage said.

"It's—I can't —"

"Tell me!" Arne shouted.

It was as if he'd shot her in the back, the way she jerked upright, the terror blooming on her face.

"He said—he said they were soul mates," Jeanie said. "He said they could only be soul mates if Jeremiah, if Jeremiah ... oh ... it's terrible. If he stopped being with other men. He said he had proof. Proof that Jeremiah, video proof, that he was with other men and he would show other people if Jeremiah didn't stop ... It was so awful. I couldn't stand it. I couldn't ... couldn't ..."

"And what did you do?" Gage said.

She bowed her head. Arne, hulking over her like an elephant, put a hand on the back of her chair.

"Jeanie?" he pressed.

"I don't know how it went bad," she said. "At first, I thought I was just going to talk to him. To—to Connor. Get him to see, to see how important it was to stay away from Jeremiah. He was a wicked boy and he was ruining my son. Turning him to the devil."

"But you took your husband's revolver?" Gage said.

"Yes. He was asleep."

"Drunk from his night out with Paul Weld?"

She nodded.

"What were you going to do?"

She shrugged. "Just to ... maybe threaten him a little. That's all. I was just going to threaten him. I'm a *Christian!* I never meant ... never ... But then, when he didn't hear me knock, I tried the door and it was unlocked. I went inside. And he was sitting there at the computer with his music loud, watching those awful things on the computer! My son and that—that man!"

"MacDonald?" Gage asked.

"Yes," Jeanie said. "Yes, him. Connor was watching it and he had the music loud and he didn't hear me. I couldn't stand it! I couldn't stand it! So I … I …"

"I don't believe it," Arne said.

She looked up at her husband, her face like crumpled tissue. "I don't even remember doing it. I don't! It was like, like I was someone else. And then, then there was all the blood. I didn't know what to do. I just—I left. I thought maybe somebody would hear me, but they didn't. Nobody came out of their rooms. I left … left him with the music on and went home. I passed a security man, that man from the paper—"

"Patrick Jantz." Gage remembered that Jantz had claimed to be at Tsunami's that night, which had obviously been a lie.

"Yes. Him. I passed him on the way out and I thought—I thought when they found the boy, all that blood, he'd remember me … the police would come for me. But they never did. I even left the gun there. I didn't even remember until I got home that I'd dropped the gun. But they never came. They never did. I kept waiting … but they never did …"

Her voice trailed off into silence. A curtain swept across Arne's face. Something had closed that was never going to open again.

"My son picked up that gun," he said, his voice quiet but holding a barely contained rage, like a lid on a boiling teakettle. "He found Connor and he picked it up. He didn't kill him. He was just … going to kill himself. He was so upset, he was going to kill himself. My son is *innocent*. He's innocent, and you let him go to jail for you?"

"Jantz, that security guy you passed, erased whatever was on the computer," Gage said. "Connor must have secretly taped them with his iPhone and Jantz took that too. Jantz couldn't make it look like a suicide because you'd shot him from behind, but he probably wiped your prints off the revolver. He didn't count on Jeremiah going berserk and attempting to shoot himself, but at the time it probably seemed like a stroke of good luck. Now Jeremiah's prints were on the gun!"

"I was going to turn myself in," Jeanie said. "I was going to do it. I was just waiting for the right—the right time."

"He knew it was you," Gage said. "That's why he decided to confess. He was protecting you. That's what I didn't understand until I had a conversation with Berry Fleicher. It made me realize how much mothers love their sons—and vice versa. I thought maybe he was just afraid of whoever was really behind the killing, that they might do something to you, but it was more direct than that. He knew it was you. If it had been Arne, I don't know if he would have confessed, but he knew it was you, somehow. Did you tell him?"

"He saw me," Jeanie said. "I was sitting in the parking lot. I was … trembling all over. It was so cold. I didn't know what to do. Then he tapped on my window. He was confused. He said he was coming back from the library and he saw me. He asked what I was doing. I just—all I could say was I was sorry. I told him I was sorry and I left."

Arne's hand, gripping the back of the chair, had turned white. Gage leaned back from the table. So that was it then. Weld was definitely a murderer, but he didn't kill Connor Fleicher. He'd killed to cover his tracks, to keep his dark secrets from getting brought into the sunlight during Connor's murder investigation. It had spiraled out of control. Even Connor's hands weren't entirely clean. Jealous when he'd found out about Jeremiah's secret sexual life, he'd tried to force Jeremiah to leave it behind by taping him in the act with MacDonald.

"My son is innocent," Arne whispered.

"Nobody's really innocent in all this," Gage said. "But of all the people involved in this, ironically he was probably the most innocent."

"And he's the one sitting in jail," Arne said.

"It doesn't have to be that way," Gage said.

"No. No, it doesn't."

They both looked at Jeanie, and she looked back, blinking heavily, a rabbit trapped in a cage. Her makeup, so perfect before, showed signs of stress—the mascara around her eyes dark and shiny, the powdery foundation on her cheeks cracking in small fissures. On the mantel, the angel inside the glass clock whirred in its revolutions, but otherwise the room was quiet. Arne pulled a cell phone out of his pocket and placed it on the table in front of his wife.

"Make the call," he said, his voice cracking.

"I don't want to go to jail," she said.

"I don't want you to either. But it has to be done."

"You'd choose him over me?"

Arne winced, like a linebacker who'd taken an elbow to the gut, and closed his eyes. He stood like that for a few seconds, immobile, a mountain of a man, and all the bravado and macho mannerisms slipped away. For a few seconds, Gage thought he saw the real Arne Cooper underneath, a pudgy boy who used his bulk to protect some sensitive and painful core, who talked a tough game but was probably more like his son than he cared to admit. It was all there in his face, a map to his heart unveiled, before he opened his eyes and glared down at his wife with cold and unfeeling eyes.

He reached down and opened the cell phone, holding it up to her.

"I didn't choose," he said. "You did."

## Chapter 25

Stepping into the cool night air and closing the door behind him, Gage saw Karen waiting in her tan Corolla at the curb. The car, cast in shadow, was parked far from the nearest streetlight, but the bluish glow of the cell phone by her ear was enough for him to see her face. She held the phone away from her ear, her expression questioning, and he shook his head and gave her the thumbs-up sign. He didn't waste time getting into the car, tossing his cane into the backseat.

"You timed that close," she said. "One more minute and I was going to make the call."

"No need," Gage said.

"She did it on her own, just like you thought she would?"

"She needed a little encouragement from her husband, but the end result was the same. Let's go. They'll be here any minute, and I don't really feel like dealing with the police on Thanksgiving. Go out this back way here, around the block and by the theater."

Sure enough, he heard sirens in the distance. She put the car in gear and followed his instructions until they emerged on Highway 101. Two police cruisers blared past, lights blinking. When they were gone, she turned onto the highway, heading in the direction of his house. He glanced at her, marveling at her wonderful cheekbones, the trim fit of her blue blouse, the tight cut of her charcoal black pants. He only looked for a second, because if he let his gaze linger, she always self-consciously touched her scar.

"Thanks for the ride," he said.

"No problem. But the meter's running, mister."

"The van should be ready by next week. Then I won't need people to chauffeur me around any more."

"Can't believe you're getting that old thing fixed. It must have cost a fortune. You could have probably bought a whole new van for the same money."

"Try two. Parts for that old Volkswagen don't come cheap. But I can't give up on it yet."

"Will you *ever* give up on it?"

"Probably not. Just like I hope people never give up on me."

She laughed at this. He liked hearing her laugh, a real laugh, not the guarded one that she'd used when she first showed up in town. He'd been getting more chances to hear the genuine thing lately. When she got out of the hospital, he'd been afraid that she'd retreat even further into her shell of remorse and regret, but something had changed after the crash. He didn't know what, and he was afraid to ask for fear that he might push it away like so much smoke if he even tried to talk to her about it, but he was immensely relieved.

They reached his gravel driveway a minute later, parking in front of the house. It loomed large and lonely, the faint light in the kitchen window the only thing beating back the darkness. He thought he caught a bit of longing in the way Karen gazed at it, and it gave him enough hope to try again.

"You know, you can move in with me anytime," he said.

She looked at him, smiling but with sad eyes. She'd been staying at the Turret House while she recuperated, turning down several offers on his part to room with him instead. More than several, really. He'd been asking every day. She'd made a couple of late-night visits that ended with tangled sheets and tangled bodies, but she'd never stayed the night.

"Part of me would like that," she said.

"You should give in to that part."

She looked at him a long time, really studying his face, and he got the sense that something was being measured, weighed. He thought that perhaps she was really thinking about his offer, that she was on the verge, which was why when she finally spoke, what she said was so devastating.

"I'm leaving tomorrow, Garrison."

He knew what she was saying, and all the implications of it, but he wanted to pretend otherwise. "Leaving on a little trip?"

"No. Just leaving."

"Oh."

"You didn't do anything wrong."

"It sure feels that way."

"No. You were wonderful. You gave me exactly what I needed."

"I'm so glad I could be of help," he said, and he hated the bitterness in his own voice and the look on her face that his bitterness elicited. He gamely tried to recover. "Are you going back to the FBI?"

"No. I can't go back there."

"Then what?"

She hesitated. "Well, I need to visit my sister in Atlanta. She's been reaching out to me, and I've done nothing but give her the cold shoulder. When we were eating our Thanksgiving dinner, all I could think about was what a bad sister I've been. I want to make up for that. It's time. And her daughters. My nieces. I think, I think I'm ready to see them too. They deserve a better aunt. After that … well, I thought I'd try my hand at being a private investigator."

"I see. Wow."

"You had a lot to do with it," she said. "You—you showed me what was possible, Garrison. Another kind of life."

"Where will you go?"

"Haven't figured that part out yet. After Atlanta, I'm just going to drive for a bit until I find someplace where it makes sense."

"Ah."

They sat like that for a moment, a veil of sadness dropping deeper over them, and Gage already felt the yawning hole that was going to be left when she was gone. He didn't want that to happen.

"You know," he said, "you don't have to drive anywhere. You could be a private investigator right here in Barnacle Bluffs. I've been thinking, you know, that I kind of like having a partner. You seem more than qualified."

She left him hanging in the balance a second, then her eyes turned shiny and bright. She leaned forward and cupped his cheeks, kissing him passionately on the lips. It was the best kiss they'd shared so far, but when she pulled away, he could already see the answer in her eyes.

"Thank you for that," she said. "It means a lot."

"But the answer's no?"

"But the answer is *not right now*. I need to find my own way for a bit."

"I see."

"Do you?"

And actually, he did. It didn't mean her answer hurt any less, but if anyone understood the need to find your own way, it was Gage. He'd been trying to find his own way his whole life, sometimes thinking he was getting somewhere, often finding he was just more lost than ever. With a last gentle touch to her cheek, he stepped out of the car onto the gravel driveway and, with a faint smile of good-bye, shut the door.

The night, as cool as it was, welcomed him like an old friend. She put the car in gear. As she passed, he thought he caught a glimpse of her face as she doubled back on the circular driveway, thought he saw tears there, but then she was gone, the red taillights disappearing around the bend. His empty house, with its half-filled crossword puzzles and bottles of bourbon, waited patiently behind him. Still, he stood there, listening. He listened to the crunch of her tires on the gravel until this sound was gone too. He listened to the hum of the traffic on the highway, the whisper of the wind in the fir trees, and even imagined he could hear the murmur of the ocean. He stood like that, listening, waiting for something, some signal that this moment was gone and it was time to get on with things, until finally the world gave it to him.

He felt the first gentle touch on his cheek, in the same spot where her hand had been only moments ago.

It was raining.

## Acknowledgments

EVERY BOOK I write always gets a bit of an assist from others. Although it's impossible to personally thank everyone who's had a hand in bringing *The Lovely Wicked Rain* into the world, I'd like to mention a few who have been instrumental.

To my good friend and fellow writer Michael J. Totten: Thanks for the early read and thoughtful suggestions. If you want someone in the writing trenches with you, Mike is your guy.

To Nathan E. Meyer, friend and frequent lunch companion: Thanks for your enthusiasm for the book and your sharp-eyed observations.

To Elissa Englund, my intrepid copy editor: A big thank you for catching all the little typos and other missteps. Any errors that remain are entirely my own.

To Garrison Gage fans: I can guarantee you that if you hadn't responded as you did to the first two books, there never would have been a third. Thank you. If you're interested in why I dropped the Jack Nolte pen name, see the Garrison Gage section on my website. It's an interesting story, but not one that every reader cares about, so I will refrain from repeating it here.

And last but never least, to my first reader and love of my life, Heidi: Thanks for needling me to write the next Gage book, more as a fan than as my wife. And for everything else, of course. I could fill a whole book and more with all my appreciation for you and it still wouldn't be enough.

## About the Author

SCOTT WILLIAM CARTER's first novel, *The Last Great Getaway of the Water Balloon Boys,* was hailed by Publishers Weekly as a "touching and impressive debut" and won the prestigious Oregon Book Award. Since then, he has published ten novels and over fifty short stories, his work spanning a wide variety of genres and styles. His most recent book for younger readers, *Wooden Bones,* chronicles the untold story of Pinocchio and was singled out for praise by the Junior Library Guild. He lives in Oregon with his wife and children.

Visit him online at *www.scottwilliamcarter.com.*

Made in the USA
Lexington, KY
27 March 2017